PR,

BLOOD ON HER TONGUE

"Chilling in its intimacy, this tale of monsters and monstrous love is a gorgeous gothic treat. I drank up every delicious word."

—Jennifer Thorne, *USA Today* bestselling author of *Diavola and Lute*

"A new gothic masterpiece. *Blood on Her Tongue* is decadent, full of gore and rot, and viscerally, relentlessly engaging. I devoured this one. Once you've tasted a little, you'll need more, then more, then more…"

—CJ Leede, author of *Maeve Fly*

"Dark, visceral, and deliciously disturbing—van Veen has woven a tale that feels like a brand new nineteenth-century classic, bristling with gothic horror and mounting dread."

—C. E. McGill, author of *Our Hideous Progeny*

"Johanna van Veen's artful and cunning use of the sublime will pull you into a sisterly web of terror, beauty, and horror, all of it sensual and dripping with the idea that death should be a kind of mutilation."

—Nicholas Belardes, author of *The Deading*

"Gruesome, at times unhinged, and deeply beautiful, *Blood on Her Tongue* is morbid in the best sense of the word. A vital addition to the gothic genre that will make you shudder with both pleasure and fear."

—Katrina Monroe, author of *Through the Midnight Door*

"Johanna van Veen weaves a seductively gruesome horror yarn with *Blood on Her Tongue*. Every page is dripping with gothic dread and undead yearning, and I couldn't devour it fast enough."

—Brian McAuley, author of *Curse of the Reaper*

"Johanna van Veen embroiders a rich tapestry of dark secrets and disturbing monsters, then delights in smothering you with it. A chilly gothic horror story that begs to be read by a roaring fire while the wind howls outside your window."

—Josh Winning, author of *Heads Will Roll*

"A heightened experience for gothic horror fans. Johanna van Veen indulges the audience with atmospheric tension and deeply flawed yet emotionally compelling characters. The taste of blood becomes sharper with every page."

—Bram Stoker Finalist Vincent Tirado, author of *We Came to Welcome You*

"Johanna van Veen takes up the mantle of Stoker and Le Fanu with this seductive tale of hunger, transgression, and the violent power of sisterhood. Sumptuous, disturbing, and sensual, *Blood on Her*

Tongue is queer gothic fiction at its audacious best. A bloody and decadent feast of a novel."

—Elliott Gish, author of *Grey Dog*

PRAISE FOR
MY DARLING DREADFUL THING

"Dark and decadent, with the haunting allure of a true gothic tale, *My Darling Dreadful Thing* is a sensation that horrifies as acutely as it delights. Johanna van Veen is a force to be reckoned with and will stain your thoughts a brilliant shade of crimson. I adored every page."

—Rachel Gillig, *New York Times* bestselling author of *One Dark Window*

"A sapphic seance of preternatural proportions, *My Darling Dreadful Thing* summons a stunning new literary voice to be reckoned with. Johanna van Veen reaches beyond the veil to conjure up a gothic shocker like no other."

—Clay McLeod Chapman, author of *What Kind of Mother*

"*My Darling Dreadful Thing* is a disquieting delight—an exciting and original gothic tale, told with tremendous flair."

—Cherie Priest, author of *The Drowning House*

ALSO BY JOHANNA VAN VEEN

My Darling Dreadful Thing

Blood on Her Tongue

Blood
on Her
Tongue

—— *a novel* ——

JOHANNA VAN VEEN

Poisoned Pen
PRESS

Sourcebooks, Poisoned Pen Press, and the colophon
are registered trademarks of Sourcebooks.

The characters and events portrayed in this book are fictitious or
are used fictitiously. Any similarity to real persons, living or dead,
is purely coincidental and not intended by the author.

Published by Poisoned Pen Press, an imprint of Sourcebooks
P.O. Box 4410, Naperville, Illinois 60567-4410
(630) 961-3900
sourcebooks.com

Cataloging-in-Publication Data is on file with the Library of Congress.

Printed and bound in the United States of America.
WOZ 10 9 8 7 6 5 4 3 2 1

For my beloved wife, Corinna, who pushes me to be the best I can be and for my sisters, Lieke and Hilke, with whom I have a very healthy and loving relationship, thus proving that normal and well-adjusted twins and triplets do exist (perhaps they only do outside of fiction?). Yay for us!

AUTHOR'S NOTE

MY BELOVED READER,

In your hands, you hold a work of gothic horror. As such, it naturally contains terror and rage and other emotional extremes, strange and frightening occurrences that may or may not be supernatural, and an atmosphere so thick you can stick a knife in it (though you can never be sure that knife will be where you left it once you return from your nightly wanderings. That is, *if* you return. It's gothic. You never know.).

What I mean to say is that you can expect quite a lot of disquieting, dark, and dreadful things from this book by virtue of its genre. I do not wish to spoil the story for you, but I do wish to warn you so that you may prepare yourself accordingly before you wander into its darkness wearing only a flimsy nightgown and holding a dripping candle to light your way that this book contains discussions and instances of sickness, death of a loved one, body horror/gore, the stigmatization of the mentally ill, misogyny, sexual abuse, domestic abuse, cheating, and toxic codependent relationships (where would gothic and queer literature be without them?).

It has always been my intent to treat these issues with the sensitivity they deserve. Because the road to hell is paved with good intentions, I have not merely *intended*; I have, among other things, done a lot of research into different mental illnesses: what may cause them, how they manifest themselves, how they affect both the person who has the illness and the people near them, as well as how these illnesses would be perceived in the late nineteenth century in the Netherlands. Additionally, I have made grateful use of a sensitivity reader (thank you, Johanie!).

Dark and creepy things lie ahead, yes, but hopefully a delightfully spooky good time as well. Please enjoy, and thank you for picking up *Blood on Her Tongue*!

Part I

"I am longing to be with you, and by the sea, where we can talk together freely and build our castles in the air."

Bram Stoker, *Dracula*

LETTER FROM MRS. SARAH SCHATTELEYN
TO MISS LUCY GOEDHART

My twin my   darling   my LUCY

All is not well with me not AT ALL well

NO

ive a <u>BLINDING PAIN</u> in my head

i didnt think it was possible to experience such pain and LIVE

i feel like taking a SPOON

to my eye and scooping it

out out OUT OUT out

anything to make

it STOP MAKE IT STOP makeitstoppleasemakeitstop

i often think but only when <u>SHE</u> allows me to think because
how can anyone think with a pain like this like something
<u>rooting</u> through your head or or or theres a word for it and i
know it but it wont come to me i think shes taking away my
words now too oh god oh god oh god ohgodohgod please no but
when she lets me i think how good it would be to be DEAD
because then at least it wouldnt hurt

*only i cant because thats what SHE wants and no matter
what i cant give her what she wants not NOT EVER
neverNEVERNEVERNeVErnevER
shesaDEMONanUNHOLYthingallVILEallUNCLEAN*
                 *i wish i could KILL her or at least
                         hurt her like she hurts me*

     seehowshelikestohaveher brainfeellike a salted slug

*see you HORRIBLE THING you can rob me of some of my
big words but i can use other words to describe what youre
doing to me*
                ithurtssomuchlucy

*please please PLEASE come to me my sweet sister i am terrified
of what i might do if you dont*

                                     Sarah

TELEGRAM FROM MR. MICHAEL
SCHATTELEYN TO MISS LUCY GOEDHART

————————————

RECEIVED AT
VEENPOORT 11:06 28/09/1887

SARAH DEADLY SICK. PLEASE COME
IMMEDIATELY. NO NEED TO SEND
WORD AHEAD. WILL ENSURE SOMEONE
THERE TO MEET YOU AT STATION NO
MATTER THE TIME. JUST HURRY. I
FEAR FOR HER LIFE.

MICHAEL

Chapter 1

THE TRAIN LEFT THE STATION at noon.

By then, so many little things had gone wrong that Lucy couldn't help but wonder whether her journey was ill-fated. Firstly, she had intended to be on an earlier train, the one that left at ten, but one of the horses pulling the carriage taking her to the station had thrown a shoe, delaying her by almost two hours. When she finally arrived, the heel of her left boot snapped off, causing her to sprain her ankle. Once she was seated within the train, she thought herself momentarily safe from the common misfortune that had dogged her that morning. This proved to be an illusion when a fellow passenger, a middle-aged woman who smelled strongly of rose water, dumped her travel bag onto Lucy's lap.

Startled, Lucy jerked in her seat. The book she had been idly flicking through, a collection of gothic tales translated from English, fell from her lap. In between its pages, tucked there carefully to prevent loss and creases, lay the most recent letters from her twin sister, Sarah. They spilled onto the floor and under the seats.

"Oh my!" the woman said. She snatched up the bag as if afraid

Lucy would make away with it. "I didn't see you," she said, by way of explanation. Then she added, "You really should be more careful, you know."

Lucy, who had dropped to her knees to gather her precious letters, only smiled wanly in response.

Offended, the woman huffed and sat in Lucy's seat. Lucy opened her mouth to tell her, then decided against it and took an empty seat by the window. She brushed away the dust and hair that clung to the envelopes, then smoothed them carefully and counted them to make sure she had retrieved them all. Merely looking at them had her feeling restless and sick, her sternum throbbing as if a piece of string had been wound around the bone and someone were trying to gather it up, pulling her along with it.

She did not have long to muse on these sensations. The only other passenger in the carriage, the woman who smelled of rose water, let out a scream a mere five minutes after the train had pulled out of the station. "Oh my God!" she shrieked, pressing her hand to her chest.

"What?" Lucy asked wildly. "What is it?"

The woman pointed. At first, Lucy had no idea at what. Then she saw a spider had crawled onto the windowpane, on their side of the glass. It was only little, barely bigger than the nail of Lucy's thumb.

"Oh," Lucy said. "Don't worry. It won't hurt you."

The woman shook her head. Her eyes had gone round, leaving the irises all rimmed with white. "Get it away from me!" she gasped, as if her fear were so potent it was choking her.

Perhaps this is another sign, Lucy thought, as she took a letter out of its envelope and placed it in her lap, though a sign of what, she didn't know, and besides, signs were cheap when you went looking for them. Better to just focus on the task at hand.

She applied pressure to the sides of the envelope, causing it to gape open, then carefully brushed the spider inside. Spiders did not frighten her, nor did any other insect, for that matter. Aunt Adelheid, her mother's eccentric older sister, had loved them and studied them obsessively. One of Lucy's earliest memories was of herself and Sarah sitting on a blanket in the garden while Aunt Adelheid dug into a patch of earth close to them. It must have rained only recently; Lucy remembered the blanket had been damp, and the soil had been dark and soft, sticking in great clumps to her aunt's fingers.

"There!" Aunt Adelheid said triumphantly. She plucked something from the ground and held it out for her nieces to see. It was a worm, nearly as long as a finger, delicately segmented, with a thick band near one end. The worm writhed in her grip. In the soft spring light, it gleamed various shades of pink and beige.

"Pretty!" Sarah cried out.

"Pretty!" Lucy agreed.

"You may touch it, but be careful! It's delicate," she said. "Some people think that if you cut a worm in half, you will have two worms. How amazing that would be! A creature that can twin itself! But that's..."

Sarah, always quick, always decisive and boundlessly curious, grabbed the worm and tore it in half.

"…nothing but an old wives' tale," Aunt Adelheid finished.

Sarah placed half the worm into Lucy's hands. It was cool to the touch, slightly wet. Sarah's own half, the one with the band near its end, continued to wriggle in her grip, its whole body curving and then straightening again as it tried to get away. Lucy's half only twitched weakly. Soon, it lay still. Lucy stared, aghast, as its vivid pink hue blanched into an unremarkable gray. It looked pathetic next to Sarah's squirming half, a poor version of what a worm should be.

A thought had come to her, horrible enough that she remembered it even now: What if she and Sarah were like those pieces of the worm? Sarah, vivid and alive, and Lucy, nothing but a weak imitation of the real thing?

No wonder people don't notice me and accidentally throw their luggage on my lap, Lucy thought, as she folded the envelope shut with the spider inside, taking care not to hurt it. Funny what things one could remember in sudden moments of stress. Not that the thought caused her any anguish, not anymore. She had long since accepted what she was and was not. In fact, the memory was almost sweet; Sarah had tried to comfort her by saying her worm must simply be sleeping and, when it still wouldn't move, she had dashed it from Lucy's hand and declared the whole thing silly, asking Aunt Adelheid if she had something else to show them, something better?

Lucy placed the envelope with the spider carefully on the empty seat beside her. She could release it once she left the train. It would be much better off spinning a web in a tree somewhere, or a lantern post, where the light might attract moths and other insects it could eat—or was this not the kind of spider that wove a web? Sarah might know...

No sooner had she let go of the envelope than her fellow passenger whacked it with her umbrella. She used such force, the envelope flew into the air. With a screech, she batted it to the floor, where she stomped on it with first her left foot, then the right. Her boots left dark marks on the paper, which was now so flattened as to make the survival of the spider impossible.

Shocked, Lucy stared at the woman. "Whatever did you do that for?" she exclaimed.

"Nasty creatures," the woman said, then shrugged. When she alighted at the next station, it was to Lucy's profound relief.

Only a few more hours, and then I shall be with Sarah again, Lucy thought as the stationmaster blew his whistle and the train resumed its journey.

Rain rattled against the thin windowpane, mingling with the soot on the glass and creating fantastic streaks of gray. Lucy frowned. She hadn't thought to bring an umbrella. No doubt it wasn't the only thing she hadn't brought and would miss; her mind had been elsewhere as she packed, and she had done a poor job. Mrs. van Dijk had offered to help her, but how could Lucy have accepted? Mrs. van Dijk was old and infirm. More importantly, she provided room and board for Lucy and paid her a small amount of money each month in return for companionship. A world in which an employer packed her employee's belongings would be a strange one indeed.

Only, Mrs. van Dijk would never have forgotten to include an umbrella.

At least Lucy had thought to bring a book, though stories teeming with women bricked up alive and haunted by chattering ghosts did not appeal to her now. But to simply sit and wait was even more unappealing, so she took out one of her sister's letters from between the book's pages, fished it from its envelope, and began to read.

When she was done, she felt nauseous, though perhaps that was partly because she hadn't eaten properly. Mrs. van Dijk's cook had made her some sandwiches for the journey, but Lucy's mother had ingrained in her a firm belief that eating anywhere in public was indecent. It did not matter that she had the train carriage to herself now that the woman who smelled of rose water had left and that she could have consumed those sandwiches slathered with butter and cold cuts unobserved.

Not that she had much of an appetite anyway. Who would, after reading something as disturbing as Sarah's final letter? If one could even call the undated sheet of paper with almost illegible scribbles that.

Lucy sighed and slipped the letter back between the pages of her book. She had read it so many times, the creases from where the pages were folded threatened to tear. Tucked in the same envelope was Sarah's drawing of the bog body. Lucy did not take it out. She had looked at it often enough to conjure it in her mind. It came to her unbidden now, and she closed her eyes in an effort to strangle the image.

When she opened them again, the train had left behind the

sprawling farmer's fields, which looked stubbled and unkempt now that the summer grain had been harvested, and wound its way through an area full of trees. Their leaves plunged the carriage into momentary twilight, snapping Lucy out of contemplating her sister's letter. She frowned and turned her head to the window.

Sarah's face looked back at her, gaunt and wild and mad.

Lucy jerked back violently, her heart pounding, only for Sarah to do the same.

Your reflection, you silly goose, she thought. The sudden darkness from the thick foliage outside had turned the window into a mirror. She almost laughed at herself in derision. Instead, she leaned closer to the glass and studied her reflection. A tendril of hair had escaped its pins, and she had a smudge of something dark that was hopefully just ink on her cheek. Worse were her eyes: there was something frightened and wild about them, like the eyes of a pursued animal. Anyone who didn't know Lucy would think her untidy and therefore a little mad. Wasn't a slovenly appearance a reliable outward manifestation of a disturbed mind?

As Lucy rubbed harshly at her cheek with her handkerchief, one thing she had not forgotten to bring, she thought, *Maybe I shall find my sister with unkempt hair and crusty eyes and dried spittle at the corner of her mouth, and I shall know for certain then that she is, indeed, a lunatic.*

She had barely finished the thought when fear grabbed her by the throat with enough force to cut off her breath. She dropped the handkerchief to her lap and buried her face in her hands to keep from crying.

Please, she thought with such fervor, a light sweat broke out all over her body and the knot at her sternum pulsed painfully, *please don't let her be mad.*

Not again.

LETTER FROM MRS. SARAH SCHATTELEYN
TO MISS LUCY GOEDHART

Zwartwater, 19 September 1887

My dearest Lucy,

You won't believe what Michael and I have been up to today! In fact, I can scarcely believe it myself. It was such a peculiar day—thrilling, yes, but also slightly frightening. Above all, though, it was incredibly interesting.

It all happened just after Michael and I had finished our lunch. One of the tenants came running to the house and told us they'd found a body while cutting peat. He hastened to add it was likely a very old body, not a recent murder victim, just one of those bog bodies peat cutters sometimes find. I have read a little about such bodies, but I'd never seen one, and neither had Michael, so the two of us hastened over to see it for ourselves.

We had to leave Katje at home; the poor girl was in great pain again. With her, you truly understand why they call it the monthly curse, don't you? I left Pasja with her. She's such a gentle dog, though you'd never think it when you saw her hunting rabbits! Enfin, I left both Michael's poor relation and my dog at home, and once I was armed with my sketchbook and some pencils to capture the body's likeness before the processes of decomposition could alter it too much, Michael and I made our way to the scene of the crime.

It didn't look much different from other fields of peat: just grassland, slightly soggy, with large squares of wet earth gouged out, leaving deep, dark pits. Bricks and slabs of peat lay drying in the next field. The air smelled of them and hot grass, this good, clean scent.

The new groundskeeper, Mr. Hooiman, met us there. He's a giant of a man, with bowed legs and a skin tanned this fascinating nut-brown color from all the work he does outside. He explained that one of the boys had found the body while cutting peat. Poor thing got a nasty shock. Nothing can quite prepare you for cutting into the earth and revealing a human hand, now, can it?

They had soon found that the hand was still attached to an arm, and the arm to a rump, and so forth. By the time we arrived, they had just unearthed the head, and did we want to see?

The first thing I thought when I saw the head was that it really didn't look much like a head. Had Mr. Hooiman not told me what exactly it was that I was looking at, I would have thought it was a deflated ball made out of pig's bladder. Something animal in origin, yes, but malformed. But as the men set to rinsing away clots of earth clinging to the head, I saw things hitherto hidden from me: tendrils of red hair, the gentle curl of an ear. I had expected a face, but the unfortunate wretch had been buried face down; I had been looking at the back of the head all the while, and felt silly for not realizing it straight away.

While the men worked, I asked Mr. Hooiman if he had any idea what we should do with the body, him having often assisted the peat cutters and therefore more likely to have experience with this sort of thing. He shrugged and said that it wasn't up to him, this not being his land. If it were though, he'd tuck it back and try to forget it.

I shivered at that and said, "Oh, but I could never! I would always know it was here, and it would haunt me. Surely we have a duty to discover who this unfortunate wretch is and who put them here? We should study the body and see what we can learn from it at the very least. We owe it to the scientific community to find out all we can."

Mr. Hooiman shrugged again. "'Tis what was usually done with the bog bodies in my grandfather's time, and his before that. If you ask me, 'tis the only decent thing to do. It may not look much like one now, but it used to be a human once, just like yourselves," he said (or something very much like it. You know how hard I try to memorize whole conversations so I can reproduce them in order for you to feel you were there, sweet sister mine, but I confess I don't always manage it perfectly. I'm sure you'll forgive me!).

Michael thanked Mr. Hooiman for his suggestions and said we had much to think about. In the meantime, it would be best if the men continued to dig the whole body out so I could sketch it in its entirety; the medical men would appreciate pictures of the body in situ. We could always rebury it later if we were so inclined. I'd stay and sketch it while Michael went to see if he could get Arthur to come. A doctor would likely see things we'd miss.

By the end of the afternoon, they had uncovered all of it: a naked human body—impossible to say whether male or female from looking at the back of it—lying face down and straight as a board. Wooden stakes had been driven through the knees, elbows, shoulders, and neck, which had set the men murmuring, some of them crossing themselves (you know Michael has never had a problem with hiring Catholics). I sketched the body from multiple angles, paying close attention to the place where it had been staked to the earth, then asked the men to lift the body out. They did so reluctantly.

When they turned it over, they gasped. There was more fervent crossing themselves, some murmured prayers. The men holding the body dropped it as if they'd been burned and wiped their hands convulsively on their trousers and jackets.

I came closer to admonish them—God only knows the damage they could've wrought—only to find myself, for a moment, quite stunned.

The body had a large piece of stone wedged between its jaws.

It couldn't have been an accident nor coincidence; the stone was of such a size that the mouth had been opened to its absolute limit to cram it in. Some of the teeth had broken in the process, and the incisors were missing altogether.

Mr. Hooiman took me aside then and explained to me that the men wished to stop working. They were afraid of the restless spirit belonging to the body. Someone buried in such a manner as this body must have been a suicide or criminal, and those make restless dead.

I didn't laugh at that, as I know Michael would have. I didn't want to disrespect the men, but I didn't want them to stop working either, not when there was still much more work to be done before sundown.

In the end, I got them to stay only by offering them double their normal wages for the day. To show them my goodwill, I sent one of them back to the house with instructions for the servants to prepare good hot food for them, and plenty of beer.

Until the food arrived, I bade them to keep working. Someone had made a crude casket, which stood propped up against a fence. I convinced some of the braver men to put the body inside it, then asked them to cut the peat around where the body had been found, to see if they could find any clothes or objects.

As they did so, I took a closer look at the body.

She was such a strange thing to look at, Lucy! Her skin looked most like tanned leather, stained the color of tea. Her body no longer seemed straight and stiff, but slightly contorted, as if she had been writhing a little before I had fixed my gaze upon her. I know it was only the uneven length of the stakes resting against the backboards of the casket that made it look thus, but it was disconcerting to behold, all the same.

I have started calling her "she," though I have to admit I still don't know for sure if the creature was male or female. When turning her over, the men had debated draping a handkerchief over her loins, presumably to protect my modesty, only the body had no sex to speak of, at least none that we could see. Bog eats bones and eyes and, apparently, also genitals!

(I'd like to warn you not to read this part out to Mrs. van Dijk, but a part of me would absolutely love it if you did. If she fires you on the spot, know that you can come live with me and Michael, as I've always said you could, just as I've always told you that the position of companion is utterly beneath you. I could give you money so you could get some lodgings nearby and employ a little maid, and it would all be very respectable. But I know, I'm flogging a dead horse here. Still, it's good to give it the occasional thrashing to ensure it really is dead.)

Where was I? Ah, yes: the apparent sexlessness of the bog body. I didn't think her nearly so sexless. She didn't have any of the usual clear physical markers of her sex, yet her face made me believe she must have been a woman, once.

That face…

It is one of the strangest, most haunting faces I have ever seen. I find it hard to describe it. I've included a sketch, but I fear it doesn't do her justice. When I studied it, it initially just looked like a wizened sack of meat, sadly crushed and misshapen. Yet, when viewed from a certain angle, that same face I had thought a deflated football at first suddenly took on a rare beauty I have only ever encountered before on paper or in marble. I know that may sound strange, since it's the face of a corpse and one greatly altered by the bog. Certainly this optical illusion disconcerted me, but it is true, and if anyone will understand, I am sure that it must be you. They say a husband and wife are one flesh, but you are my twin and thus my other half.

Well, I gazed upon it, and I wondered what she would have looked like in life, before the bog tanned her to leather and dyed her hair red and consumed her eyes, before her jaw had so savagely been opened and a rock thrust inside her mouth, breaking her teeth down to pearly pips. Merely looking at it gave me a phantom pain in my jaw, and I resolved to remove the rock then and there; who knew what we might find once it was gone from her mouth? It wouldn't be easy. I feared I might damage her teeth and jaw even more in attempting it, and that would rather defeat the purpose.

But I couldn't very well leave her like that, now, could I?

I felt around the bit of rock, reached into her mouth with my fingers. The inside of her mouth felt damp, like the mouth of one still alive, and I shuddered, but did not pull away. Instead, I began to extract the stone from her jaw, doing it gently at first, then with a bit more force, grimacing at the sound of her teeth grinding against the stone. I tried to get a firmer grip but cut my knuckles on the broken stumps of her teeth.

I pulled my hand back with a cry. Little cuts gaped on my knuckles. Already blood as dark as the water from the bog flowed freely down my palm and wrist. It had stained her teeth pink.

~~The peat cutters have got it all wrong.~~ "~~She's not hungry, just thirsty,~~" ~~I thought, and then laughed at my own silliness. I sucked on my knuckles, the harsh taste of blood mixed with the smokiness of peat blooming on my tongue.~~

Don't bother trying to read that last paragraph. It's just morbid nonsense. You know that I sometimes fall prey to very peculiar flights of fancy, especially after my darling little Lucille... But I don't need to go into that now.

Well, I had a strange turn, probably due to the sun beating down on me and that damnably creepy illusion that made the bog woman look beautiful for a moment and then the shock from cutting my hand on those little teeth of hers. I stood sucking at the cuts, frowning at the pain, when Michael and Arthur finally arrived.

Arthur was immediately drawn to the body. He paced around the casket, studying the body from all angles, then asked to look at my sketches to see how we had found her. Next he began to touch her, feeling her throat and jaw, then the joints staked through, muttering all the while.

"Well? What do you make of it?" Michael asked.

I went to him and threaded my arm through his. I felt very tired all of a sudden.

"Fantastic!" Arthur said. His cheeks were flushed, and he

looked like an excited schoolboy. "I think the body is at least a century old, but look at those hands! I can take fingerprints as easily as I could from my own hand. Bogs truly are remarkable."

"Have you ever seen anything like it?" Michael asked.

Arthur shook his head. "No, but I've read some accounts. Bog bodies are rare, but such finds are not entirely unheard of, though it has been a long time since one was found in Dutch soil. If I remember correctly, the Germans had more luck and found a body like this in Schleswig-Holstein some fifteen years ago. They recorded the find and the subsequent autopsy meticulously. We might do the same here. Imagine the secrets we might uncover!"

He and Michael stood talking for a long time then, both growing animated by the prospect of discovery. I said little. I'm afraid I'd started to feel tired and a bit faint, probably from lack of food and the pain in my hand; though my knuckles had ceased bleeding, they still smarted abominably, the pain hot and pulsing.

After a while, the food and drink arrived, and Michael went around paying the men. Soon, they were almost merry, yet none of them stayed much longer. The light was fading fast, and they wished to get on home. Michael employed the bravest of them to help carry the casket back to Zwartwater; the cellar, being dry and cool, will help preserve the body, and with some small adjustments, it'll be an excellent place for Arthur to perform an autopsy, which he wishes to do as soon as possible. I think he would have taken a knife to her out in the fields, or else this very night, if we had let him.

As Michael and I walked home, I asked him again what we are to do with the body. He has his heart set on an autopsy, as has Arthur. Strangely, I find myself torn. There is no denying that opportunities like this seldom come along and we might learn all manner of things from this body, yet I find the prospect ~~revolting~~ *distasteful, though I am not sure how I can account for these feelings. I've never been one to stand in the way of scientific discovery, so why should it bother me now? Perhaps I shouldn't have tried to think of the body as a human being.*

What do you think, Lucy dearest? To cut or not to cut?

I'll stop this letter now. It's quite long as it is, and you know how Michael loves to tease me about how often I write to you. Besides, my hand smarts from where I cut it, and though writing isn't exactly agony, it isn't quite pleasant either. An apt punishment, perhaps, for being so immodest as not to wear gloves outside the house! Mother would have had a fit, had she been alive to see me sit in that field with my hands and wrists exposed for all the workers to see, but then, she was never one for drawing, which is very hard to do when wearing gloves. Pencils are so very slippery.

I only wish you could have been there with me to see it, Lucy mine. I wish to know if you would have been able to see the beauty in that strange face, too.

I'll truly stop now.

Arthur sends you his love (I know you are not the marrying type, but should you reconsider, know that he'd make a fine husband, and you a very fine doctor's wife! But you mustn't mind me. I'm flogging yet another dead horse. Truly, I sometimes feel I've got enough of them to pull a whole carriage!).

Give Mrs. van Dijk my regards. Better yet: tell her I think she's positively cruel for keeping my twin away from me; only think that you and I could have seen the excavation of this body together if you still lived with me!

Your loving sister,
Sarah

Chapter 2

LUCY ARRIVED AROUND SIX IN the evening. She had rarely been so relieved to see the stone letters, now much faded, above the front door, spelling out the house's name: ZWARTWATER.

She had thought it an odd name for an estate until she had seen it for the first time, now almost five years ago, when her parents had still been alive. Michael had invited both sisters to stay with him, Sarah because he was courting her and Lucy for the sake of propriety. The house had been built on soft ground unsuited for stone so heavy, which made the whole structure sag to one side. This, in combination with the west wing, which had been built much more recently in a different style, gave the house the appearance of having suffered a stroke. There was beauty in it still, the way imperfect things can be beautiful, but it was a beauty of a dark and fading kind.

The ground was so soft because the land had used to be bog, now largely drained. Yet the draining had lowered the land considerably and brought it much closer to the groundwater, which meant the soil could only take in a little liquid until it became swollen and sodden. Thus, every fall of rain turned the earth to mud and created large puddles. In summer, these functioned as nurseries for insects; until the discovery of Peruvian bark, the locals had been riddled with malaria. In autumn and winter, when the sun was weak and often hidden, the grounds of the estate were pockmarked with large expanses of water that didn't shrink for days, often even weeks. The dark soil colored the water black.

Black water. *Zwart water.*

A fitting name, yes, but an ominous one, too, Lucy had thought that day five years ago. The thought came back to her as soon as the house appeared through the sheets of ceaseless rain, and it lingered as a servant led her upstairs to see her sister. Normally, Sarah would have fetched her from the station with the horse trap, or she'd be waiting for her in the hallway, pacing impatiently, then running for the door as soon as she heard the creak of the carriage outside, laughing with the joy of being reunited with her twin.

No laughter now. The only sound came from Lucy's broken heel and her kid gloves. The leather creaked and strained at the seams every time she opened her hand, then closed it around the banister. The rain had ruined them, as it had ruined the silk of her dress. Despite Michael's assurances, no one had been waiting for her at the station. Rather than wait for the stationmaster to send someone up to the house, she began walking herself, her broken shoe and the rain be damned. Anything was better than waiting. The servant driving the horse trap found her after only fifteen minutes, but by then, her clothes had already been ruined. It was a waste, but she could not find it within herself to care. There would be other gloves, other dresses. She had only one sister.

Arthur was waiting for Lucy outside the sickroom. He was a tall thin man with blond hair the color of honey, though his mustache was much darker. He grew it in the hope it lent him a sense of authority; his face was a boyish one, the cheeks round and red. A kind face, Lucy had often thought, the sort of face you'd be happy to see at your bedside when you felt weak and unwell. It suited him.

They had grown up together, she, Sarah, and Arthur. Their parents had been friends and moved in the same circles. Arthur was almost five years older than Sarah and Lucy but made a good playmate, patient and kind. Because he had three older brothers, he had to make his own way in the world, and he did so by going to university and studying to be a doctor. He joined student societies, and there he met Michael, the only son of a noble family who stood to inherit the large family estate once his father passed. For men like Michael, university was often not a time to learn but a time to drink and whore and gamble before they married and took up their responsibilities as heirs.

Yet Michael was serious in his studies and pursued knowledge doggedly even when his father died and left Zwartwater to him. Though he had never been able to settle on a single subject and therefore became a jack-of-all-trades, master of none, university had drawn him and Arthur together. That, in turn, led Michael to the Goedhart twins. He and Sarah were engaged within three months of their first meeting, then married as soon as Michael finished his studies. He had secured a position as a country doctor for

Arthur, which was unglamorous, the pay poor and the work hard, but it had the advantage of keeping them close together.

It all seems so long ago now and yet no time at all, Lucy thought tiredly. Arthur smiled at her, took hold of her left hand. He did not flinch at the feel of the sodden leather, but he did say, in a soft, concerned voice, not quite the same he used with patients but not very much different either, "You are very wet."

"I shall change once I've seen my sister," she said.

"You might catch a cold. Your lungs…" Again, he did not continue.

Briefly, she closed her eyes. When she opened them again, she gave his fingers, which she still held in her gloved hand, a little squeeze. "I shall change once I've seen my sister," she repeated, not unkindly. "Now tell me: What exactly ails her?"

"A fever of the brain; she has a blinding pain in her head. As a result, she can't keep anything down. You must try not to be frightened when you see her; she's much changed. Ever since last night, she is often unconscious, and when she isn't, she raves, so you mustn't be startled if she says strange things either."

"Is it like last time?" Lucy asked.

Arthur hesitated, then said, "In a way. It shall pass much faster, since her fever is the culprit this time, not her mind fracturing. When the fever breaks, she'll be her old self again."

"What sort of strange things does she say?"

He was quiet for a moment, rubbed his face in that harsh way men can often be seen to do but women never, and said, "She seems convinced there is someone, a woman, who means her harm."

A hot little coal of worry and dread burned in Lucy's breast. The sensation traveled all the way up to her throat, causing her to swallow thickly. The thought of her sister in pain had been agony; knowing she was confused and frightened as well was, quite frankly, unbearable. "What woman?"

Arthur shrugged. "I'm not sure. It doesn't matter. It's not real."

"It's real to her. Please," she said, "let me see my sister."

Together they went into the room, which was not Sarah's own but a guest room rarely in use. The curtains were closed, plunging the room into darkness; the only light came from the fire roaring in the hearth, which made the room hot and stuffy. Immediately, Lucy's clothes began to steam. She could see very little in the dark. But she could smell: her own wet clothes, plus soap and syrupy medicine administered with silver spoons. Underneath those scents was the stench of an unwashed body sweating, and underneath that, the sweet whiff of rot.

As her eyes adjusted, she could make out the solid shapes of the furniture: a silk dressing screen with its painted flowers; a chest of drawers; a little writing desk with dainty legs. Its chair had been moved next to the bed and was currently occupied by a young woman with close-cropped dark curls. She wore a simple dress, as befitted her station as a poor relation to Michael subsisting on his charity. Its color was impossible to guess in the queer half-light. She got up when she saw them and went to Lucy to embrace her. She felt hot to the touch.

"Katje," Lucy murmured.

"It's good you are here," Katje whispered, then smiled. She was a nervous creature, with a twitch around her mouth and a tendency to look one in the eye only in little bursts. Lucy did not care for eye contact either, and so she did not mind.

"How has she been?" Arthur asked.

"A little restless," Katje confessed. "She kept tossing and turning."

"Did she speak?"

"Sometimes, but her words were slurred, and I couldn't make them out. I think she talked in her sleep." As a child, Sarah had often walked in her sleep, and many things besides. The habit came back to her occasionally, often in times of stress.

"Nothing more?" Arthur asked.

Katje shook her head.

They all spoke in hushed voices. *As if we are in the room of one already dead*, Lucy thought, then shuddered violently, painfully. She moved past Katje, to the bed in which her sister lay, and bent over to look at Sarah.

The disease had ravaged her. Before, they had been so alike that no one could tell them apart, and looking into a mirror had made Lucy uneasy because the face staring back at her should have belonged to Sarah but did not. Now there could be no confusion. Whereas Lucy looked reasonably healthy, Sarah was gaunt and sick. She had lost weight so rapidly, her skin hung loosely around her bones, like a piece of cloth inexpertly draped over a frame.

Lying on top of the covers, Sarah's hand was a strange thing, almost translucent yet not threaded through with veins as one might expect when the skin grows thin as onion paper. *Waxen* was the word that popped into Lucy's mind. Sarah's lips, too, were almost white, save for a sore that bloomed red and brown in the right corner of her mouth. Apart from that little wound, only her cheeks retained any color: they were a shocking pink—not the shade of a healthy blush but that of a patch of badly scalded skin.

"Sarah, I'm here," Lucy said, gently taking hold of her hand. Up until Sarah's marriage, which had taken her to Zwartwater and thus far away from Lucy, they'd used to hold hands all the time. With clasped hands they had slithered out of their mother; perhaps that was why nothing had more power to soothe Lucy than Sarah's slim fingers twining with hers. Sarah, always restless, always eager and quick and laughing, had a habit of toying with Lucy's fingers, of moving them this way and that, and stroking her knuckles and the dips in between. When Sarah had married and Lucy had slipped her hand into her sister's, the golden wedding band had felt wrong at first. It was not quite cold but hard and unyielding, biting into the flesh when firmly pressed against.

This hand, so slight and limp, didn't feel like it belonged to her sister at all.

The shock of it was enormous. It drove the breath from Lucy's body, made her throat smart. Stinging tears welled in her eyes. As she bent closer to her sister to press a kiss on her burning forehead, gravity coaxed them from her eyes, and they fell: one to land in Sarah's hair and lie there unbroken, and the other to drip on the bridge of Sarah's nose, where it balanced precariously, then slid down the left side, following the curve of her nostril.

Sarah's eyelids twitched. Slowly, she opened her eyes. They were very large and wet in that dry sunken face.

Like the face of the bog woman in her drawing, Lucy thought, and instantly felt thoroughly chilled.

"Lucy," Sarah murmured, "are you really here?" Her breath was foul, stinking of sickness and hunger and thirst.

"I am," Lucy said, then gave her sister's hand a firm squeeze.

Her sister's mouth stretched to the sides, drawing her lips taut, causing the sore to crack and weep, and revealing her teeth. In childhood, she had lost the one next to her upper-right incisor. It had been replaced by a fake made of porcelain, its shiny white surface incongruous with the other teeth; Sarah's love for tea had slightly discolored her natural ones. In that cadaverous face, her teeth were huge, as were her eyes, now opened very wide in terror. "Leave, at once," she begged, clutching at Lucy's hand with such strength that the little bones ground together.

"But I've only just arrived. I've come to nurse you." Lucy said.

"You can't stay. She's killed before and will kill again if I let her. I've seen it, Lucy. I've lived it. She's hungry. Oh, I've never known a hunger like hers!" she said. Her eyes, fever bright, gleamed wetly.

Fear, primal and deep, froze Lucy to her very marrow. Had Arthur not gently disentangled her hand from her sister's grip and moved her to the side so he could tend to his patient, she might have stood like that forever, still and stiff, her heart lurching sickeningly.

"Like I said, she doesn't know what she's saying," he said softly. Then, with a brighter voice, he coaxed, "Sarah, you aren't well. You must drink this." He brought a glass to her lips.

"No! You're lying to me. You're trying to feed me that disgusting mush again, bread softened in milk. You want me to eat. You know I mustn't," she moaned, twisting her face away.

"It's only water. Feel how cool it is." He held the glass gently against her forehead.

She pressed hard against it and moaned, and the sound was suffused with such deep pleasure, it embarrassed Lucy.

Arthur said, "I know. Now drink up; it'll soothe the fire in your brain."

Eagerly, Sarah clasped his arm to guide the glass to her mouth. And then she bit him.

Chapter 3

IT HAPPENED SO FAST, LUCY did not understand at first.

With a cry, Arthur tried to pull back, dropping the glass and spilling its contents into Sarah's lap. She didn't even seem to notice. All her attention was on preventing Arthur from pulling away. She had a firm hold on his wrist and wouldn't let go. Her mouth stayed fastened on the inside of his lower arm, her lips pulled back, revealing her large teeth sunken into the soft flesh.

"Sarah!" Lucy cried out. She grabbed her sister by the shoulders so she could wrench her from Arthur, yet those bony shoulders and emaciated arms belied her sister's strength. Sarah would not be pulled away. In fact, she didn't seem to care that Lucy was yanking on her, nor did she care that Arthur was trying to pry her fingers from his wrist. She chewed and she drank.

In the end, it was Katje who saved them by upending the jug of water from the bedside table over Sarah's head. Sarah cried out and shied away, her teeth bared. The lines between them were colored pink.

Arthur stumbled back, clutching his wounded arm. He tripped

over a stool, then sat heavily and without dignity. Blood trickled from between his fingers. The smell of it was thick in the air: salt and metal.

Sarah, meanwhile, had recovered from the shock of the cold water. She took up the drenched sheet and sucked at the spot where Arthur's blood had dripped and spoiled it, crouching over it like an animal, shivering with cold or perhaps with pleasure.

Lucy felt as if she might cry. The soft little noises of Sarah's sucking, the quiver in her throat as she swallowed, the harsh glitter of her eyes glimpsed through the mop of her dripping hair—all of it was horrible and wrong.

"I'm so sorry," Katje said. Her mouth was twitching from amusement to horror and back again. She bent over Sarah and tried to wipe her face with a corner of the sheet.

"That's no use. The sheet is soaked. We must get her out of those wet clothes and in front of the fire. Let's pray the shock of such freezing water to her system won't prove fatal," Arthur said, the words clipped, his voice rough. He made to help lift Sarah out of bed, but Lucy blocked his path.

"Let us do it. With your arm like that, you're of no use to anyone," she said, then went to pull the bell rope to summon one of the maids. For a moment, it looked as if Arthur would argue, but when he spoke, it was only to excuse himself.

Together, Katje and Lucy helped Sarah out of bed. They undressed her and put her in a dry shift and nightgown. That done, two maids carried in a divan of purple velvet, so Lucy laid Sarah on it and covered her with blankets. During all this, she was still and quiet. When Katje mixed a draught to make her sleep, she drank without complaint, the corners of her mouth twisting at the bitter medicinal taste.

"I shall stay with her," Lucy said.

Katje shook her head and said, "You need to get out of those wet clothes and get warm. Sarah wouldn't want you to sicken. You can sit with her then, though she'll be fast asleep soon and will want for nothing we can provide."

Lucy thought of arguing, but Katje spoke sense, and she needed a little time alone to think. When she stepped out of the room, into the cold and damp of the hallway, she took a shuddering breath and tried to press what she had seen just now deep inside her, where all the painful things went, large and small: the worm Sarah had torn in two; the woman on the train crushing the spider; Michael, always Michael...

Arthur, meanwhile, had not progressed beyond the hallway either. He leaned heavily against the wall as he tried to bind his handkerchief around his arm. When he could not do it with one hand, he cursed under his breath. His face was ashen, his fingers unsteady. Lucy wondered if he might faint.

"Let me," she said, taking the scrap of fabric from him. The wound was an ugly thing, ragged and horrible, but the flow of blood was slowing, and its place on the middle of his lower arm meant it would not impede his movements. Yet to know it was Sarah who had made it...

Better not to think of that and focus at the task at hand. She folded his handkerchief and pressed it against the injury, causing him to hiss in pain. "I'm sorry," she said.

"Don't be. You aren't responsible for Sarah. At the moment, I

fear Sarah isn't even responsible for Sarah. Mark my words: if this
fever breaks, it might well be she won't even remember what she did."

"It's much worse than I expected," Lucy admitted. She took out
her own handkerchief and wound it around his arm before securing
his handkerchief in place.

"Then I must apologize. I should have done a better job preparing you."

"Nothing could have prepared me for this. There. All done."

She did not linger, for she did not wish to hear him chastise
himself, nor did she wish to talk any more of what had just happened. People sometimes thought her cold and reserved, arrogant,
even, but in truth, she was merely quiet and pensive. As a child, she
had been painfully shy with everyone except her aunt and sister.
She'd had something of a stammer, which had made her loath
to speak. This speech impediment as well as her tongue-tiedness
had since been overcome, but old habits die hard, so she remained
largely quiet.

Despite Michael's assurance that she need not write ahead,
they would be ready to receive her at all times, her usual room had
not been prepared. Most likely Michael had simply forgotten to
tell the servants, or if he had, he had not known what orders to give;
running the household was Sarah's domain, and he did not like to
interfere with it.

However it had happened, the room had not been aired, and
the fire in the grate had only just been lit, giving it no time to dispel
the cold and damp. But her things had been brought up, and it was a
place where she could be alone and unwitnessed, so she did not mind.

Her room was known as the Silver Room, so called for the wallpaper, which was patterned with silver waves, and the wood of the fruit trees that had been used for the fireplace and wainscoting, which glowed a lovely silver if the light hit the material in a certain way.

How well this name suits it in such dreary weather, Lucy thought. The scant autumn light was blunted and cooled by clouds so dark, they seemed bruised. It silvered the windows, which were awash with rain, and made running patterns on the wall. It was like sitting in a sea cave.

She peeled off her gloves, now merely damp rather than sodden, then took off her hat and began to pull out the pins that kept her hair up. Tendrils of it, damp and twisted like rope, slithered down her neck and shoulders. When it was all down, she combed it with a silver-backed brush that belonged to her sister. In this queer light, her hair seemed as silver as the brush, though in reality it was merely an ashy blond.

I could be a mermaid or sea witch, combing my hair and counting the souls of the drownèd damned, she thought as she looked at her face in the mirror, which was speckled black because the abundance of water that had given the estate its name meant the house was often intolerably damp, and dampness spoiled things, wore them out.

She braided her hair. She'd have to put it up for dinner but was suddenly so exhausted, she couldn't be bothered. Besides, she didn't even know if dinner would be served the proper way. They might send her a tray and have her eat in this room, which she generally enjoyed; that way no one could see how much or how little she ate except for the servants. Yes, why go through the trouble of serving dinner when there was only Michael to enjoy it, now that Sarah was too ill to leave her bed? Only, he wouldn't be alone, not tonight, though if the room was any indication, no one would have taken her into account when preparing dinner.

She should just ask Michael and make sure. But he was not here, else he would have welcomed her. He was probably outside, the streaming rain be damned, walking so fast that his legs burned, trying to outrun his fear and worries, the way he had done when his little daughter had lain choking and crying as she died of scarlet fever.

Lucy sank onto the nearest chair and sat pinching the bridge of her nose in an effort to stem the tears. The images and half-formed thoughts she had been so careful to push down now rose to the surface, forcing her to witness them.

Lucy had been prepared to see her sister sick and suffering, and she had been prepared to withstand and ignore all the little indignities that came with it: the smells, the fluids, the helplessness. But she had not thought the illness would reduce her sister to a kind of demented beast, biting their lifelong friend and lapping up the blood like a dog. She kept hearing the soft sucking sounds Sarah had made as she had gnawed on Arthur's arm and when she had taken the blood-splattered cloth into her mouth.

How was it possible that Sarah had gone from a healthy young woman to this emaciated, rabid creature in less than two weeks? For she had been healthy then, excited and productive. It almost beggared belief that a mere fever of the brain could wreak such changes. Yet some diseases ravaged the way fire did, swiftly and without mercy. They had seen that with Lucille, hadn't they?

Lucy could ask *why* all she wanted, but that way lay no satisfaction, only madness.

After a while, she pulled herself together enough to take up a buttonhook and set about unbuttoning her boots. When this was done, she rolled down her left stocking, revealing skin whitened with cold, the toes tinged blue. She took her foot in hand and squeezed and rubbed it to get the blood flowing again, wincing and gasping at the pain. Yet she welcomed the throbbing and burning because it let her mind focus on something other than the display she had just witnessed.

The knock on the door came when she sat massaging her other foot to life, tears blinding her.

"Who is it?" Lucy asked.

"It's Katje. May I come in?"

"Yes."

She slipped inside, closed the door behind her, then leaned against it. She had a mark on her cheek.

Arthur's blood, Lucy thought, feeling as if she might heave.

"I thought you might need help undressing," Katje said. She tried to look Lucy in the eye, then let her gaze wander, as she usually did.

"That's thoughtful of you, but I could ring for one of the maids." Lucy did not know the exact relationship between Katje and Michael, bar that she was some sort of poor relation who depended on his charity. Such women were supposed to be loyal companions, help rear the children, nurse the sick—in short, to make themselves useful in any way. But they were members of the family still, not servants, and so, in much the same way Lucy was not expected to help Mrs. van Dijk with her hair and clothes because she was a companion and not a maid, Katje could not be expected to help Lucy now.

"It's no trouble. I do it for Sarah all the time. She likes it better when I undress her than Magda. She can be rough and impatient, you see." And Katje smiled, temporarily stilling the spasming around her mouth. She came to Lucy and began to unfasten the hooks and buttons of her dress. Katje had rather beautiful hands, long and thin, the wrists delicate, the sort of hands an artist might wish to make a plaster cast of so he could model his sculptures and paintings on them. As she worked, she hummed a little song in a high-pitched voice, then giggled nervously at nothing at all.

She really is a nervy creature, quite strange, Lucy thought.

It's because she was brutalized as a child, Sarah had told her once. *I don't know the details of it, nor do I wish to, though I can imagine. Suffice to say she suffered abominably. When Michael's mother heard of it, she did the proper thing and took the girl in.*

Such suffering was bound to leave a mark. It was really quite extraordinary, Lucy thought as Katje undid the buttons at her cuffs, that the girl was merely odd and overly anxious, but still capable of love and kindness and decency; in her place, Lucy feared she might have become emotionally damaged to the point of numbness or perhaps even cruelty, the way her mother had after Aunt Adelheid had died. *The way I will if Sarah… But that shan't happen, and as long as I have her, I can survive and withstand anything.*

They did not speak as Lucy undressed, and the air grew heavy between them with what they had witnessed but did not speak of. As Katje laced her into her corset, Lucy broke the pregnant silence between them, asking, "Have you seen the bog body? The one they found two weeks ago?"

But that is not what I wanted to ask at all, she marveled as soon as the words had left her mouth.

Katje's hands stilled. She was quiet for so long that Lucy had already given up on the idea that she'd speak, and then she did. "You mustn't speak of that to Sarah, you know," she said.

"Why is that?"

"It upsets her." Katje inhaled slowly, carefully; Lucy felt her breath stir the little white hairs on the nape of her neck.

"But why?" Lucy pressed.

"Did Doctor Hoefnagel tell you that she's scared of someone?" Katje asked, and her breath ruffled those little hairs at her nape in the opposite direction.

"Yes. He said he didn't know who she could be, though."

Katje giggled nervously. "Did he? And him so learned, I thought it would be obvious. Poor Sarah is terrified of the bog woman."

"Oh," Lucy said. A pain rose in her stomach, insistent as nausea, sharp as a pang of hunger. "That makes sense, I suppose." It truly did. Sarah's letters had grown bizarre and disturbing—perverse, even—only after the bog body had been found.

"There. All laced up," Katje said. She picked up the dress of green velvet Lucy had chosen, helped it over her head.

"But have you? Seen the body, I mean?" Lucy repeated.

"No." Katje did not look at her but bent her pale face over Lucy's arm to do up the buttons of her sleeve. Her fingers trembled against the inside of Lucy's wrist. She seemed on the cusp of saying something more when the front door slammed shut with such force, the water in the pitcher on Lucy's bedside table rippled.

A man roared, not unkindly, "Will someone take this bloody dog from me?"

Then Michael has come home at last, she thought, briefly closing her eyes.

Zwartwater, 21 September, 1887

Darling Lucy,

Today, Arthur and an old schoolmate of his, a specialist in decomposition named Doctor Rosenthaler, conducted the autopsy. I helped them, not by sketching, but by taking down everything they said and did.

I wish I hadn't. I'm uneasy in mind, both troubled and frightened, and it's all because of that blasted bog body! We should have put it back in the ground, as Mr. Hooiman suggested.

Too late now, though.

The beginning of the autopsy was unremarkable. It was mainly a rehashing of things you and I already know: When was the body found? Who found it? When did they find it, and how? What did it look like? As I made my notes, Doctor Rosenthaler kept exclaiming what a wonder the body was, what a miracle its preservation. His delight was really quite endearing.

"*How old do you think she is?*" *I asked, but he shook his head and said he could not yet say. He was rather disappointed that we had found nothing in the surrounding peat; most bog bodies have at least some clothes buried with or near them, and those would help pin down when she had been murdered.*

"*But the lack of clothes is interesting in and of itself,*" *he rallied. "It makes it likely she was sacrificed, or else sentenced to die. The poor souls who wander into the bogs and drown by accident tend to be dressed. Of course, the stakes driven through her joints also point in that direction.*"

He suggested those stakes were to keep the body submerged. He made a joke about pickles, then grew serious again and said that the staking may have been used as a form of torture if the poor wretch was still alive when they were driven in.

The doctors were less certain as to the significance of the stone in her mouth. Doctor Rosenthaler thought it might have been used to gag the woman, though he had to concede it was a strange way to keep someone from crying out, dangerous and cruel. Arthur suggested it was a form of punishment. The lack of incisors, they ignored almost completely.

All the time, I had to keep myself from laughing at their silliness. It seemed to me perfectly clear why her murderers had crammed a rock in her mouth. "It's to keep her from eating," I said at last, when I could stand their discussion no more.

They both gave me such a funny look, you'd think I'd have said something utterly strange!

I elaborated: "The staking, the forceful thrusting of the

stone between her teeth, the pulling of her incisors, burying her face down, all of it was done to confuse her and keep her tied to the earth and render her unable to use her mouth in case she came back."

"Came back?" Arthur asked, still not understanding.

I explained to them patiently that the little research I had done before the autopsy suggested this was the sort of thing people used to do to the corpses of suicides and others who were deemed in danger of becoming revenants, or who were thought to have become revenants already. To be fair, that sort of thing hasn't happened in our country for almost three hundred years, but travel stories are rife with it.

"Where would we be without your help?" Arthur laughed when I was done.

Finally, he and Doctor Rosenthaler began to touch the body. No part of her was to be left untouched. They looked at her fingers first, scratched under her nails to see if there was anything but peat crusted under there. They combed her hair for the same reason, doing it very carefully so as not to rip it from the scalp. Her loins were inspected very carefully to try and determine her sex, but neither of them wanted to commit. I joked that they were being bad sports, seeing as they had a fifty percent chance to be right, and weren't those good odds? But they refused to be drawn.

"We'll know once we've had a look at the organs," Doctor Rosenthaler said and picked up a knife, and I thought privately that he was no fun at all; I can't stand men without humor.

"Won't you need a saw to cut through her bones?" I asked as he set about making incisions in her chest.

"The body from Schleswig-Holstein didn't have any bones left. The bog consumes them," Arthur told me.

"Is that why her head is so dented? Because there's no skull to help it keep its shape?" I asked.

"Perhaps, though a fierce blow to the head could have caused it to become misshapen, too. The weight of the peat may have crushed it further." He made a quick sketch of the different parts of the skull for me and explained how they are separate when we are born, to allow the head to be squeezed through the birth canal, and only fuse together and harden with time. Dear Arthur! He so loves to explain. He would have made a fine schoolteacher. His boyish enthusiasm is infectious.

Yet, throughout his talk, I was very conscious of the sounds Doctor Rosenthaler made as he hacked away at the bog woman, the squelching and the scraping, opening her up so he could plunge his hand inside and draw her secrets from her, and I felt a strange sensation running along my sternum. It wasn't quite a pain, but it was unpleasant, the way you can experience a phantom pain when you see someone suffering horribly. She won't like this at all, I thought suddenly. I had to admonish myself then for being fanciful. Really, you'd think I'd never seen a creature being dissected before! Of course, those were only mice and dogs and, once, a calf, but mammals all look remarkably similar once you've opened them up; it's only their size and the number of nipples that differ.

Meanwhile, Doctor Rosenthaler was prying open the bog woman's chest, draping fronds of hide-like flesh over her upper arms. This accomplished, he held up a lamp and stood peering into the cavity, doing nothing. He had a mighty frown that seemed to be carved into his forehead. "Arthur," he said after a while in a small voice, "I think you should take a look."

Inside, the bog body was completely empty.

"Perhaps the bog ate her organs, just as it ate her bones," Arthur proposed, but Doctor Rosenthaler shook his head. Other bog bodies did not look like this one. Arthur said that perhaps the murderers had removed the organs before throwing the body into the bog, but she had no mark on her bar the one Doctor Rosenthaler had made.

"There must be a rational explanation," I said. "The Egyptians used to draw the brain out through the nose. They'd thrust a hook into the cavity of the skull through the nostrils, and move it about until the brain was all cut up and could dribble out."

"And which hole do you suggest they used to extract several meters of intestine, two kidneys, a liver, two lungs, and a heart, Mrs. Schatteleyn? Through the mouth? Or through the anus?" Doctor Rosenthaler asked me curtly.

Had I been less uneasy, I would have told him spitefully he had forgotten to mention the bladder, esophagus, womb, and ovaries, and that women have an extra hole in which a hook can be inserted very well, as most men can attest to, but a lady *can't say such a thing unless she wants to be thought crude and unwomanly, or worse, mad.*

"Sarah is right. There must be an explanation that we are currently not seeing," Arthur said soothingly.

They went on with their work, much quieter now. They took some measurements, then closed her back up. It all happened rather quickly, since there was not much else to do and not much to look at.

Then there was only the head left.

With a hammer and chisel, Doctor Rosenthaler carefully broke the rock inside her mouth and extracted it piece by piece, dropping them on some cloth so he could glue it back together later. His hands were not quite steady. Afterward, her poor lips were covered with dust, which Arthur wiped away carefully with a bit of damp cotton wool.

He looked into her mouth and said, "She lacks a tongue. Do you think it was torn out?"

Doctor Rosenthaler replied, "There's no sign of a wound. I bet the same mysterious process that consumed the organs could make short work of a tongue, which is, after all, no more than a strong muscle."

"But then why not the rest of the body, too? She doesn't lack muscles, just organs."

"My dear man, if I knew, I'd tell you, but I'm as much in the dark as you are," Doctor Rosenthaler said. Despite the coolness of the cellar, he had sweat beading on his forehead and glistening in his sideburns.

They took measurements of her head, then prodded the dents with the back of their tools. Arthur repeated his earlier remarks about the possibility of the head being staved in, which might well be the cause of death. That, or the stake driven through her neck.

Nothing left to do but look inside her head, then.

Doctor Rosenthaler opened up the top. A smell filled the room, so strong that even Arthur and Doctor Rosenthaler gagged, and throughout their careers, their noses have been abused by all manner of filth. I had to press my sleeve to my mouth. My eyes watered. It was unlike anything I'd ever smelled before, and I struggle to describe it. It came right through the fabric of my sleeve, burned inside my nose and throat and mouth, almost like a physical thing.

In the end, we bound cloths soaked in lavender water over the lower halves of our faces. That scent was also overpowering and cloying, but we were able to bear it better than the stench coming from the bog woman's head.

As Arthur carefully folded away the part of the scalp covered with hair, something fell out. He managed to catch it in one hand, then made a soft noise at the back of his throat.

"What is it?" Doctor Rosenthaler asked.

"The brain, I think."

"What do you mean, you think?"

"It doesn't much look like any of the other brains I've seen. It's much too small. It feels strange, too."

I'm no doctor, as well you know, Lucy dearest, but it's

impossible not to have picked up a thing or two when living close to Arthur, and I can assure you that the thing Arthur held so gingerly in his hand did, indeed, not look much like a brain. It fit easily in Arthur's palm and was the same color as a walnut. It was wrinkled like one, too, but threaded through with something that looked like grayish fleshy roots.

"A kind of mold, perhaps?" Doctor Rosenthaler suggested.

"Does mold survive years and years of being submerged in the bog?"

"Perhaps it only started growing after the body was exhumed. Some types of fungi can grow very rapidly."

"If it's even fungi," I said. I didn't think the doctor's explanation was very satisfying, and neither did he, but none of us knew enough about mycology to dispute it.

Arthur shoved her brain—or what was left of it, at any rate—back into her head, his face contorted by disgust, then set about sewing her up. Afterward, he scoured his hands with hot water and carbolic soap.

The bog woman currently remains in the cellar until we decide what to do with her.

What am I to make of all this, sister mine? Is this as unsettling to you as it is to me? Because the bog woman's death and burial, her lack of organs and tongue, her altered brain are unsettling, aren't they? Or is my mind making morbid what in truth is merely strange? There haven't been many bodies like this, so who is to say there is even anything unusual going on?

I am trying to calm myself, as you can probably tell. ~~It's not an easy thing, having a mind that can't always be trusted. I've found myself thinking of Aunt Adelheid a lot these past few days, and I am terrified, more than I can possibly say, that we might share the same fate.~~ Write to me quickly, darling, and help assuage my fears and worries. Better yet: come and visit me soon, that I may hold your hand in mine, rest my cheek against yours, and be comforted by you.

With all my love, always,
Sarah

Chapter 4

FROM WHERE LUCY STOOD IN the upstairs hallway, she couldn't see Michael's face, though she could see his boots were caked with dull mud. Water streamed from his coat, leaving cloudy puddles. He had his hat and a silver-topped walking stick in one hand. With the other, he held a piece of dirty rope whose end was looped around the neck of a shivering Italian greyhound: Pasja. The skin covering her haunches rippled as if trying to dislodge a fly. Her fur, normally a soft gray, was smeared with mud and stained green in places from grass.

"She caught the scent of a hare. I had a devil of a job to catch her after that, and when I finally did, the leash snapped, and I had to do it all over again. In the end, I hauled her halfway home by the scruff of her neck, until I met Mr. van Eyck, who was so kind as to fetch me some rope," he explained to the servant who took the hat and cane from him.

A different servant began to wipe Pasja down with great sheets of newspaper. The dog whined softly.

"Tough luck, girl," Michael told her coldly as he unbuttoned his coat. "That should teach you not to run off and make me look like a fool." But once he had struggled out of his sopping coat, he stooped next to her and scratched her between the ears. His hands were similar to Katje's: long, beautiful. When he made to stand, he looked up and caught Lucy's eye.

"Lucy," he said softly.

His face was a curious one, not at all handsome, yet interesting. With the skin so white as to almost seem bloodless and the wide-spaced black eyes, it had something of the shark about it. The effect was heightened whenever Michael opened his mouth; he had two extra teeth in his bottom jaw that had grown behind the row of regular teeth. When they'd been newly married, Sarah had once mentioned offhandedly in a letter that she had asked Michael to have them extracted, for they were pointed and sharp and he often cut his tongue on them, but he wouldn't hear of having two good teeth pulled, so Sarah had carefully filed them for him. The implications—that Sarah may have cut her own tongue on them as she and her husband kissed, and that his kisses must often have had a tang of blood to them—had not been lost on Lucy. She had closed her eyes and run her tongue over her own teeth, and in doing so, she had thought that, if she had been married to Michael, she wouldn't have minded.

She might, in fact, have enjoyed it.

Lucy came down the stairs and let him kiss the back of her hand. His lips, rain chilled, did not merely look bloodless but felt bloodless, too. His lips parted, and she felt the press of his teeth. Gooseflesh rippled all over her body. She withdrew her hand hastily, then cupped it with the other one. The skin he had kissed tingled. She dug a nail into it, but that only drew more attention to the spot. *You damned little traitor*, she told herself silently.

"Had I known you'd be here already, I would have come home sooner," he said.

"But you couldn't because Pasja was hunting," she said. At the mentioning of her name, the dog came over to Lucy and sniffed the hem of her dress and her proffered hand.

"She's been quite out of sorts lately," Michael said.

Haven't we all? Lucy thought but did not say, for there were servants still with them, so she could not speak freely. It was the same during dinner. She wished she had simply asked to have a tray in her room instead, as Katje had done; small talk did not come easily to her, especially not now, especially not with him. It would have been easier if Arthur had been there, but he had other patients to attend to.

It was not until they had tea in the library that they were alone at last. By then, she felt both high-strung and exhausted.

"How's Mrs. van Dijk?" Michael asked. "Very peeved to find herself without her companion, I'm sure? I heard she can be rather possessive."

"She doesn't like it when people speak ill of her."

Pasja lay in front of the roaring hearth, basking in the heat. When Lucy spoke, she thumped her tail against the carpet in lazy arcs.

"She'd be mighty strange if she did, though I meant nothing with my remark," Michael responded.

She poured some milk into her cup. It spread through the dark tea like a cloud. The porcelain seared her skin. The sensation was not quite pleasant, but it soothed her. "You really mustn't. She has been good to me."

After her parents had died, both of them without warning and within two weeks of each other, it had become apparent that there was very little left of the family wealth. This did not matter much for Sarah, who was already safely married, but it had meant the end of life as Lucy had known it. Becoming an old woman's companion was far from the future Lucy had imagined when growing up, but it was respectable and meant she didn't have to rely on her sister and brother-in-law for money.

Michael slung one long leg over the other. "Let's not talk about old Mrs. van Dijk. I know you well, and you've been burning to ask me some questions."

Lucy wasted no time. "Why was I not called for sooner?" she asked.

Michael spooned some sugar into his tea and stirred it vigorously, the spoon grating against the delicate rim. "Because none of us realized how ill she was. After the autopsy, she locked herself away in her room with her books and her papers, took her meals there. You know what your sister is like when something piques her interest."

"And there were no signs?"

"No." He frowned. "Well, Magda did tell me she wasn't eating well and had asked for laudanum because she had a headache, but you know what maids are like: prone to hysterics and exaggeration."

Magda had never struck Lucy as prone to hysterics and

exaggeration. She did not tell Michael this but resolved to talk to Sarah's lady's maid soon.

"Besides," Michael went on, "you know as well as I do that Sarah often forgets to eat when she's working on a project. As for the headaches, she had suffered from those before, especially when reading a great deal. Arthur suggested she try wearing spectacles." He chuckled darkly. "Spectacles! For an inflammation of the brain! So you see, dear Lucy, that none of us understood the true extent of her illness."

I should have known from her letters, Lucy thought. Guilt churned in her stomach. "When did you know something was wrong with her?"

"Some three days ago, when she began to talk incoherently." He leaned closer to her, his voice pleading. "I assure you, Lucy, that I did everything I could, but when she began to deteriorate, she did so very quickly. I wrote to you as soon as I realized how serious the situation was."

She resisted the urge to rub her eyes; she felt dog-tired all of a sudden. "I know you did. I'm just trying to understand how all this could have happened. For her to become so desperately unwell in so short a time…it has rattled me."

"Of course it has."

"Have you engaged a nurse?"

"No."

"Katje can't take care of Sarah all alone."

He took a sip of hot tea. His Adam's apple moved beautifully up and down his throat. "That's why I wrote to you."

"I'm not trained."

"Yet you did very well last time she suffered from a temporary bout of insanity."

A memory clawed its way up from the hurtful place: Sarah dressed in a dirty shift, her nails split and weeping, murmuring things that weren't quite words, crooning over a stinking bundle in her arms…

Lucy's throat contracted almost convulsively. For a moment, she could not speak. When she did, her voice was queer, slightly strangled. "Grief can make us do the most peculiar things."

He laughed without mirth. "You know very well it wasn't just grief. Plenty of women lose children, but they don't do what Sarah did."

But I wasn't talking about her, she thought.

"It was sick, and unnatural, and perverse. I had to go to great lengths to hush it all up. If it had come out, I would have had no choice but to have her committed, your irrational fear of the asylum be damned."

She wanted to say that no, it wasn't irrational, he knew what had happened to her aunt Adelheid, but she knew better than to interrupt him. It was one of the things he absolutely could not stand.

"If you hadn't been there," he continued, "I think I might have lost my mind."

"Don't," she whispered.

He frowned, gulped down the rest of his tea, poured another cup. "Well, you can understand why I'm loath to hire a nurse. One can never know if they are truly discreet. With you, I need not fret."

No. I've proven I can keep a secret, haven't I? She put her cup down and bent over the dog to fondle her so she need not look at him. "Poor Pasja. You must miss your mistress."

"She's been quite out of sorts lately," Michael said, "slavering and shivering and barking at nothing."

Lucy squeezed a silky ear softly between her fingers. The dog closed her eyes in ecstasy. "She seems fine now."

"It's because you're giving her attention. Everything is heaps better if you're being stroked. You're a bit of a slut, aren't you, Pasja?" he said, then gave the dog a playful shove with his foot. She looked at him with mournful wet eyes.

"Maybe she'd feel better if she were allowed to stay with Sarah."

"Oh, not at all," he said, and she looked up at him, at his strange, dear face, which looked stranger still with the light of the fire dancing upon it, carving black shadows on his cheeks.

"What do you mean?"

"She currently can't stand being anywhere near Sarah. She barks her head off, shows the whites of her eyes, pulls up her lip. If I didn't know any better, I'd think the madness was catching."

Pasja placed her head on Lucy's knee, whined softly. Lucy hadn't realized she'd stopped stroking her. "But you know better?" she asked.

"It's the smell of the bog body. For some reason, it makes the dog fly into a frenzy. You should've seen her after the autopsy: she was so frightened, she could've just about torn Arthur's throat out when he bent over to try and pet her. To be fair, he did smell awful. They all did. Such a charnel-house stench. I wouldn't be surprised if it still clings to Sarah in some way. You know she attended the autopsy, don't you?"

Lucy nodded. "She wrote to me about it and about how the body was found." She hesitated, then said, "In truth, I found her letters somewhat troubling. She found the body so very...interesting."

"Interesting? She has been obsessed with it from the moment we found it. She was adamant she assist in the autopsy Arthur performed." Michael took a sip of his tea, made a face, put the cup down roughly. Tea slopped into the saucer. He didn't see, or didn't care, because he leaned back in his chair and went on. "I shouldn't have allowed it. I can see that now. It's not natural, this fascination with something so broken and ugly. Aren't women supposed to have a natural inclination toward the beautiful and the healthy, like plump babies and silky dogs and men with good teeth?"

Lucy smiled. Michael's ideas about what was womanly and what was manly were always so rigid, some of them so oddly specific, it was hard not to be amused by them. Had he been in a kinder mood, she might have teased him. Instead, she said gently, "Aren't men supposed to have that inclination, too?"

Michael scowled and made a jerky sweeping motion with his hand, as if to brush her words away. "A hankering for the macabre certainly is unnatural in either sex, I give you that, but more so in a woman than a man. That's why I wouldn't be surprised if that damned leathery corpse is at the root of Sarah's current madness. An unnatural act may very well lead to unnatural thoughts."

"Katje thinks the woman Sarah is so terrified of might be the bog woman."

Michael steepled his fingers under his chin as he considered this. The flames of the fire were reflected in his eyes, little writhing flickers of yellow. "She might be right. The body certainly obsessed her in the days before she fell ill and thus would make a logical subject for her mind to fix upon now that it is diseased. Then again, trying to find logic in the ramblings of a lunatic is, in itself, a kind of madness."

"Sarah is no lunatic," Lucy said sharply.

"Forgive me. I meant only someone whose mind is disordered."

"*Temporarily* disordered."

Michael sighed heavily. "That's what we hope, isn't it?"

Lucy let Pasja's ear run between her fingers to calm herself. There was something almost sinfully pleasurable in caressing the dog's ears, which were soft and furred on the one side, hot and naked and beautifully veined on the other. "Where is the body now?"

"Gone."

"Gone how?"

"It did not keep."

"I thought Arthur would smoke it like a ham after the autopsy?"

"Decomposition got to it first."

"But surely something remained?"

"Only some dried strips of skin I wouldn't even give to my dogs. Arthur sent them to his old university. I doubt they will have any use for them, but one never knows. Why, you look rather disappointed. Had you hoped to see the body for yourself?"

She remembered Sarah's drawing: the twisted face with its

mouth opened farther than a human mouth should be able to open, the tendons of the cheeks and jaw stretched taut. It had no eyes, just two holes Sarah had colored in with ink, making them appear endlessly deep. It was the face of a dead thing, but in that drawing, it had not looked dead. Instead, it had seemed possessed of a sinister sort of intelligence.

What could she have done in life to deserve such a death?

Lucy suppressed a shudder. "No," she said. "No, I don't think I would." She finished her tea in silence, then excused herself and went upstairs to the sickroom.

Chapter 5

LUCY FOUND SARAH FAST ASLEEP. Katje had placed a damp cloth on Sarah's forehead, from which water had trickled, plastering the little wisps of hair that grew at her temple to her skin. The hollow of her throat was wet with sweat.

"How is she?" Lucy whispered.

"She's been asleep, mostly. She woke some two hours ago. I gave her some water. She won't hold anything else down."

"I shall sit with her," Lucy suggested.

Katje shook her head and said, "I've given her another sleeping draught. Doctor Hoefnagel said the most important thing right now is to try and get the fever to break, and for that, she needs to sleep as much as possible. She won't wake for hours yet. Better you get some sleep, too. You must be exhausted."

Lucy took Katje's hands in hers and squeezed them. "What about you, though? You probably haven't slept in days."

"You mustn't worry about me. I don't need much sleep; I never have."

"Then I envy you. All the same, starting tomorrow morning, I'll nurse my sister."

Lucy kissed Katje on the cheek and bade her good night. Yet despite Lucy's fondness for sleep and the long day she'd had, her mind was restless, and she knew she would not be able to sleep if she went to bed now. Better to stay up and tire herself out a little more, try and ensure a dreamless sleep.

Because the servants hadn't prepared the room properly, there was no paper at the writing desk. Rather than ring for a maid to fetch her some, Lucy went to Sarah's room; her sister always had some sheets of paper at the ready.

The room was cold and smelled slightly of damp and dust. Funny how a mere week of disuse could do that. Sarah's beloved things were all there: her crystal bottles of scent at the vanity, her boxes of jewels, the little writing desk with its carved legs. A ream of creamy paper with the Zwartwater letterhead lay on top, as Lucy had expected. Next to the stack of paper rested a lovely pen made of silver, which had Sarah's name engraved on the cap. Lucy had its twin. They had been presents from Michael for their twenty-first birthday, though Sarah's had been accompanied by an emerald ring; Lucy's had come with a notebook bound in calf's leather with beautiful marbled paper at the beginning and end instead.

Apart from the pen and paper, the surface of the writing desk was covered with pamphlets, torn envelopes, books, and journals. Sarah's interests were broad, and her desk reflected that: Fashion plates were used as bookmarks in a medical handbook. A piece of paper, rather dirty, with a labeled drawing of a human tooth on it had been crammed into a torn envelope on which Sarah had begun and abandoned an equation. A newspaper clipping about the discovery of a new kind of bat in Mexico lay crumpled and smudged on top of a treatise on ticks. This last one must have been of particular interest to Sarah; the text was heavily underlined, the margins full of scribbles.

Lucy let her hands glide over it all with fondness, marveling at her sister's mind. From a young age, it had been clear Sarah possessed a fierce intelligence. Sums held no difficulty for her, and she could memorize any text she had read and reproduce it after having read it through only a few times, often months later and with startling accuracy.

Her hunger for knowledge had been ferocious, especially regarding the natural world. Lucy had loved holding her sister's hand and listening to her talk about moths, or orchids, or stickle-backs, or whatever creature or plant obsessed her that week. Sarah maintained to this day that the best gift she had ever received was an ant farm Aunt Adelheid had made for her for Saint Nicholas Day. Aunt Adelheid loved moths most of all insects, but she was also a knowledgeable amateur myrmecologist. When she'd discovered one of the maids had a talent for drawing, she'd let her assist her in her studies. One of the most vivid memories Lucy had of her aunt was of her sitting at the table with the maid, their heads so close together as to almost touch as they pored over a drawing of an Indian meal moth, smiling and whispering at each other.

They did say madness and genius were sides of the same coin. It was just a bitter, hurtful shame that some greater power kept tossing Sarah's coin, as it had done with Aunt Adelheid's. All Lucy could do now was hope it would be thrown again—and this time definitively land on the side of genius.

Lucy tore her eyes away from the cluttered desk to the silver-framed picture that kept watch over it all. She had expected to meet the level gazes of her parents but found instead the dead stare of her niece.

With her black curls and large blue eyes, Lucille had been rather pretty in a doll-like way. A funny little girl who loved to laugh. Once she had learned how to talk, she'd rarely stopped. Lucy remembered all the times she had held Lucille on her lap, rocking her a little, holding her hot little hands in her own, and listening to her emphatic babbling.

The picture had been taken after Lucille had passed away from scarlet fever. The photographer dressed her in white. Then he propped her up on the sofa and surrounded her with flowers before placing a rose in her hand. He painted eyes on her closed lids; her own eyes had gone cloudy already. Others exclaimed how beautiful she looked, like a little angel. Why, one could not tell she was dead at all! Sarah laughed and said it was the only picture they had that wasn't blurred, because her darling little daughter had been such a lively thing and could never sit still, and wasn't it funny that her sweet child looked most alive when she was dead?

Lucy often wondered if these comments about Lucille had triggered Sarah's madness, the seeds of which she had always carried with her, as Lucy probably did, too. She had heard their father say as much during the only fight between her parents she had ever heard, just moments after Aunt Adelheid had been taken away to the asylum.

Perhaps Lucy was to blame for those seeds of sickness germinating in her sister. Every gardener knew plants would only grow in the right conditions. As others had gushed over Lucille's picture, Lucy should have spoken out, told them that it didn't please her, but she had not wanted to add to her sister's pain. How could she insult the memory of Sarah's daughter by saying the last photograph that had ever been taken of her was, to Lucy, deeply unsettling? Her niece, looking not quite alive, but not quite dead either.

Little Lucille in limbo.

Lucy turned away, wishing she hadn't seen it. More than a year had passed since Lucille had died. Had the picture begun to comfort rather than hurt? She did not know, had not known the photograph was here either, and that unsettled her. She and her sister did not keep things from each other as a rule.

She pushed it all away and counted out sheets of writing paper. That done, she hesitated, then took the little book on ticks with her. Its spine had been broken rather roughly, and after having lain forcefully open for days, it closed with reluctance. It was not the sort of thing she usually read, but it would be better suited to lull her to sleep than the gothic tales she had brought with her.

Back in her room, she penned a quick letter to Mrs. van Dijk to let her employer know she had arrived safely. About Sarah she said very little, only that she was indeed seriously ill. The letter would go out with the morning post and reach Mrs. van Dijk before the day was out. Lucy then wrote in her diary. Like Sarah, she had kept one since the age of ten.

Finally, she crawled into bed with the book on ticks. It had a thin red ribbon sewn into it to use as a bookmark. Lucy took the end of it into her mouth and sucked on it as she read, which her mother had always told her was a disgusting habit fit only for a hussy, because the sucking leeched out the dye and painted her lips red. She did not suck on ribbons for their color, though; she simply liked the sensation of the thin wet silk on her tongue and against her lips.

The first thing Lucy noticed about the book were the margins. They were filled with Sarah's beautiful handwriting: references to other pages and different texts, observations, questions she had. As Lucy got further into the book, the handwriting deteriorated. It became ever more slanted, the letters running into one another to the point of near illegibility. Lucy read what was scrawled on an empty page between two chapters:

Ticks are a benign sort of parasite becausetheyonly take a little
blood butotherparasites take more fromtheir   host
likethis fungus this PARASITE auntadelheid told me about
before they took her away

        liketheymighttakeMEaway

                it attacks ants and it takes over the
            the the   whats the word
    whycantithinkofthe right

                    word

A sickness settled in Lucy's stomach. "Don't worry, Saartje. I won't ever let them take you away," she whispered. She curled her hands into fists, letting her nails dig into her palms. Her poor sister had been terrified these past few days, and Lucy had not been there to comfort her.

Lucy read on. The notes on the next few pages were badly smudged, as if Sarah had tried to scrub away the words. Halfway through, she had stopped annotating altogether. The final note, made next to a paragraph about the amount of time different species of ticks could go without blood, had been made with such vehemence, the thin paper had torn. Lucy had to squint at it, then bring it close to her face to make out what it said.

like the BOG WOMAN

Lucy flung the book away and sat with her heart drumming in her chest, her hands growing clammy. "She's sick. A temporary madness caused by a fever of the brain. She wrote that when she was already ill. There's nothing sinister about the bog woman," she told herself out loud.

But Sarah thought that thing was thirsty, some part of her said, *and then it made her cut her hand on its teeth and wet its mouth with blood.*

This was such a morbid thought that she almost laughed. Instead, she did her best to push it all far out of her mind. The last thing this situation needed was hysteria and superstition. Those were probably the exact things that had led to a poor woman being staked down in black water with her mouth full of stone and broken teeth.

Or was there something else at play?

The manner of her death would have required planning. Stakes had to be sharpened, a tool to drive them in had to be brought along, and a place for the staking where they would not be disturbed and the body not be discovered had to be found. Her death also required at least two people: one to hold her down and one to do the staking and the cramming in of the stone.

Lucy shuddered. It was all so horrible, so vile, so downright *evil*. The perpetrators must have been half out of their mind with fear or else have had a thirst for violence. A pity it had all happened so long ago. There could be no solving it now, no justice for the poor woman, not even any dignity now that her body had been reduced to nothing but leathery strips floating in formaldehyde in some professor's study.

They should have given what remained of her a decent burial, Lucy thought, then realized that, despite her best efforts, she was dwelling on dark and macabre things. She got up, picked the book up from where she had thrown it, and thrust it into one of the drawers in her nightstand so it was out of sight, then crept back into bed.

The rain had stopped, but the wind still blew. It came in great gusts that wormed themselves into every little nook and cranny, whistling and whining, sounding eerily like either a child or a young woman keening. Sleep would not come. She was still too frightened, too perturbed.

To hush and distract herself, she spun herself a little tale.

I'm walking in some dark woods, the branches overhead lacing together like clasped hands. I'm not alone. He's walking behind me, his footfalls soft, for he's the hunter, and I'm his prey. When I come to a clearing, he will be upon me, one arm around my waist. I'll be his caught thing then, to do with as he pleases, and the shock of it will send a wave of color sweeping across my cheeks. Soon enough, the color will drain from my face, only dredges of it remaining in the bite marks he'll leave. Those will damn him when I'm found, eventually, for no one else has two extra teeth in their lower jaw...

Lucy reached the point of orgasm quickly and quietly, for the fantasy pleased her. This was how she wanted and how she felt she deserved to be had: rather brutally, in the dark, in the dirt, by her sister's husband.

Chapter 6

AT SOME POINT DURING THE night, Lucy woke with a start. There was no disorientation, no fear, just guilt and shame. Here she was, comfortably in bed—quim still slick from indulging in what should never be thought about, for onanism is a sign of madness, and what woman desires her sister's husband?—while Sarah lay wasting away in a stuffy room. Though *wasting away* sounded gentle, like something a plant might do. Lucy could find nothing gentle in a sickness that sucked the flesh off your bones, blinded you with the pain in your head, and made you raving mad to the point where you bit your childhood friend, and all that in just a few days.

She got up, put on her dressing gown and slippers, and picked up a lamp to light her way. As a child, she had been afraid of the dark. Her nurse didn't allow her to have a candle next to the bed for fear of fire, but Aunt Adelheid sometimes snuck in and sat with her until she fell asleep, a flickering candle held between her hands, the hot wax running down her fingers. When Lucy asked her if it hurt, Aunt Adelheid told her she loved the sensation of wax cooling on her skin.

"Dipping my fingertips in the hot wax of a just-extinguished candle is one of my many vices, I'm afraid," she'd said, then laughed.

The house was dark but not quiet. It groaned and clicked, as if it felt Lucy scrabbling about inside, her hand to the dark wooden paneling of the hallway so as not to lose her balance, and wondered what she was doing up so late, when all should be abed.

Katje shot up from the divan on which she had been sleeping as soon as Lucy opened the door. Lucy pressed a finger against her lips. *It's only me*, she mouthed.

Katje giggled softly. "Oh, but you gave me a fright!" She would not look at Lucy. Instead, she lay back down. She rolled herself into the sheets as if they were a shroud, then curled up tightly.

She really is strange, Lucy thought as she killed the light, removed her dressing gown and slippers, and crawled into the bed. She took her sister into her arms. The feel and weight of her were alien, as her handclasp had been. She pressed her nose against Sarah's neck and inhaled her scent. It was tainted by sweat and sickness, but underneath all that, she still smelled like Sarah. The familiarity of it made her throat and chest ache. They had often slept like this before Sarah had gotten married, for warmth and comfort and safety.

On the nights when the governess extinguished all the lights and Aunt Adelheid wasn't there with a dripping candle to keep the darkness at bay, Sarah would hold Lucy close and whisper facts in her ear. It had been hard to be scared when her twin explained the best way to bathe an orchid or debated whether a mouse or a frog was the best test subject for galvanism.

As if remembering these nights, Sarah began to mutter. The words were unintelligible, but they came in a steady patter, with the occasional pause, as if she were listening to another and answering him.

"Hush. You're talking in your sleep again," Lucy whispered.

"I'm not asleep," Sarah said, the words still slightly slurred but understandable now. She sounded offended.

Lucy smiled. "Aren't you? My apologies, Sarah."

"That's quite all right, but I'm barely Sarah."

"You're talking nonsense, darling. You must be quiet now and sleep."

"But there's so much to do."

"No, there isn't. Katje and I and the servants will take care of it all, you silly sweet. You've got nothing to do at all but to get well, and for that, you must sleep. Hush and shush," Lucy said, then clapped her hand over Sarah's mouth. The lips parted. Lucy felt the tip of her tongue against the base of her fingers, and then, very gently, Sarah's teeth closed around a bit of skin. Lucy pulled her hand back. "Don't be disgusting," she said.

"I'm not. I've got such a hunger and thirst in me, is all. The water was so deep and dark…" Sarah whined.

A little chill swam up Lucy's spine. "You're safe now, I promise," she said. No use denying her sister's delusions; that would just distress her. Best to soothe her. "Shall I fetch something for you? Some laudanum for your head?"

"No, no! I don't want to be drugged. I must eat. I'm starving." She murmured something Lucy didn't quite catch, something about the black water outside.

Lucy ignored this. "What would you like?"

She sensed her sister smile. "Meat. I want it pink on the inside. I want it tender and juicy. I want the blood to run down my chin as I eat."

"You're being silly again. You haven't been able to hold anything down for a whole week. Meat is the last thing you should be thinking of right now. You'd be spewing up your guts before you could swallow. Why don't you try and drink something first?" Lucy asked, trying to keep her voice light.

Sarah grunted and shook her head. "No more water! Please, no more, not ever! The bog, the bog…"

"No water, I promise," Lucy said quickly; Sarah had grown loud, and Katje stirred uneasily in her sleep. Lucy did not want to wake her. "How about something to eat? I can ask the servants to make some pap for you, or some bread soaked in milk, or some beef broth."

"Food not even fit for an invalid," Sarah grumbled; at least she did not shout.

"On the contrary. It's very fit for an invalid. Anything else would be too stimulating."

"Do you mean to starve me out? I'll have to eat and drink you up if I don't get something good soon, and I don't want that because I love you more than anyone."

"That's good to know. I love you, too, very much so. Now be quiet."

She murmured something Lucy couldn't make out, twisted around for a bit until her arms could snake around Lucy, then hushed and grew still.

The next morning, Lucy rang for Magda to help her get dressed. Magda was a large young woman with sloping shoulders, a round face, and an air of discontent. Lucy chattered a little about the weather (rain, again) while Magda did her hair, then said, "These past few days must have been strange for you with your mistress so unwell."

Magda merely shrugged; Lucy could see her do so in the mirror.

"I believe," she went on, "that you may have been one of the first to realize my sister was unwell. You went to Michael about a week ago to tell him you were worried about her, isn't that so?"

"And what if I did?" she asked brusquely, pausing with her hand full of Lucy's hair to look at Lucy in the mirror with narrowed eyes.

"I'm not accusing you of having done anything wrong, Magda." Lucy tried to soothe her. "I'm just trying to understand what has happened to my sister in the days leading up to her illness. She's… well, she's very sick, as you well know, and I've never seen anything like it before. As her lady's maid, you could observe her better than anyone. What about my sister's behavior worried you?"

Magda returned to the work of pinning locks of Lucy's hair to her scalp. "I don't know. It was just a feeling at first. She didn't eat well, and she had headaches, but that wasn't out of the ordinary, especially when she was working on one of her projects. I told her before she shouldn't be looking at all those books when it was dark out, that she'd just ruin her eyesight, and then where would we be? But she never listens to me. When she asked me for laudanum, I told her she should try spectacles instead. I shouldn't have said that. She flew into a rage and locked her door against me."

Lucy winced. At her worst, Sarah could grow unreasonably angry at little things, especially when a project consumed her. It was one of her least favorable qualities. "Did that upset you?" she asked.

Magda shrugged, but there was something hard and defiant in the set of her mouth, the gleam of her eye. "I shouldn't have tried to be smart, now, should I? My mother always did say I have a lip on me and it'll make me come to grief one day, because talking back is fun and witty when you're a fancy lady but just plain disrespectful when you're a maid, but I can't help being anything else than the creature the good Lord made me. And you know your sister better than I do, Miss Goedhart; she's quick to anger but also quick to grow calm again. Why, within an hour, she had me running around fetching all manner of things for her as if she'd never been mad with me at all!"

"What sort of things?"

"Books, mostly."

"What sort of books?"

"All sorts." She finished pinning the last lock of Lucy's hair in place, then set about brushing down the dress Lucy had laid out the previous evening.

"Anything about bog bodies?" Lucy asked lightly, tracking Magda's movements in the mirror.

Magda shrugged again. "There might've been. Some of the titles were in other languages."

Lucy remembered the heap of books and tracts on her sister's desk and the little book about ticks with its broken spine, her sister's increasingly incoherent notes scribbled in the margins.

Like the BOG WOMAN.

She felt cold all of a sudden and wished she had not asked Magda to put up her hair; it would have been nice to draw it around her now like a cloak and be enveloped in its warmth. "Do you know what Sarah was writing about? Could it have been about the bog body that was found here?"

"Stand up please, miss. I can't fasten your corset with you sitting down. You know, I saw that body when they brought it inside, and I found it a sorry sight. Most of the other maids didn't want to go anywhere near it because they spook easily. Not me. I've seen dead bodies before, haven't I, what with my fifteen siblings, nine still living? And this was nothing to be scared of. It looked more like a leather sack than a proper body."

"Was my sister writing about it?" Lucy insisted.

Magda shrugged. "Mrs. Schatteleyn wasn't in the habit of telling me what she was working on. A lady's maid is not expected to assist her mistress with anything that requires a brain." There was something hard, almost angry, in the way she said this.

"But what do you think she was working on?"

Magda had picked up Lucy's dress and guided it over her head, careful not to disturb the hair she had so carefully pinned up. "Something about insects. At least that's what the books she wanted me to fetch for her were all about, the ones whose titles I could read." She frowned. "Although, now that you mention it, she did want a specific book about fungus, but I couldn't find it. I thought maybe one of the footmen had borrowed it, and I thought to myself I'd go and look for it later, only Mrs. Schatteleyn flew into another rage when I told her I didn't have it, and she slapped me, and then she bit me. That's when I knew there was something wrong with her again."

She rolled up her sleeve and showed Lucy a half circle of marks on her lower arm. The skin had broken in places and was scabbed over; in other places, Sarah's teeth had only left behind bruises, now colored a sickly yellow.

Gooseflesh rippled up Lucy's neck and throat. "You didn't tell Michael that she'd bitten you. Why didn't you? My sister shouldn't have done this to you." Her voice came out high, distraught. Normally, she would have thought twice about showing emotion in front of a servant, let alone acknowledging to a servant that her sister had wronged them—her mother had warned her that such behavior would ultimately lead to insubordination from the servants, and a woman who would let her servants bully her wasn't worthy of respect—but the bite marks had shocked her. Sarah could be quick to anger, especially when someone distracted her when her mind was consumed with work, but that anger usually expressed itself verbally. If she had ever before physically hurt a servant, Lucy was not aware of it.

Magda shrugged again. "I tried. I began to tell him of all the things that were wrong with Mrs. Schatteleyn, but he didn't let me finish. He doesn't like us maids. Most of us, that is."

"Did you tell anyone else about this? The housekeeper, maybe?" Lucy asked.

"Why would I? If a maid goes running to the housekeeper every time her mistress slaps or pinches her, why, no work will ever get done. Mrs. Schatteleyn can't help that she's not a docile lunatic. I do think a good wallop every now and again would make her a lot more manageable, but I know better than to lay a hand on my superiors."

If she talks about Sarah like that to a social superior like me, then what sort of things does she tell the other servants and all those siblings of hers? To protect Sarah, it was vital that as few people as possible knew about her current mental state. The very fact that only a handful of people knew about Sarah's previous bout of insanity was the only thing that had kept her from the madhouse.

"Mind you," Magda went on as she did up the last hooks of Lucy's dress, "I do hope this won't go on for much longer. An invalid for a mistress is hard enough, what with all those soiled sheets and nightgowns, but to have a mistress who is both an invalid and a madwoman, well, that's more than I get paid for. I…"

Lucy interrupted her sharply. "Magda, that's no way to speak of my sister! Have you no compassion?"

Magda's eyes hardened. It was as if a brick wall came crashing down between them.

Now she'll never trust me with any information about my sister again, Lucy thought. She closed her eyes for a moment. When she opened them, she said, "I did not mean to bark at you just now, Magda, but you must understand…"

"Oh no, don't apologize, please, Miss Lucy," she said coldly. "The fault's all mine. I forgot for a moment who I was talking to. It won't happen again. Now, is there anything else you need me to do for you?"

Lucy shook her head.

"Then I shall go and see if Mrs. Schatteleyn needs my help, won't I?"

When she had gone, Lucy rested her head in her hands. "Oh, Sarah," she said softly, "what on earth is wrong with you?"

Over the next two days, Sarah deteriorated further. She did not speak anymore in her sleep, did not toss and turn. She just lay in bed, her eyes closed, breathing shallowly and quickly, looking simultaneously ancient and incredibly young, the child she had been and the old woman she might not grow into mingling on her face. When she woke, she was delirious. She was often frightened, cried occasionally. Once, she asked after Lucille and tried to get out of bed because she believed the child was calling for her. She was so weak, she could not stand. Had Katje not slung her arms around Sarah, she would have fallen. She refused food, complaining that she wasn't well and shouldn't eat. When they tried to spoon some broth into her mouth when she was sleeping, she was sick with such violence, Lucy feared she'd die on the spot. From that moment on, she wouldn't drink anymore either, causing her lips to split and her tongue to swell grotesquely.

Lucy witnessed this one-woman horror show of the body, and because it was her beloved twin sister who performed it, it hurt almost more than she could bear. To say it broke her heart was an understatement: it maimed a tender, vital part of her. Worst was that there was nothing to do but the small tasks of the nurse: stoking the fire, preparing wet cloths, keeping the room clean.

Michael visited every few hours, but he was ill at ease. "Sickrooms are no place for a man, unless he's the patient. I'm useless here," he muttered once, violently stabbing the poker into the fire, causing a rain of sparks. One hit him on the back of the hand. He cursed and sucked the skin, a fierce scowl on his face.

How like a demon he looks, Lucy thought.

"You mustn't think your visits are useless. Sarah knows you're here, and that will give her strength and courage," Katje said.

"I don't think she knows anything at all. Look at her! If you'd told me I was looking at a corpse, I'd believe you. How can anyone look like that and still live?"

"Don't speak so!" Katje begged him. "What if she can hear you?"

"Then I'd like her to know that it is all right if she stops fighting. She needn't live on my account. I would not ask that much of anyone."

In that moment, Lucy hated him. The intensity of the feeling shocked her. She tamped it down quickly and harshly, yet when she spoke, she couldn't stop emotion from bleeding into her voice. "You are upset," she told him. "I understand. But for my sister's sake, you must not speak like that. If she can hear you, it will only hurt her. If she can't, there are still Katje's feelings to consider— and my own. I must believe Sarah will get well. I simply must. If there is no hope, well…" Tears blurred her vision, burning her eyes like salt. She could not finish her sentence and crouched over her sister's hand instead, pressing it against her cheek to warm it. Sarah did not merely look like one already dead; with her cold hands, she felt like one, too.

Michael was quiet for a moment, then cleared his throat and

said, "You are right. I apologize. I have no wish to dash anyone's hope, and as long as she still breathes, there's hope yet. Forgive me, both of you. All I can say in my defense is that it doesn't come easy to me to be helpless. It isn't natural for a man."

The other times he visited, he was quiet and did not stay long, but he came, and he tried, and for that, Lucy was grateful.

It was easiest when she was alone. She did not have to pretend she was anything but half out of her mind with fear. She tried to write in her diary to soothe herself, but all she could think about was how desperately unwell her sister was.

That, and the bog woman.

The whole case frightened and sickened her, but she could not deny it drew her, too. She could see how Sarah, who always had been driven by a hunger for knowledge, had grown obsessed with it.

Soon, though, the bog woman merely depressed Lucy. Without any clues as to the woman's identity or when she had even lived, the reason for her murder and burial remained a mystery, and unlike Sarah, Lucy did not have an appetite for those.

She mainly sat and held Sarah's hand in the hope the sensation would penetrate into some primal part of her psyche and let her know Lucy was there with her, prompting her to talk to Lucy.

Such waiting was its own kind of torture.

"This won't do," Arthur said on the third day. "To get better, she must eat and drink. The body cannot heal itself without fuel. If we can't get any fluids into her, she'll die."

"But she can't hold anything down. A sip of water is about all she can manage, and lately, not even that," Katje said. She twisted the stuff of her dress between her long fingers. She had such dark rings under her eyes, they looked bruised.

Arthur thought for a moment, his fingers steepled, the tips touching his mustache. In the firelight, the hairs gleamed like gold thread. He sighed, dropped his hands, and said, "If she can't stomach anything, we must give her a blood transfusion. I see no other option to nourish her." He touched his injured arm for a moment, then said, "Perhaps, on some unconscious level, she realized that, too."

It was such a kind thing to say, implying Sarah had not bitten him in some feral frenzy but out of a desperate need to secure her own survival, that Lucy felt all tender toward him. She began to work at the buttons on her cuff. Arthur saw, smiled, and stilled her hand. "Men are stronger, as is their blood."

"But she and I are the same."

"If she needs another transfusion, I shall keep that in mind. For now, I will do this by the book, and the book recommends using the blood of a healthy man." He turned to Michael, who nodded, took off his jacket, and rolled up his sleeve. Katje bound a handkerchief around his arm until the veins stood out clearly, all swollen with blood. "An excellent nurse," Arthur said, then made a little bow. Instantly her cheeks flooded with red, and her mouth twitched something fierce.

Michael winced when the needle went in, then looked away to his wife. "Funny, isn't it? Not so long ago, doctors believed an abundance of blood could make people sick, and they bled them to restore the balance of the humors. I still have tenants who demand to be bled when they feel unwell. Yet here we are, pouring more blood into the patient to make her better. One can almost under-stand why some prefer religion to science. At times like these, I, too, find myself hankering after the safety that constancy brings." A light sheen of sweat had sprung up on Michael's forehead, and his face had taken on the color of whey.

"Transfusions are not as novel as you may think," Arthur replied. "Doctors have been performing them for decades. It isn't normally done anymore, mind; we are supposed to give transfu-sions only in case of acute blood loss, and saline solution is pre-ferred rather than blood. For reason we don't yet understand, a blood transfusion sometimes kills the patient."

"Then why do you use blood?" Lucy asked. Her mouth had gone dry with fear, her hands cold.

"Have no fear, Lucy. I know what I'm doing." Arthur tried to soothe her. "Doctor Blundell writes of a patient who suffered from a canker of the stomach that left him unable to eat or drink. He injected him with blood from several healthy men, and the patient felt less faint and was able to take food once more. That is the effect I'm hoping to achieve. Besides, whatever is causing Sarah to fail so rapidly seems to have diminished the amount of blood in her body; that would explain her paleness and why she is so short of breath. I wonder if a transfusion might not strengthen her a little."

Once he had extracted a pint of blood from Michael, he injected it into Sarah's arm. She did not respond to the needle slipping into her vein.

Lucy held her sister's hand and squeezed it so hard that the fine little bones in her own hand hurt. *Please*, she thought, *you must get well again, if not for your own sake, then for mine. I can't do without you. You can have my blood, if you need it. You can have my flesh and bones, too. You can have it all, as long as it keeps you here.* She kissed her sister's knuckles one by one.

"I must take my leave of you all now, but I shall come again this evening. Please send for me earlier if there's any change. Michael, you must rest now, and eat and drink plenty," Arthur said as he packed up his bag.

"When shall we know if it worked?" Katje asked.

"Difficult to say. I've got no experience with this procedure and am afraid I don't know. The most important thing now is to keep her comfortable."

He thinks she's dying, Lucy thought, and whatever tenderness she had felt for him drained away.

Chapter 7

BUT SARAH DID NOT DIE that day, nor the one after. Arthur gave her some of his blood the same night Michael had; the next day, Lucy donated some of hers, and the day after that, Katje did the same. The blood seemed to do her good. It brought a little color back into her face, which made it look heartier.

Less like the face of one dead or dying, and more like the face I've known since the womb, Lucy wrote in her diary. She balanced the book in her lap, wrote with her right hand, and held her sister's with the left.

She still sleeps most of the time, but Arthur tells me that this is only to be expected with one who is as ill as she is. "It's not a bad sign, Lucy," he told me just now. "Her body is fighting the infection and needs all its energy to do it, energy she would otherwise use in being awake. She might yet pull through."

Dear Arthur! I've no doubt he would lie to me if he thought it would spare my feelings. That man lives to be kind. But I don't think he'd think it a kindness to deceive me about the severity of

Sarah's condition, and if all hope were lost, surely he would not have continued with the transfusions, dangerous as they are?

Oh, but the mind can be such a dark place to be caught up in. If only I could unburden myself to someone other than these pages! But that must never happen again; well I know it. And yet, I can't help if I sometimes desire for Michael to

"You'll ruin your eyesight," a weak voice said.

Lucy sprang up. Her diary fell to the floor, splaying open, bending some of the creamy pages, and her pen rolled underneath the bed, but she didn't care. "You're awake," she said stupidly, pressing her palm against her sister's brow. It was still warm but no longer searing hot. A good sign. With luck, the fever would soon break completely, and then the worst would be over.

"I'm thirsty," Sarah said. She was still so weak that she could scarcely lift her own hand. Lucy helped her sit up and held a cup for her, stroking the matted hair at the back of her sister's head. It was greasy from where it had touched the pillow but strangely brittle and dull everywhere else. There was a smell to it, animalistic. Strands of it came away, which Lucy tucked into her pocket so Sarah needn't see. Perhaps they should have shorn her head.

Sarah drank quickly, noisily. She finished one cup, then another.

"No more for a few minutes, or you might be sick again," Lucy said. "Is there anything else you'd like me to get? I could ring for some broth if you're hungry. I could even toast a bit of bread for you, if you think you could hold it down."

"Not yet."

"How's your head?"

"Better. It doesn't throb so abominably anymore."

"That's good. You seem very lucid today. That, too, is good."

"Lucid for Lucy," Sarah joked.

"And the fever hasn't burned through your terrible sense of humor either. Better and better! I shall have someone fetch Arthur. He'll be pleased to see you're yourself again. Michael, too, of course." She made to move across the room to pull the bell rope, but Sarah gave a little cry and grabbed her hand.

"No!"

"What is it?"

"I…I just don't want to see anyone but you yet—and Katje."

"All right," Lucy said slowly, sinking onto the edge of the bed again.

"It's because I'm not well."

"But, Saartje, everyone knows that. You've been very ill for over a week now. You had us rather worried."

Sarah swallowed. Something clicked in her throat. "But I'll have to put up a brave face for them, Lucy. With you and Katje, I don't have to pretend."

Lucy took Sarah's hand in hers, brought it to her mouth, kissed it. "Do you want me to read to you? I could get a book from your room or one of those treatises you love so much."

"I just want you to hold me for a while," Sarah said, so Lucy did. Their hands slotted together as they always had. It felt wonderful to sit like that, not saying anything, just holding each other as they had done even when in the womb, sharing a placenta.

Sarah toyed with Lucy's index finger, squeezing the joint, bending it. After a while, she asked, "Have I really been that sick?"

"Oh yes. Can't you remember?"

Sarah shook her head, winced. "My limbs are heavy, I'm dog-tired, my stomach is a sore pit the size of a walnut, and my head feels strange, so I know I must have been, but I don't remember being sick."

"What do you remember?"

Sarah's brow ruffled as she racked her brain. In combination with the pallor of her skin, which spanned across her skull tight as the skin on a drum, this made her look almost ancient. "I was reading a book and making notes in the margins. I already had a headache then, absolutely splitting, so strong that I felt I'd faint. It wasn't like anything I'd ever had before: It was sharp, like being stabbed. It was persistent and almost continuous. Does that make sense?"

Lucy thought of telling Sarah what she had written in her letter, how she'd thought the bog woman was giving her headaches and was doing things to her brain, but Lucy kept quiet; if her sister didn't remember, perhaps that was for the best.

Sarah spread Lucy's index and middle finger out as far as they would go, then snapped them shut. "Initially, the pain was focused in one part of my head, but it began radiating out in tendrils, as if something were digging its roots into my brain. It had also started to affect my vision, like those migraines mother suffered from, but there was no nausea. In fact, I felt ravenous, but I knew somehow that it was imperative I didn't eat, as if a headache is something you can starve into submission. Well, I was trying to read, but the words danced on the page. I threw my pen down because I couldn't understand what I was writing anymore, and the pain was such that something had to give, and then I woke up here and saw you scribbling away in your notebook."

"Nothing in between?"

"Only dark dreams, disturbing but already fading. I believe I dreamed that I bit Arthur." She laughed at that.

Lucy said nothing, just dropped a kiss on her temple. A chunk of hair had fallen, leaving only the little wisps of baby hair, delightfully soft.

Sarah still toyed with her fingers, gently twisting some of the flesh at the base of Lucy's ring finger. The frown had crept back onto her face.

"What are you thinking so hard about, hm?" Lucy asked, pressing her free thumb between her sister's brows to smooth the skin there.

"I feel like I've forgotten something important."

"Any leads? Anything I might do to jog that memory of yours?"

"It was from before I fell sick. I had this realization. It really was frightfully important. I remember my heart beating so fast, the blood pounded in my ears, and it hurt because all sound had started to hurt at that point."

"Such an exciting discovery, then?"

"No, I wasn't excited. I was frightened." Sarah shuddered suddenly, with such force that her elbows drove painfully into Lucy's rib cage. "Lucy," she asked slowly, "what book was I reading when I became ill?"

Lucy hesitated, then said, "I can't know for sure, but on your desk, I found a treatise on ticks you were in the process of annotating."

"What is the last thing I wrote? Do you know?"

"Just some notes on ticks, Saartje. Nothing special."

"So you've seen it? What did I write?"

A light sweat had sprung up all over Sarah's body, giving off a slightly sour smell and dampening her nightgown, yet she was cold, not warm. Lucy took her hands and chafed at them to warm them, but Sarah pulled them away and turned so she could look her sister in the eye. "*Tell me,*" she said, emphasizing each word, "what, exactly, did I write?"

"I don't remember," Lucy tried, but Sarah saw right through that.

"Don't lie to me! You don't know, can't know, how important it is that you tell me honestly. What did I write?"

Lucy did not look at her sister as she said, "You wrote something next to a paragraph detailing how long ticks can survive without blood. You wrote that, in this, ticks were somehow similar to the bog woman."

Fear passed over Sarah's face like a dark cloud. It tightened the muscles in her face. A tendon in her throat stood out like a rope pulled taut.

"Oh, Saartje!" Lucy exclaimed. "Don't you see it's nothing but sinister-sounding nonsense? You were already sick when you wrote it. Whatever you think it means, I can assure you it's nothing of the sort."

Sarah didn't seem to hear. "I think she's inside my head, and she's eating my brain," she whispered. She closed her eyes, let out a shuddering breath.

When she opened her mouth, she screamed.

"Get it out!" she wailed. "Get it out, get IT OUT, GET IT OUT—GETITOUT! OH MY GOD, GET IT OUT!" She clawed at her head, driving her nails into her scalp, tearing the skin and ripping out strands of hair.

Lucy clasped her wrists and tried to pull her hands away, but her sister bucked and fought like a demented thing. "Stop it!" Lucy begged. "Please, stop it! You'll only hurt yourself. You're frightening me."

Sarah did not heed her. Lucy didn't think her sister understood a word she was saying. The whites of her eyes showed. Some capillaries had burst, creating spiderwebs of red that were hair thin but very vivid.

Then while the left eye stayed staring straight ahead, the right eye began to turn away of its own accord. The iris disappeared behind the eyelid, which did not quiver but remained open, the delicate veined skin wadded like a piece of tissue paper, leaving visible only eggshell white threaded with red and pink. When it began to bulge like something was trying to push it from its socket from the inside, Lucy let go of her twin and backed away.

She knew she had to do something, but she was so terrified, she had no control over her body. As she retreated, she tripped over a footstool and fell. She knew, dimly, that her ankles and elbows and wrists should smart, but if they did, she didn't feel it. She just lay there, staring, feeling like she might die of fright.

Beyond that, she felt nothing at all.

All the while, Sarah kept screaming. The words had slurred into one long ragged howl, deeply animal and unlike anything Lucy had ever heard her sister make before. Her writhing caused her to tumble from the bed, and for a moment, the howling was reduced to a high-pitched wheezing because the fall had knocked the breath out of her, but it soon started up again, unbroken until the point where Sarah stopped clawing at her face and instead began to slam the heel of her hand against her eye.

Whenever her hand connected with her eye, it did so with a horrible meaty sound of flesh meeting flesh—*cornea? Jelly? Oh God, what is an eye even made of exactly, and why is hers trying to squeeze out of her HEAD?*—that turned the wailing into a low whimper. Soon, there was an awful rhythm to it.

Wail.

Slap.

Whimper.

Wail.

Slap.

Whimper.

Wail...

If you don't stop her, she's going to smash her eye to pulp.

The thought came cold and clear, cooling some of the burning fear that still held Lucy enthralled. She staggered to her feet and looked wildly for something she could use to bind Sarah's hands.

On the bedside table, among the bottles of medicine, the damp cloths, and the half-empty glasses smudged by fingers and lips, she spied a spool of bandages. She had to step over Sarah to get there. Lucy stumbled over one of her limbs and crashed against the table, the edge digging hard into her belly. Her fall knocked over half the bottles and a half-full glass. Water ran over the surface of the table. Breathless, she reached for the bandages, to snatch them out of the way of the liquid.

Her fingers closed around them with a horrible wet crunching.

The screaming stopped.

For a moment, utterly confused, Lucy stared at her hands, at the white strip of fabric that bulged from between her fingers. It was just a spool of bandages. Her hands were fine.

I didn't make that sound, she realized.

But if it hadn't been her, then it must have been Sarah.

Shock traveled down her spine with the swiftness of a bucket of water upended over her head, freezing her. She couldn't turn around. As long as she stayed like this, looking at the puddle of water spread and drip down the table, the fabric of the bandages rough against her palm, whatever had happened hadn't *really* happened, because she had not seen it.

But she had heard it, as she heard Sarah now, her sobbing little gasps, all rough and choked and interspersed with moments of nothing. And Lucy smelled this sudden stench of blood mixed with something meaty. Underneath, it smelled slightly fecal.

It took an enormous amount of willpower to turn around and look. When she did, she felt a phantom pain in her head, but it was very soft, almost not a pain but a kind of faintness.

As Sarah had been rolling around the floor, writhing in pain, she must have come upon Lucy's pen, the one she had dropped when she'd realized Sarah was awake. It was the one Michael had given Lucy for her birthday, made of silver, the tip wonderfully sharp. Sarah had found it, and she had rammed it into her eye, driving it in with such force that only the end was still visible.

The eye itself had burst like a soft-boiled egg.

Chapter 8

IT WAS ASTONISHING, REALLY, HOW much work a death demanded.

Michael had to talk to the vicar to arrange the service and Sarah's interment in the family crypt. The woodworker had to come and measure her so she would fit perfectly into her casket. Black-bordered cards needed to be sent out to notify people of her passing, and an obituary needed to be written and placed in the newspapers to that same end. Black clothes made of bombazine and crepe had to be ordered. Until those had been sewn, the mourners had to be able to wear black, so dresses and shirts and trousers had to be dyed. Ingredients needed to be ordered, menus planned, food cooked for those who attended the service. Mirrors and paintings were to be taken down, or turned to face the wall, or covered in swathes of fabric.

There was, of course, also the body to take care of. Lucy could have left this to someone else, as was usual—no one expected the direct family to arrange anything, grieving as they were—but she couldn't stand the idea of someone else laying out her sister's body.

She was perfectly capable of doing it herself, anyway, seeing as it entailed little more than washing and dressing it; the only people who would even think about embalming a body were Catholics, and then only for their sainted dead, or Americans.

Together with Katje, she washed Sarah carefully, bound her jaw, then brushed what was left of her hair and put it up carefully. None of her clothes would fit her emaciated frame anymore, so Lucy and Katje set about altering a dress. She hung pearls in her sister's ears. Her wedding ring was too large for her thin fingers, so Lucy secured it with a piece of string.

The veil they draped over Sarah's face was white and trimmed with Brussels lace. The work was very fine; no doubt the nun who had labored over it had sharp eyes. Yet, in time, such small work ruins the eyes, and she would be blind before she reached middle age.

Fitting, Lucy thought as she looked at her sister's face. Though the veil hid the worst of her injuries—the bruises, the half-moon marks her nails had left at her temples and hairline, the little bald patches where the hair had fallen or been torn out—it could not mask the damage done to her eye.

Through the weft, it was possible to see the meaty mess, which had glistened at first, then turned dull and brittle. She asked Arthur if he could try and stitch it up, but he shook his head and told her that both the upper and the lower eyelid had been torn beyond repair. Whatever skin was left was too thin; piercing it with a needle and then trying to drag some black thread through would only rip it further.

During the first night after Sarah's death, the wound secreted a

little fluid, which the veil absorbed. Lucy did not see it in the weak
light of the candles, even though she sat up all night to watch over
her sister and keep her company. They had laid her out in one of
the lesser-used rooms downstairs; no one had much wanted her
to stay in the room in which she'd died, which would now, Lucy
supposed, be forever tainted, forever haunted.

She watched over her sister alone. Katje had wanted to stay, but
she sobbed and even moaned to the point where Lucy couldn't stand
it anymore. She hadn't expected this from Katje. Such an excess of
grief was appropriate for a woman who had just been widowed, not a
girl who had just lost a friend. Lucy told her to go and sit with Pasja
instead. The dog had been slinking around the house with her tail
between her legs, shivering and occasionally whimpering, getting in
everyone's way; she needed someone to be kind to her.

When Lucy tried to remove the veil to wash away that slightly
putrid bloom of yellow, it had already crusted, so it would not come,
stuck to what was left of Sarah's right eye. Lucy put her head in her
hands and took a deep shuddering breath.

"I'm sorry, Sarah," she said. "I should have sewn you an eye
patch of silk or perhaps black velvet. With your pearl earrings, you'd
look half a rake, but I suspect you might have enjoyed that." Sarah
had always had a sympathy for the villains of each story, for the
lost and the damned. No one but Sarah could have been so deeply
attracted to the bog woman, and that attraction had no doubt been
in part due to the way she'd been buried, shunned and condemned,
after dying in agony unforgiven and unshriven.

The manner of their death may have been similar, but their

graves would not be. It was the first thing Michael had arranged. "We shall say she tried to rise from her sickbed, but weakened as she was, she fell, and in falling, she hit the bedside table in such a manner that the pen was driven through her eye. A horrible way to go, very strange, but not a way to condemn," he said. His face was tight, his voice forcefully flat.

"Suicide committed when temporarily insane is not an offense according to the law," Arthur said softly.

"The fact that it is not punishable by law doesn't mean it is in any way desirable. I can do without the stigmas of insanity and self-murder tainting my name and that of my wife," Michael snapped.

And so they had told a bunch of half-truths to give Sarah a proper funeral. Lying did not bother Lucy. For her sister's sake, she would do much worse—and do it gladly.

"Though it wasn't exactly a lie, now, was it?" she murmured. She clasped her sister's hand in hers. It was cold, the fingertips already discolored, the joints stiff. Soon, that stiffness would disappear, and if she held the hand long enough, it would not feel cold anymore either, and then she might fool herself that it wasn't a dead woman's hand she was holding.

"You thought there was something inside your head, and you wanted it gone. You destroyed yourself in attempting to remove it, but that destruction was not your goal, merely a side effect." She crouched over her sister's body, pressed her cheek against the back of that cool stiff hand. It was not a comfortable position, since she had to contort her spine and twist her head, but what did she care for comfort now? "Though if God disagrees and you are damned and restlessly must roam, please, Saartje, *please* come and haunt me," she whispered.

If only I could cry, she thought, *I think I might feel a little better.* Her eyes burned like two blue coals, and the unshed tears seemed sharp as flint. It was not that she could not stomach pain; indeed, she welcomed it, for anything was better than the numbness that pervaded her entire being. It was not natural to feel so little. The moment of horror had come, the limb had been severed, but the pain had not yet registered. It would come, she knew; it could not be avoided.

Waiting, always waiting, she thought bitterly. She imagined Hell as an eternal waiting room whose doors would lead to planes of pain hitherto not experienced. In such a case, the absence of pain was not bliss but part of the torture, as indeed it was to Lucy now.

She rubbed her cheek harshly against her sister's hand, wanting the feel of it to be ground into her very cells. "Why," she hissed, "why did you have to die and leave me all alone? You were all I had. Selfish, selfish! Did you not know you left me but one wish in life, and it was that I might die before you did so I'd never need to know this pain?"

Her cheek burned with the friction, and the top layer of Sarah's skin began to slough off, leaving her hand looking tender.

Lucy continued. "Perhaps it was selfish of me to want this. You may have been my leader, and gladly did I let you rule me, but I always did think I was the stronger one. I am still convinced that I can bear this pain of separation better than you could have. I didn't want to, though. In this *one* thing, I wanted to be spared."

A hand on her shoulder made her jump.

"I'm sorry. I did not mean to startle you," Arthur said. He had his hands raised, as if she were a skittish horse he wished to calm.

She lay her hand against her throbbing cheek to shield it from his sight. She found a wisp of Sarah's skin clinging to it, thin as cobweb, almost translucent. She held it between her fingers, unsure what to do with it. For a moment, she thought she really might cry after all, though not from grief but from shame. What kept her from it was the fact Arthur seemed even more embarrassed at having witnessed such a violent, intimate display of emotion. "Why are you here?" she said, and the words came out harsh, raw, accusatory.

"I came to see how you were doing. You've been sitting up with Sarah all night, I've heard."

Always a gentleman, Arthur.

"During the wake, she must not be left alone." She smoothed Sarah's sleeve, which Lucy's rubbing had rucked up and wrinkled. Her sister's hand, as predicted, felt hot and alive, but the warmth was fleeting, and soon only the patch she had chafed at held no warmth.

When it became clear she would not say anything else, Arthur cleared his throat and said, "Forgive me, but you look exhausted."

Now that, she thought, *a gentleman wouldn't say*. A doctor before everything else, then. "These past few days have been trying," she said.

"And the days to come will be trying, too, even more so if you don't take good care of yourself. You may not feel like it, but it is vital that you do. Lucy," he said, and he spoke with the voice of a friend, not a physician, "you must try to sleep."

"On the contrary. I think sleep is the last thing I could possibly need," she said, smiling a little. People described sleep as a respite from grief, only for the blow to land afresh upon waking. It had never been so for Lucy. When little Lucille had died, she had dreamed, some days after the funeral, that she held the little girl in her arms. She was quite cold, but when Lucy began to rub her little hands and blow on them, she warmed quickly. Soon, she was moving her arms and head, murmuring something unintelligible.

For all appearances, she was a living child.

But she is dead, Lucy thought as she rocked her niece, then again as she toyed with her little fingers, as she dropped kisses on her silken head. *She is dead and buried.* And because she knew this with unwavering certainty, it did not matter that she didn't know she was asleep and dreaming: she was not able to rejoice at the weight of the child in her arms, at her scent and the words she slurred in her sleepy voice.

It had been similar when her parents had died; she had dreamed about them incessantly then, too. She knew with cold dread that it would be far worse with Sarah. The horror could be strangled during the day but not at night. Lucy had never been able to rouse herself from a nightmare, so she would have to endure until her mind could take no more and woke up, the sheets wet through with her sweat, fear seeming to choke her heart inside her breast.

"I can give you something to make your sleep dreamless," Arthur said.

She hesitated. "But Sarah shouldn't be left alone."

"Magda could come sit with her."

"Magda has too much to do to sit with her mistress's corpse."

"That may be why she'll consent to it. Servants don't usually get to simply sit. Katje would do it gladly, too, of course."

"Katje is currently weeping her eyes out."

"The girl has taken it hard," Arthur conceded.

Why do we all insist on thinking of her as a girl? She's almost twenty-two, isn't she? That's only three years younger than I am, she thought dispassionately. She rubbed her eyes, then hissed as her ministrations made the dry pain flare up. "I can't think right now," she said.

"That is why you must sleep. Come, no more arguing. As a doctor and your lifelong friend, I dare say I know what is good for you."

He mixed a draught for her, which she drank obediently, then took her up to her room. Already she felt drugged and slow.

Once in bed, she realized she still held the fine web of Sarah's skin between her fingers.

She rolled it into a ball. It was very small, no larger than the back of a pin. Afraid she'd drop it and lose it between the heavy sheets, she did the only thing she could think of to keep it safe: she popped it into her mouth and held it under her tongue.

One last thought crossed Lucy's mind before sleep dragged her under: *If this is what death tastes like and death is as it tastes, then it is a dull thing indeed.*

Chapter 9

GRIEF MADE PEOPLE DO STRANGE things, yes, but it also made strange things happen to people. During the days leading up to the funeral, Lucy found that time did not behave as it should. Hours would sometimes pass at the blink of an eye. At other times, the blink of an eye seemed to take hours.

She helped with the arrangements as well as she was able. When she wasn't doing that, she sat with her sister's corpse. She felt very protective of it. Whenever people came to say their good-byes, she watched them anxiously, scanning their faces for signs of revulsion or alarm, her whole body tense, her breathing shallow and quick. Many of them she did not know and therefore could not trust.

Worst was when they wished to touch Sarah. She had awful, intrusive visions, waking nightmares, really, of someone gripping Sarah's hand and accidentally twisting off a finger or someone bending over Sarah, placing their elbow on her belly and resting their weight on it, only for the skin to burst and the elbow to sink into her all the way to her spine. Bizarre thoughts, unrealistic and paranoid, but they had a hold on her and would not leave her no matter how hard she tried to reason them away, which she couldn't, not always, and wasn't that a sign Lucy herself was perhaps running mad?

A day before the funeral, Mrs. van Dijk arrived. She would spend the night with them, seeing as she was elderly and lived far away, and thus she could not be expected to make the trip to Zwartwater and back to her own home on the same day.

"Let me look at you" was the first thing she said to Lucy after she had kissed her cheeks thrice. She held Lucy at arm's length and studied her. "God, you look awful. Black doesn't suit you. It washes you out completely, and you're already such a pale, colorless creature."

"How kind of you to come," Lucy murmured.

"Bring me to your sister, that I may say my goodbyes to her."

Mrs. van Dijk held her by the arm, both leading Lucy and gripping her for support. Due to a childhood bout of polio, she had one withered leg that was much shorter than the other, the foot small as a child's and twisted as a root. She had to have special shoes made with an extra-thick sole to even out the difference, but she walked with a pronounced limp nonetheless and had to use a cane. She had a collection of them at home: canes made of ivory and of polished wood, some tipped with silver, while others were simple and austere. She had brought a black one now, the top carved to look like a raven's head.

When they reached the coffin, Mrs. van Dijk sucked her teeth. They stood there for a long time, until she said, "Well, that's quite enough of that, I think. She doesn't make a pretty corpse, I'm afraid. Poor thing. Her suffering must have been immense. I hate to say it, it sounds very callous of me, but now that I've seen her, I do think death must have come almost as a mercy."

"She was recovering when it happened," Lucy whispered.

"Was she? You wouldn't say that from looking at her. It's hard to imagine her looking worse than she does now. Of course, it doesn't help matters that she has been dead for the past three days. Those open windows and buckets of ice can only do so much. You look about ready to faint. Come and sit down. There's a dear. I've got some smelling salts on me that might revive you."

She waved the foul-smelling things under Lucy's nose, and Lucy began to cough. At the back of her throat, she tasted flowers, and underneath that was the sweet, meaty taste of rot. She coughed to the point of retching.

Mrs. van Dijk gave her firm slaps between the shoulder blades with a beringed hand, which did nothing apart from stamp Lucy's back with the van Dijk's family seal. By the time the coughing fit was over, she had a burning pain in her chest, was red in the face, and felt exhausted.

Mrs. van Dijk patted her shoulder. "There, there. All better. Nothing like a good coughing fit to get the circulation going. Now, do tell me: How are you holding up?"

"As well as I'm able." Lucy choked. She picked up a lily—vases of fragrant flowers had been placed around the room to mask the scent of putrefaction—and stroked the fleshy petals in an effort to distract herself from the itch in her chest; if she wasn't careful, she'd start coughing again. A little pollen, fine as dust, powdered the back of her hands. She wiped it away, but it had already stained her skin yellow.

Mrs. van Dijk tutted and handed her a handkerchief. "Come, no need to lie to me. That answer will do very well with others, but you are my companion. I know you better than that."

Lucy scrubbed at the back of her hands until they looked bruised. "All right. I shall be honest with you. I feel maimed and… and mutilated, but also a little numb. The pain has yet to come, I think. I fear it will obliterate me when it does. I wish I were dead."

"You poor dear. Death is a kind of mutilation, yes. A piece of you died as surely as your sister did. I remember that very well when my dear husband died. And to imagine it must be even worse for Michael…"

Anger rose in Lucy's throat like bitter bile. Was this what others thought, too? That the blow was hardest to bear for Michael? He had loved her sister; of this she had no doubt. But he had known her for only a few years and could replace her when the time was right, whereas Lucy, who had known Sarah from before they were born, could never find another sister. He hadn't been present at her death either, so he had been spared the horror.

She passed her hand over her face to compose herself. It was scented with the lily she had crushed. *I shall associate this scent with Sarah's death forever now*, she thought, just as she would the smell of blood and meat. She stood, then brushed the thick scraps of lily petals off her skirt. "Forgive me. I don't make a very good companion at the moment."

"You do look pale as a sheet. Maybe you need to lie down for a bit?" Mrs. van Dijk's voice was tainted with disapproval—apart from polio and other childhood illnesses, she had never been sick a day in her life, a fact in which she took great pride—but Lucy assented readily to the suggestion.

She did not go to her own room, though, but to Sarah's. There she lay on the bed and buried her nose into the sheets, trying desperately to get a whiff of her sister's scent. The sheets had been washed and smelled of nothing much at all, so she sat in front of the vanity instead. She pulled back the gauze that had been draped over it to keep Sarah's wandering spirit from becoming entrapped, then looked at her reflection.

Mrs. van Dijk was right; black did not suit her. She looked wan, sickly, with bags of grayish skin underneath her eyes. The horror and sleeplessness had stamped her face with lines that hadn't been there before, furrows between her brows and lines that ran from her nose down past her mouth. To conjure Sarah's face, she smiled, but that only served to make her look slightly unhinged.

After Aunt Adelheid had been committed, their father had ordered to have all her possessions removed. Only the ant farm she had given to Sarah escaped his notice. In the weeks that followed, their mother would stare at it for hours, her pale face reflected by the glass. She and Adelheid hadn't been twins, but now Lucy wondered: Had her reflection given her some sort of comfort because it had looked, at least a little, like her sister? Sympathy for her mother swelled inside her chest.

After all, once they close Sarah's casket and inter her, the looking glass will be the only place I can find my sister, she thought. It was a gruesome thought, painful as a blow to the belly.

She sprang up and tried to throw the sheet back over the mirror, but haste made her clumsy, and she pulled the mirror down. The silver-backed glass cracked with a sound that was almost beautiful. Shards shivered to the floor.

Lucy cursed softly. She took hold of the frame and put it upright. Most of the glass remained inside, but a large piece in the bottom-right corner had cracked and broken and lay in fragments on the floor. She gathered the fragments carefully and bound them in her handkerchief. That done, she turned the mirror around so its reflective surface faced the wall. When she straightened and brushed down her skirts, she found a piece of wadded paper. It must have been hidden behind the mirror. As she unfolded it and smoothed it out with the flat of her hand, she found the ball actually contained three sheets filled with Sarah's meticulous small handwriting. The first one was dated the twenty-second of September—almost two weeks ago.

I've been sleepwalking again, Lucy read. *It used to happen pretty often to me when I was a girl. Lucy often had to fetch me from the school-room, or the dining room, or wherever it was I had wandered off to, and guide me back to bed without waking me. My wanderings became...*

The door opened. Michael stood on the threshold. He had not expected her, and in that tiny moment before he realized he wasn't alone, she saw rage in his eyes, then, when he saw her, a flash of fear. They stood staring at each other, both stricken and afraid. "Lucy," he said at last, and the fear made way for relief, only to be replaced by anger once more. "Goddamn, woman. It's a good thing I've got a strong heart; you scared me half to death just now. For a moment, I thought you were…"

"I'm sorry," she said.

His gaze traveled past her and landed on the broken mirror. He closed the door behind him and strode toward the vanity. The corner of the mirror had chipped the wood. He rubbed at the flaw with his thumb, clicked his tongue in annoyance. As he let his hands wander over the frame to see if that, too, was damaged, Lucy slipped the balled-up pieces of paper with Sarah's writing into her pocket.

"This was a wedding present. It's ruined now," he said.

"I'm sorry. I didn't mean to break it."

"Fuck!" he shouted, then kicked the mirror with such force, it slammed against the wall, breaking the glass even more.

Lucy backed away from him until she felt the edge of the writing desk cut into the small of her back. She clutched the tabletop, bits of paper crinkling against her sweating palms. She could not stand shouting. When Michael raged like this, she was afraid of him. Her eyes burned.

Now, isn't this silly, she thought clearly through the guilt and the misery and the fear. *I can't seem to cry for Sarah, but I feel as if I might cry for angering Michael.*

She rubbed her eyes harshly with her fingertips, ruffling her lashes unpleasantly, but everything about them ached abominably: the balls felt hot and dry, the lids as if they had been cut.

He turned and came to her. For a moment, she thought he

might strike her, but all he did was take her face between his hands and gently, gently blow on her eyelids to soothe their smarting. He had been chewing peppermint; she smelled it on his breath. It made her eyes prick painfully, but also made them feel cool and fresh.

"You must not mind me. I can be beastly. I'm not truly angry about the mirror," he said.

"Then what has angered you?" she asked. His blowing made her eyes mist over, and as a result, his features were blurred to her.

"Mrs. van Dijk told me she intends to take you back with her tomorrow."

She placed a finger against his mouth so he would stop breathing on her eyes. "But I'm not ready. I've got nothing packed. It's too soon…"

"That's what I told her, but she insists on having her little slave back."

"You know it isn't like that, Michael."

"I know that the work is beneath you and that you know very well you needn't put up with it. There's a place for you here and always has been."

"And you know very well I couldn't stay."

"I disagree." He kissed one eyelid, then the other, then the first one again. His tongue darted between his lips, hot and wet, to lick up a tear that had tangled in her lashes.

"We mustn't," she murmured. She clasped his wrist. He was hirsute, and the hair grew thickly and darkly on his arms and knuckles, but the place where the bone protruded at his wrist was quite hairless, the skin very soft and smooth. Always sensitive to sensations, she ran her thumb over it and found it delightful.

He began to kiss her on the mouth.

She shuddered and turned her face away. "We mustn't. We really mustn't," she said.

He took hold of her chin and made her look at him. "But we want to. Don't deny this. You have craved the meat and the madness of it as much as I have."

She smiled. "And therein lies the trouble, doesn't it? We knew it wasn't right, that it was unforgivable, but we did it anyway." She tried to keep her voice light, but the tears lay hard like pips underneath the skin of her throat, softly strangling her.

He stroked her neck with his thumb, doing it rather harshly, leaving marks behind that were at first white, then flushed red as the blood came rushing back. "You may have thought it wrong, but you didn't deny me before."

"Things were different then. Lucille had just died, and Sarah wasn't coping well, and you were lost and hurt. I didn't mean to...to fornicate with you. I only ever meant to comfort you." She winced at the word *fornicate* even as she said it. It sounded so grand, so severe and biblical. It hadn't been like that at all.

"What a filthy word," he said, as if he had read her mind. He kept stroking her throat. Her skin throbbed under his attentions. "You say things are different now. Perhaps they are. But answer me this, Lucy, and answer me honestly: Do you think I am not in need of comfort now as much as I was then?"

"Don't ask me!" she cried. She dug her nails into his wrist to still the hand that chafed at her throat. "Why must you grasp after me so? You married Sarah; you made your choice! Stop straining after what you can't and shouldn't have."

"Oh, darling," he said, digging his thumb painfully into the soft tissue underneath her jawbone, "don't you know that, of all the sins that taint me, greed is the strongest? I always want what I shouldn't have. But I think you know what that feels like."

When he kissed her again, she did not resist—did, in fact, lean into it.

He gathered the fabric of her skirt in one hand, pressing the heel of the other between her legs. Her hips rose of their own accord, and it felt so sweet that she gasped. He began to massage her, slowly at first, then, when she had caught up with the rhythm, a little faster.

When he parted her and slid his middle finger against the velvety flesh, he pressed his mouth against her hair and groaned. "Oh, Lucy, my darling, you're dripping wet," he said.

She tried to say something but could only sob. He had to let go of her skirt then and draw her to him to keep her standing; her knees were trembling something fierce and were close to buckling. She clutched his lapels to stop herself from falling. Her cheek lay against his chest, the silk of his cravat against her temple. Through the layers of fabric, she could feel the steady thud of his heart, which increased slowly the more she gasped, the more she bucked and strained against his hand.

Release struck her like lightning. For a moment, she was aware of nothing but the pure delight of her orgasm rippling through her.

He held her fast as she rode it out. When it was done, he began to move her to the bed.

Shame stabbed at her. "Michael, not here!" she begged, trying to pull from his grip.

"I'm a gentleman, Lucy, but I'll be damned if I don't get what I am owed," he growled.

"But not here!" She pinched the web of skin between his index finger and thumb brutally. He cursed and instinctively shoved her from him. The force of it made her cut the inside of her cheek on one of her teeth; a little blood pooled into her mouth, rich and hot and horrible. She swallowed it, gagged. The taste of it unleashed something in her, and she felt wild with want.

"My God, Lucy, are you hurt?" Michael asked, his eyes wide. "I didn't mean to shove you so roughly, but you took me unawares. Let me look at you, my darling!" When he drew her close to check her for any injuries, she slotted her mouth over his and ran her tongue over his extra two teeth.

———

When they were done and he had given her his handkerchief to wipe away the sticky mess coating the inside of her thighs, the smell of it almost thick enough to get rid of the phantom smell of Sarah rotting and bleeding, she felt so revolted with herself, she wished she had a knife—*or a pen*—so she might cut herself and thus be punished.

Michael stood at the window, retying his cravat. His reflection in the glass was queer and blurred; she could not read it. But he could read the self-hatred and the guilt and the shame in her face, for he came to kiss her.

She twisted away.

"Suit yourself," he said, not unkindly.

She came to her feet. Her legs were still weak with pleasure. She took care to walk into the corner of the writing table as she made her way through the room, relishing the sharp pain of a bruise blooming.

At the door, he took hold of her arm and said, "You may think I'm using you. I'm not. If this were just about sex, I would rather rut with one of the maids. It's less complicated that way. But I care for you, Lucy, more than I suspect you know."

She looked at his fingers, so long and white against the black of her sleeve. "Please let go. I need to sit with Sarah. These are the final hours that I may." *And I chose to spend some of that precious time coupling with her husband in her bed. I am* vile.

Fornicating had been the right word after all.

As she took her place next to Sarah's corpse again, the pages she had tucked into her pocket rustled. She took them out, smoothed them over her thigh. To distract herself from her self-loathing and guilt and grieving, she began to read.

When she was done, she sat very still for almost a quarter of an hour, her eyes large but unfocused, her face and lips blanched. The pages fell from her lap, startling her from her trance. She gathered them with shaking hands. "Don't worry, Saartje. I'll take care of this," she murmured.

Without looking at her sister, she left the room. Upstairs, she collected Sarah's final letters, the treatise on ticks, and a pair of sewing scissors, then took them to the library, where a fire was roaring in the grate. With the scissors, she cut the threads that had been used to sew the pages of the tick treatise together and ripped them from between the cover. She then set about cutting all the paper to pieces.

Halfway through, a sudden panic that someone might come in and read those infernal words took hold of her, so she dropped the scissors and tore the pages with her fingers before feeding the fire by the handful. The clothbound book cover did not burn so easily; it smoked and stank. She beat at it savagely with the poker until it submitted to the flames.

The only evidence of Sarah's madness left now was Sarah's maimed eye. Tomorrow she'd be interred, thus hiding it from sight. Within a few months—possibly sooner, if the winter cold did not come early this year—nothing would be left of her face but bone and stringy bits of tendon. Only Lucy would know the true extent of her lunacy then. She'd have to shoulder that burden alone, just as she would have to face everything alone from now on.

She folded her hands together, and though they were exactly like Sarah's, they didn't feel like her sister's. They were just her own hands, one desperately gripping the other, seeking a sensation that would never come again.

---

22 September 1887

I've been sleepwalking again.

It used to happen pretty often to me when I was a girl. Lucy often had to fetch me from the schoolroom, or the dining room, or wherever it was I had wandered off to, and guide me back to bed without waking me. My wanderings became fewer the older I got. Since my marriage, I can count the times I've walked on a single hand, and whenever I did, Pasja wouldn't let me get far: she'd paw at me and softly nip at my hand to wake me, and if that didn't work, she'd scratch the door connecting my room to Michael's until he woke and could help me instead.

When little Lucille died, I didn't walk at all. Then again, her death turned me into an insomniac, and I had to take a tincture Arthur prescribed and Michael prepared for me himself every night to preserve my sanity, so perhaps that's why I never wandered then.

But I did so last night, and I am frightened and horrified and revolted.

I blame myself. If I hadn't insisted I attend that autopsy, the smell of that bog body wouldn't have clung to my hair and clothes, driving Pasja into a frenzy. Who could blame her? That charnel-house stench was almost more than I could bear, and her nose is so much more sensitive than mine. She kept pacing and whining, occasionally sniffing my hands and growling softly, the hair on her neck and back raised. She has never shown me any aggression, but she showed me her little white teeth more than once. I couldn't keep her with me, not like that. I asked Katje if she'd mind having the dog with her for a night, and so I was all alone.

I dreamed that I was in the cellar with the bog woman. I don't remember getting there, but dreams usually begin in medias res, so it didn't scare me. She was lying on the table where Arthur and Doctor Rosenthaler had cut her open and unsuccessfully tried to unravel her secrets. She didn't look at all like her old self, dyed and cut and broken. She was whole, her joints not staked through, her chest firmly closed. Yet, with the uncanny knowledge of the dreamer, I knew it was her and knew this was what she had looked like in life.

When I touched her, she was cold, and she was cold because she was naked. I lay down next to her and gathered her in my arms to warm her, pressing her body against mine. Her skin was soft and supple under my hands and quite white, quite cool, yet under my attentions, it began to redden.

When I opened my eyes, I saw that she had done the same and was smiling at me. She clambered on top of me and kissed me. Soon, I was consumed with desire. I wriggled underneath her. Delighted, she writhed on top of me. She pressed her mouth to my neck, and I felt not the press of her teeth as I saw them, whole and a little yellow, but the raggedy bite of teeth chipped and broken. She pierced my skin and lapped at the drop of blood that welled. Her tongue was wet and hot, and though the small wound throbbed and stung, there was a pleasure in it, too.

When I was weak from her attentions, she kissed me again, more deeply than before. I caught a whiff of peat and stagnant water as something seemed to slither from her mouth into mine, something cool and soft. It tasted sweet and strong and rich, like blood, like rot.

I felt a deep sense of revulsion so strong that I gagged. She clamped her hand over my lips and nose. I tried to fight, but I was still weak, and I couldn't help but wonder if she had seduced me for that exact purpose.

She stroked my throat until, convulsively, I swallowed what she had spat into my mouth. It went down slowly, pain-fully, for though it was smooth and soft, it was also large, about the size of a child's fist. It clung to the meat of my esophagus. I coughed, retched, but down it went.

I woke up gasping for breath, my throat aflame and my limbs cramped with cold.

For a moment, I didn't know where I was. Then I realized I was sitting in front of my bedroom door. I went inside and locked it to keep myself from wandering again. I crawled into bed and closed my eyes, but I couldn't sleep, from fear and cold and the rawness in my throat. I coughed softly, but that only made it hurt more.

There is a logical explanation for this. My mind, so consumed with the bog woman ever since we found her, turned to her in my sleep, and my sleeping mind, unfettered by morality, gave me a dark and disturbing dream about her.

In writing all this down, I have purged myself of it. I must now try to forget that any of it ever happened. I shall rip out these pages and destroy them.

As for the body: I don't much care what happens to it now, as long as it is removed from here.

Chapter 10

THE DAY OF THE FUNERAL dawned.

The undertakers took Sarah to the local church in a black hearse drawn by six black horses. Something had spooked them; they foamed at the mouth, rolled their eyes, dug at the earth with their hooves. Soon their coats were glossy with sweat. The driver had the greatest trouble to keep them from bolting. By the time they arrived at the church, he, too, was sweating profusely. One of the horses had champed at the bit so hard that its mouth was bleeding. The blood came slowly but thickly, mixing with the foam that slathered its chest.

Sarah was placed in a little room located at the back of the church to allow her nearest relatives to stay with her and say their goodbyes before the coffin would be closed forever and carried into the main part of the church for the service. To this end, the room had two doors: one leading to the church itself and one going out. It faced north, which made it cold and dark. There was a soft, sad smell to it, of dust and damp and neglect, even though it was clean.

Only Michael, Katje, Arthur, and Lucy went inside. Mrs. van Dijk, who had ridden with them because she insisted it was ridiculous to send another carriage solely for her humble self, wandered around the church as she waited for the service to begin; they could hear the tap of her cane on the flagstones.

"Awful woman," Michael muttered. His face was a tight mask, even more bloodless than usual. It made a bruise under his jaw, not quite hidden by his cravat, seem particularly vivid. *Did I do that?* Lucy wondered.

Lucy thought of saying Mrs. van Dijk really wasn't that bad, merely loud and opinionated, but what was the point? Michael considered both those things faults in a woman; Lucy would not change his mind. Besides, this was neither the time nor the place to argue.

She turned to Katje, who was crying softly into a handkerchief of black lace. Unlike Lucy, the state of mourning became her: she looked fetching in black, which matched the dark color of her cropped curls and her milky complexion very well, and she could cry without sound in a manner so pretty, it was almost disturbing. Katje had been crying almost constantly for the past few days, but rather than turn her face blotchy and ugly, it made her eyes, though rimmed with pink, glitter in an arresting way.

How horrifying. Is there anything more dangerous to a woman than to be beautiful when weeping? Lucy thought.

Katje caught her watching. She looked away, then back to Lucy again. Katje said, in a soft voice choked with tears, "I'm sorry. I must be making a spectacle of myself. I don't mean to. It's just that I loved

Sarah very much. She was so good to me. With her, I didn't think of myself as poor and strange and broken."

When Lucy opened her mouth to contradict her, Katje added, "No need to deny it. I know that's what people think when they see me. But Sarah…she could look past all that and see me, the real me, I mean, the creature I am underneath, and it made me so…so *happy.*" She smiled. Her mouth trembled and twitched, making her look vulnerable and a little mad.

"She could be good at making people feel comfortable and seen, if she wanted," Lucy said. She swallowed, looking away.

"She was a very fully realized person, wasn't she?"

"I suppose so," Lucy hedged, although she knew Katje was right. Sarah *had* been a fully realized person, almost as if in herself complete. It was that exact quality that had made her so attractive, for it was rare. Lucy hadn't possessed it. Even with her twin next to her, she had often felt like only half a person, insubstantial and unfinished. That watery quality, that blurredness, must have been especially pronounced when she had been with Sarah. No wonder Michael had preferred her to Lucy.

Lucy took the handkerchief Katje offered her. She folded it, making it smaller and thicker until it would be folded no more, then shook it out again. The tears still hadn't come, but they felt close to the surface and perhaps would finally flow before nightfall.

She had repeated this process of folding and shaking the hand-kerchief thrice when the time came to close the coffin.

I shall never see my sister again.

Panic turned her insides to water. For a moment, she thought she might faint. The blood drained from her face and hands. When she bent over the coffin to kiss her sister's forehead for the last time, her lips were so numb, she did not feel the fine weft of the veil, nor the cold skin underneath. As she straightened herself, the world rocked. Her heart throbbed. It was the only thing she could feel.

Arthur appeared at her side and took her by the arm. He steered her to the only window in the room, which was small, the glass strangely yellow and warped. "Slow breaths," he said.

She had wadded Katje's handkerchief into a little ball and held it tightly in her fist. Her hands were wet with sweat. It had saturated her gloves, dampened the lace of the handkerchief. Arthur took it from her, moistened it with the water from one of the vases, then dabbed her forehead and temples with it. The water had a bitter, chalky smell to it.

"I'm fine. Don't fuss," she murmured, but she did not resist when he peeled down one of her gloves and pressed the handkerchief against the inside of her wrist, nor when he put his arm around her as Michael screwed down the lid of the coffin. He did it quickly, like it was either distasteful or simply unbearable. When it was done, his face contorted, only for a moment; then the pallid mask slipped back into place.

After, they had to take their place in the pews at the front of the church, but Lucy still felt weak and sick. "Just leave me here. I'll join you in a minute," she said, then gave a little smile.

When they had left, she sank to the floor and buried her face in her hands. They were clammy and smelled brackish.

"I can't do this," she muttered, but she knew she could because she had been doing it for days, was, in fact, doing it right now. In a little bit, she'd get up, shake out her skirts to dislodge potential grains of dirt and dust, and enter the church. There she'd sit in one of the wooden pews designed to be as uncomfortable as possible to keep the congregation awake. She'd take a hymnal and let it lie open in her lap, the onion-thin paper wrinkling under her fingers. Once the service began, she'd stand when bid, then sit again when ordered to. She'd listen to the vicar talking about Sarah, praising her for being a good wife and mother, and then she'd think that he hadn't known her very well at all, because if he had, he'd talk about her bravery and intelligence, how funny she could be, how insufferable, how lovely, lovely, *lovely*...

Faintly, the sound of scratching.

She dropped her hands, furrowing her brow as she listened. It came again: nails scrabbling against wood. Perhaps mice or even rats. Not so strange a thing to hear near Sarah. Unless frozen in ice, every corpse eventually proved itself a banquet for certain kinds of insects, birds, and rodents. The smell of Sarah's corpse—despite the tub of ice placed underneath her coffin and the windows opened to let in the cool air, she had begun to stink—would attract all kinds of animal life. A natural process, yes, but that didn't mean Lucy could just leave the mice to it. They could have Sarah once she was interred in the family crypt but not before.

She listened closely, trying to locate the sound. It came intermittently, softly but steadily. She picked up a Bible, then crept around the coffin with it held aloft so she could kill any mouse that dared show itself. Soon her calves cramped, but she kept creeping,

straining to hear the scratching over her own breathing, the rus-
tling of her skirts brushing over the ground, and the soles of her
buttoned boots grating against the floorboards.

It's coming from inside the coffin, she realized. Her mouth
flooded with saliva as her stomach contracted. She pressed the
back of her gloved hand against her lips as she fought not to vomit.
If she found a rat eating its way through Sarah's belly or nibbling
her fingers or face, she feared she'd start screaming and never stop.
There was only so much the mind could take before it cracked.

Then came the realization: What if it wasn't a rat, but her sister
making that noise?

She rested her forehead hard against the cool lacquered wood
of the coffin, pressing her hand flat against it. Her heart was tearing
through her chest.

"Sarah?" she asked. The name came out hushed and strangled.
She cleared her throat, then touched her knuckles softly to the
wood. Her hand had left a ghostly imprint of moisture. "Sarah?"
she repeated.

The scratching stopped.

"Sarah, please knock if you can hear me."

Nothing, just the beating of her own heart and the muffled
voices of people in the other room. She sighed, leaned her elbows
on top of the coffin, and ground her eyes with the heels of her hands.

Softly, hesitantly, a knock.

It was muffled by the velvet that clothed the inside of the
coffin, but it *was* a knock; nothing but a rap with someone's knuckles could have made it.

Emotion seized Lucy by the throat. "Oh, Sarah!" She sobbed, then laughed. "Don't worry. I'm going to get you out of there."

She grasped one of the thumbscrews used to screw the lid shut. It was silver-plated, beautifully wrought in the shape of a vase with flowers. Lucille's had been shaped like little doves. Funny how such things came back to mind. The ones used on her parents' coffins had been plain. One didn't expect such elaborate, beautiful things when one buried a Protestant, but Michael had the tastes of a Catholic.

She tried to twist the screw open, yet it wouldn't budge. She put the tip of her finger in her mouth, then used her teeth to tear off her glove. When she gripped the screw again, it felt so cold that it burned. Again she tried to twist it, first to one side, then to the other because she suddenly wasn't quite sure which side was right. Not that it mattered; it would not move.

Damn Michael and those beautiful hands of his straight to hell! What need was there to screw on the lid so tight? The law ensured a regular supply of bodies to the universities; unless the body was in any way unusual, there was no need to fear it would be stolen by resurrection men and sold for anatomy. And what fear could there be that the coffin's occupant wanted out? That was what the wake had been for: to ensure Sarah was truly dead and not merely coma-tose. Not that it had helped, because here she was, feebly moving around inside, scratching against the wood with her weak hands.

Of course, there had been that incident with Lucille…

Lucy grabbed a silver candlestick and bashed it against one of the screws, which bent it. She tried to twist it, but it was firmly stuck. She bit off a scream of frustration, resisting the urge to drum her fists against the side of the casket.

"Don't be afraid, Saartje. I'm going to get someone. I won't be long!"

She had not quite made it out of the room before she ran into Arthur. The jolt of it was sickening; she had not expected him, had not even raised her hands to cushion the blow.

"Steady!" he said.

She clasped his lower arms, making him wince; the wound from Sarah's bite had not quite closed. Lucy winced in sympathy but did not let go. "Arthur!" she breathed.

"I've come to see if you feel a little better. The service will begin in a quarter of an hour. The coffin should be in the front of the pews by then, but I didn't want the undertaker and his men to disturb you." His kind eyes crinkled at the corners in concern. "You're still looking mighty pale. Do you feel feverish?"

"Black washes me out; ask Mrs. van Dijk. You must come with me first, though. I need your help. God, am I glad you're here."

His face lit up at that. He was all ruddy cheeks and twinkling eyes and smiles when happy or pleased. It was a shame he had not yet married a pretty little girl who lived to delight him.

"I'm always happy to assist," he said.

"Then you must come with me. She's alive!" She squeezed his good arm so hard, her fingers turned white.

"Who is?"

"Sarah, of course. Who else?"

He took a deep breath, as if gathering himself, then placed his hand on top of hers. "Lucy, I know this must be very difficult for you, but your sister truly isn't alive anymore."

He talked in that soothing doctor voice of his, the very same he must use on patients who were sick and confused. She had the sudden urge to hurt him, really hurt him, by gripping his lashes and yanking them out or scratching at his eyes. She clenched her hands into fists. "I heard her," she said.

"Corpses can make sounds. They can sigh or groan. Sometimes they can even move, but those things are caused by the processes of decomposition, nothing else."

"She didn't sigh or groan. She was scratching the inside of the coffin lid. I heard her nails against the wood. I thought it was a rat at first, but rats don't knock when you ask them to."

"Lucy,"—*if he says my name like that one more time, I really can't be held responsible for what happens next*—"you have been under a lot of stress lately. You are grieving, and you haven't been sleeping, and…"

"I'm not mad!" she cried. Tears of shame and frustration welled. She dashed them from her eyes with hatred and impatience, then took a shuddering breath. With a lowered voice, she repeated, "I'm *not* mad. Twins are not identical in everything."

"I'm not suggesting you are. I'm only saying that the mind can play tricks upon us, especially when it has suffered such a massive blow as yours has. There's a family in this village who lost a child, and when it had just happened, the father told me he kept seeing the little boy from the corner of his eye, always dashing out of sight. He's a decent fellow, calm and stoic, with very little imagination."

"I'm not hallucinating. Sarah was scratching the wood, and then she knocked on it when I asked. She's in there, Arthur, and she's alive!"

His hand was hot on hers. He stroked a single line along her knuckles with his thumb, very softly, very gently. "Marry me," he said.

She blinked; she couldn't have heard right. "What?" she asked.

"Marry me, Lucy."

"I don't understand."

Those ruddy cheeks of his turned a deeper shade of pink. "Come, don't act as if I'm speaking a different language! I've asked you to marry me."

She had the curious feeling that she wasn't properly aligned with her body anymore. Everything felt either too sharp or too dull. She shook her head a little, as if trying to dislodge a drop of water from her ear. "You're not speaking sense."

"On the contrary, I'm speaking more sense than I ever have. Don't you see that marriage would be the sensible thing? You've received the worst blow in your life. As your husband and your doctor, I'll be able to take care of you in ways no one else ever could."

Was this truly happening? Was she really listening to her childhood friend pleading his case for marriage when she had just told him her sister was scratching her hands bloody, trying to get out of the coffin in which she'd surely be buried if they didn't act? Reality had never felt as thin as it did in that moment.

"Of course, in becoming my wife, you'll be somewhat restored to your proper place in society," he went on. "I know being a doctor's wife is not exactly as prestigious a position as you must have hoped for before your parents died, but you must concede it is much better than being an old widow's companion."

Tears of frustration and anger made her vision swim. "Why does everyone assume I hate working for Mrs. van Dijk? Is it that impossible to believe I actually enjoy being her companion? And must I remind you it was you who found me that position in the first place?" She tried to extract her hand from his, but his fingers clamped around hers, not with enough force to hurt—he'd never hurt her—but with insistence.

"You weren't raised for servitude, Lucy. It pains me to see you reduced to it. I would've saved you from it sooner, only I didn't have enough money then to keep a wife, and I would never have you live in poverty. You weren't raised for that either."

"I wasn't raised for a lot of things, like burying my sister after she has attempted to destroy herself with the pen that was a gift from her husband for my twenty-first birthday, yet that's exactly what'll happen if you don't help me!"

"Of course, there's also the matter of my loving you most ardently," he said softly. He had long lashes. She rarely noticed them, they were so pale, but in the yellow light falling through the window, they seemed as sharp and defined as hoarfrost.

"But you can't marry me," she said.

"Why not?"

"Because madness runs in my family, and mad people shouldn't have children."

"Your father didn't think so."

"My father didn't know until it was too late."

"Michael didn't think it a problem."

That's why he now has a dead wife. "We weren't exactly forth-coming about Aunt Adelheid at first." Their parents had never spoken of Aunt Adelheid after she had gone. They had told their daughters to do the same, lumping her together with all the other things one didn't speak about because they were shameful, like defecating and their neighbor's psoriasis. The worst was that Lucy could understand why they had excised Aunt Adelheid out of their lives as one would a cancerous mole: no one would marry a girl who had a mad relative.

"We shan't have children, if that's what worries you," Arthur said and smiled magnanimously.

"But, Arthur, I don't love you like a wife should love her husband."

"But you are fond of me?"

She pulled at his arm in an effort to get him to follow her. "You know I've always been fond of you."

"I won't ask any more of you than that, Lucy."

"Why must you ask me at all? Why must you keep pressing, when I've told you that I can't think, not with my sister alive and terrified in that coffin?"

"I know these sensations are very real to you, but that doesn't make them so," he said, a little coldly.

She wanted to stamp her foot, or grab him by the lapels and shake him, or scream in his face—anything to make him stop patronizing her. She tore her hand from his grip and pushed her fists hard against her face instead, knuckling her closed eyes till they smarted. When she dropped her hands and opened her eyes, she felt a little calmer.

"I've got no need of Doctor Hoefnagel now," she said, "nor of the man who desires to be my husband, but of plain Arthur, my childhood friend and confidant. I am telling you I heard my sister move inside her coffin. Perhaps it is as you say, that my nerves are frayed and none of it is real. But what if it is? Could you live with yourself then? All you need to do to help me is come with me and open my sister's casket so we can look inside and ascertain that she is truly dead. I tried to open it myself, but I lack the strength in my hands. It'll only take a minute." She gave him a tremulous smile.

"And then you'll consider my proposal?" he asked.

"And then I'll consider your proposal," she assented.

That seemed to decide him. He squared his shoulders, patting her hand affectionately. "I shall assist you then."

Unscrewing the lid proved to be a slow business. Multiple times, Arthur stopped and shook out his hand, then rubbed at the flesh of his fingers, which was at first livid and then red and pink and purple, stamped with the pattern on the thumbscrews. He did not humiliate her by complaining, nor by saying they needed to hurry, that they would be missed and hold up everything and how would that look? He did curse once, when his fingers slipped on the silver. He got out his handkerchief and wrapped it around the screw, and that helped.

As he worked, Lucy wrung her hands with such force, the skin at the base of her index finger split. It hurt like hell. Her whole body did—her nerves were acutely sensitive to the point of pain, as if she had received a large electrical shock. Perhaps it was as Arthur had said. Perhaps she was overwrought, crazy with grief.

Only, she didn't really believe that.

Finally, Arthur loosened the final screw. Lucy hurried to his side, then helped him lift the lid and prop it against the wall. She thought her heart would burst in her chest, it beat so quickly.

When they turned around, Sarah had sat up.

She blew at her veil, then brushed it impatiently from her face. Her fingers were studded with splinters and left a red smear on the veil, which stuck to her mangled eye and drifted back, thus revealing only for a moment her colorless lips peeled back from her teeth, the porcelain one painfully white among the gray ones.

"Finally," she said. "I'm fucking starving."

Part II

"Do you not think that there are things which you cannot understand, and yet which are, that some people see things that others cannot?"

Bram Stoker, *Dracula*

A YOUNG LADY ALMOST BURIED ALIVE

Lady Sarah Schatteleyn, the beloved wife of Lord Michael Schatteleyn of the Zwartwater estate in Drenthe, was reported deceased in this newspaper some six days ago after a short but violent sickbed. That this was not in fact the case was proven just before her funeral sermon.

Her loyal twin sister, who had not left Lady Schatteleyn's side during the wake, found it impossible to tear herself away from her sister even when the lid was screwed down, sitting with it as long as she was able before decency would compel her to take her place in the church.

Just before that moment arrived, she heard scratching. Initially, she suspected mice, until she heard that the sound came from *inside the coffin*! She compelled the local physician to help her open it to ascertain whether the lady had truly died. Upon doing so, they found Lady Schatteleyn cold and still. They were in the process of replacing the lid when the woman's hand shot out and clasped her sister's. Both then uttered piercing shrieks: the sister one of terror, and Lady Schatteleyn one of such acute agony, it broke the heart of anyone near enough to hear it. Both then fainted; such is the affinity between twins.

Cases of premature burial are rare. More often than not, the fear of premature burial turns out to be unfounded. In 1884, a man in Cabrils, Spain, dug up the body of a young girl whom he— erroneously, as it turned out— believed had been buried alive (it must be noted that the man was later committed to an asylum on account of him being feebleminded; even after the girl had been reburied, he kept insisting she was still alive).

Cases may be rare, but they are not unheard of. Just two years ago, a young woman was buried alive in Michigan, the USA. Unlike the Michigan case, in which the woman in question did not look deceased—it was this very fact that made her fiancé disinter her swiftly after she was buried, only to find that the poor woman, now truly dead, had been buried alive; her bloodied hands, the torn lining of the coffin, and the look of terror on her face that until then had worn an expression of beatific peace all attested to that—Lady Schatteleyn never gave the appearance of being anything but deceased. Yet she was fully conscious as her body was washed, shrouded, and placed in its coffin, though unable to move, or utter a sound, or in any other way signal to those around her that she was still living.

According to her physician—

the same one who helped unscrew the coffin lid—she must have suffered from a severe case of catalepsy brought on by the brain fever that preceded it. She also used to sleepwalk frequently as a child, thus making her more susceptible to catalepsy and other such disorders.

Lady Schatteleyn is currently at home, where she is recovering from her horrific ordeal. Well-wishers are asked to write but not to visit; her delicate state of health requires her to rest and avoid all kinds of excitement that might bring about another fever.

Chapter 11

"GOD, JOURNALISTS ARE SUCH SENSATIONALISTS. They do love to put their noses where they don't belong. A bunch of half-truths and exaggerations. As if Arthur would ever discuss my wife's medical history with some eager hack writing for a third-rate newspaper," Michael said, after he had read the article out loud to those gathered at the breakfast table. He threw the paper down in disgust, then wiped his stained fingers on a napkin.

"But the article does paint our darling Lucy as a hero, as indeed she is," Katje said, smiling.

"At the expense of Sarah's privacy and my own."

"My dear man, how on earth would you have kept it quiet?" Mrs. van Dijk said. "Try and see it in a positive light. That journalist chap did you a favor. He made it very clear you don't want any company. Nobody with any decency would dare visit unannounced now."

"That doesn't stop the other journalists," Michael retorted.

"Well, no one has ever accused a journalist of having much decency. That would be deadly in their profession."

"If I see another one of those bastards sneaking around, I'll put the dogs on him. I told Mr. Hooiman he's free to shoot at them, too."

"Rather harsh, don't you think? Those men are only trying to make a living."

"Let them do it elsewhere!" Michael said hotly.

Lucy closed her eyes. She wished she could place her hand lightly on his and tell him he shouldn't let Mrs. van Dijk rile him so, but she couldn't do that with others present.

Katje, whose face had been spasming between a range of different expressions as she listened to them argue, broke the silence by giggling nervously and saying, "Oh, but those are lovely earrings, Mrs. van Dijk. Emeralds suit your coloring very well."

"They're just paste, but thank you," Mrs. van Dijk said. She brushed her skirt as she spoke, absent-mindedly plucking at the silvery dog hairs that clung to the fabric. All her clothes were covered with it, since she had taken pity on Pasja. The little dog had been slinking around the house, tail so far between her legs that the tip brushed her ribs, the whites of her eyes showing. The day after the almost funeral, as Lucy tried to put on her leash to take her out to walk, she growled and bit her hand, drawing blood. Michael grabbed his cane to give the dog a thrashing despite Lucy's pleading, would perhaps even have dragged her outside and put her down—saying how *a dog that bites people can't be suffered to live*—if Mrs. van Dijk hadn't intervened. For once, she hadn't spoken, had simply scooped Pasja up, tucked the dog under her arm as one would a book, and taken her to her room.

Pasja stayed in Mrs. van Dijk's room now, where she spent

most of her days lying on a pillow, sleeping fitfully, or chewing at her paws. She cleaned them carefully, catlike, digging between the toes with her beautiful pink tongue.

When Pasja lay quietly like that, occasionally thumping her tail, it was impossible to imagine the dog had bitten Lucy. The wound wasn't deep, but Arthur looked at it twice every day for signs of infection and rabies after he was done visiting Sarah.

Lucy wished he wouldn't. He hadn't pressed her for an answer to his proposal, and she, coward that she was, didn't bring it up because she didn't want to see the hurt on his face when she inevitably rejected him. She loved him too little to make him a good wife and too much to let him settle for her.

Not that she had much time to think about it with Sarah being near. It had been almost a week now since she'd been miraculously restored to life. Michael was at least partially right when he said journalists were sensationalists, because the journalist who had written that article in *De Nieuwe Murmerwolderse Courant* had tried to make his piece more interesting by fabricating details. There had been no piercing shrieks, no matching fainting fits.

Instead, Sarah repeated that she was hungry before tearing the veil from her face. It came away with a horrible wet ripping sound, and her ruined eye wept black and yellow fluid. The reek of it—sweet, cloying, so strong that it was almost physical—made them gag. Sarah's good eye rolled back, and she slumped in her coffin, her bony elbows knocking against the sides, the sound muffled by the lining of red velvet. Lucy hastened to her sister's side, took her in her arms, kissed her brittle hair, and wiped away the sludgy tears with her handkerchief while trying not to look too closely at what remained of the eye. Sarah tried to fend her off with weak hands, whimpering, but that was good, because it meant she was alive, alive, alive…

The first thing Lucy did when they returned to Zwartwater was sew a number of eye patches for her sister. She had sewn them once before, for Aunt Adelheid. She and Vera, the maid she had trained to be her assistant, had gone out one hot summer night with a lit lantern and a butterfly net to catch moths. For their trouble, they were rewarded with several moths as well as copious mosquito bites and, in Aunt Adelheid's case, an infected eye; something had flown in, and in a reflex, she had rubbed her eye hard, grinding the insect to pulp rather than dashing it away. Within a day, the eye reddened and swelled and wept pus. Any other woman might have been mortified, but Aunt Adelheid only laughed and said that, though it was a damn shame she wouldn't be able to catch moths for a while now on account of her not being able to perceive as much depth with only one eye, she'd always rather fancied being a pirate. When she had healed, she'd confessed to Lucy she was almost sorry she would not be wearing an eye patch anymore, for Vera had found it wonderfully rakish, and was there anything more pleasurable in life than impressing a woman?

Lucy could only hope that, in time, Sarah, too, would come to love wearing an eye patch. Unlike Aunt Adelheid's, her eye would never heal. The eyelid was still tattered, but occasionally, when Sarah blinked, the wounded eyelid moved, too, and Lucy could hear the scrabble of her lashes against the velvet. It sounded eerily similar to Sarah scratching at the inside of her coffin.

Arthur had taught Lucy how to clean the wound. Though it gave her that strange fluttery feeling in her head and belly, she bit down and did as she should; she could not bear the idea of Magda or any of the other servants being revolted by her sister. Lucy washed the wound twice a day, then packed the now-empty socket with cotton wool. On the second day, Arthur removed what remained of the eyeball to prevent rot from setting in; by then, a kind of fungus had already begun to grow, so he burned it.

"I know how it must sound, but it's a lucky thing she used a pen to destroy her eye and not her fingers," Arthur had said as he'd prepared his instruments for the operation.

"Because of possible infections?"

He shook his head. "No, because of the angle of penetration. The pen went in at an angle of almost ninety degrees to the eye. Had she tried it with her thumb, she might have rooted around and gone down past the occipital bone, which can cause convulsions or even death. I've seen it happen once during a bar fight. It wasn't a pretty sight."

He looked her over, then said, "If you are ever attacked, remember that eye gouging is extremely effective at incapacitating an attacker. For someone as small and slight as you, it's probably the best way to defend yourself. Thrust hard and thrust deep. You must crush the eyeball or at least cause severe hemorrhaging if you are to take out your assailant."

She remembered the sickening crunch and the jelly of Sarah's eye running down her cheek like yolk, and thought she might be sick. "I'll keep it in mind," she'd managed to say.

Sarah's eye socket did not seem to be healing yet.

"But it might be too early for that yet. For days, she teetered on the brink of death. It mustn't be wondered at that her body's processes are tardier than what we might expect in a healthy woman," Arthur had told her when she'd brought it up. He'd smiled at her, reached out to press her hand and soothe her, then seemed to remember he was still waiting for her to tell him whether she'd be his wife and dropped it again. "Try not to fret. There are no precedents for cases like this, you know."

Yet Lucy couldn't help but feel that her sister wasn't behaving the way she should. This feeling was exacerbated when she went to Sarah's room to have tea with her, only to find Sarah had taken a pair of scissors to her hair and hacked it off. Strands of it lay in her lap, hung in the crook of her elbow, and clung to the fabric of her nightgown.

Lucy pressed her hands against her mouth. The muscles in her throat clenched so hard, it took a moment before she could speak. When she did, her voice came out pained and childlike. "Saartje, what on earth have you done to your hair?"

"I cut it."

"I can see that, but why, in God's name? And who gave you the scissors?"

"I can't afford to spend energy on growing hair."

"Did Arthur tell you that?"

"I didn't need him to tell me."

Lucy picked up a strand and twisted it between her fingers. "But you love your hair," she said helplessly. "It'll take you years and years to grow it out again."

"It can't be helped. It was all brittle and damaged and horrible. This way, it'll grow back much faster."

With this, Lucy couldn't argue. "Still," she said, as the hair rustled dryly against her fingers, "you could've asked me to help you. You needn't have given yourself a fever cut. Give me the scissors, and I'll snip off whatever hair you missed." She held out her hand. For a moment, she wondered if her sister might argue, but Sarah extracted a pair of embroidery scissors from between the sheets and handed them over without complaint. They were made of silver, plain but sharp and shockingly cold.

"These aren't yours. Who gave them to you?" Lucy asked.

Sarah's face was curiously still, almost more like a marble effigy than a real face. "Don't treat me like a child. I don't care for it."

"I'm not treating you like a child."

"Yes, you are. You and my husband and the doctor treat me like a fucking child! Do you think I'm stupid? You're watching me all the time. You talk to me in that special sort of voice you use only when you think I'm insane again. You've even removed sharp objects from my room. As if I'm likely to put a pair of scissors through my other eye, or a pen, or a knife—or a needle or a pin or a fork or, God help us all, a fucking teaspoon!"

Lucy looked at the scissors in her hand, fit her fingers in the handles, and opened and closed the blades. They snicked together beautifully. "There's no need for you to be angry with me, and there's no need to swear either. You never much used to."

"Well, I've changed. A pen through the eyeball will do that to a person."

Sarah, screaming. A wet crunch, followed by a soft trickle. The meaty stink of it. How easily those sensations rose in Lucy's mind, how hard to push them back into the darkness again.

"That's why we're so careful with you. We don't mean to infantilize you; we're merely worried. Surely you can understand that? Now, please don't talk about it anymore," she said in a small voice.

She cut off the remaining locks, and there was only the sound of the scissors snipping, the swish of the strands of hair falling into Sarah's lap, and the droning of a bluebottle at the window. It thudded against the glass, was still for a moment, then flew up again, buzzing.

When she was done, Lucy slipped the scissors into the pocket of her dress. She gathered the hair, then put it in a twist of newspaper. "Would you like to keep it?"

"Whatever for? There's no need to braid it into bracelets and necklaces anymore. I'm still alive, after all."

Lucy took her sister's bony hand and brought it to her mouth to kiss it. It was the one she had rubbed against her face so vehemently that the top layer of skin had sloughed off, though flaky patches remained, mainly at the knuckles. A line of dead skin, the edges translucent and raggedy, ran across Sarah's wrist like the thinnest strip of lace, marking the place where the skin had torn and come away. Like the eye, this had not yet begun to heal.

"And for that I'm more grateful than I could ever say. You know that, right? That I love you more than anyone else in this world?"

"Of course I know that," Sarah murmured, resting her cold cheek against their clasped hands.

"Shall I ring for tea? Cook made some of those watercress sandwiches you love, and some little cakes, too."

Anything to get her to eat.

Despite her assertion that she was—*fucking*—starving, Sarah had barely been eating since she had almost been buried, which struck Lucy as yet another strange thing; surely someone as starved as Sarah should want to do nothing but eat?

Magda brought up a tray with cups and a steaming-hot pot of tea, as well as an étagère with sandwiches, cakes, small bowls of berries, and bits of apple shaped like triangles. Back when Lucille had still been alive, all fruits had needed to be carved into stars, or she wouldn't eat them. Lucy remembered holding her godchild in her lap, helping her take sips of her cup of milk and feeding her bits of pear and hothouse melon with sticky fingers, the air around them perfumed by the sweet juices.

The dull pain of missing her niece brought tears to her eyes. Under the pretext of spooning cream in her tea, she bent over her steaming cup to hide them. She watched the cream unspool, creeping through the liquid like tendrils of fog. By the time her tea paled into an even color, the tears had gone.

She brought the cup to her mouth, readying herself to take a sip.

It was then that the bluebottle, which had ceased throwing itself at the window a minute before, landed on Sarah's eye. Not on the lid nor the soft creased skin underneath; it landed on her remaining eyeball.

And she did not blink.

It sat there, rubbing its front legs together in the way flies were often observed to do, as if washing them with the fluid that coated Sarah's eyeball, and she did not instinctively blink to get rid of it. She did eventually raise a hand to her face and plucked the fly out, then crushed it between her thumb and index finger, but the movement was deliberate, precise, not the quick panicked dashing one would expect from having something in one's eye.

That is not normal, Lucy thought, then shuddered so violently that her jaws snapped shut.

A crack, very loud to her. The feel of something smooth and hard against her tongue. Tea dribbled down her cup and into her lap, hot at first but quickly cooling. She lowered the cup, staring at it in astonishment, her heart racing. A piece was missing. For a second, she was utterly confused. Then she realized what had happened: she had bitten through the rim and now held a piece of it in her mouth.

She probed it with her tongue. Sharp pain lanced the tip, strong enough to bring tears to her eyes. She gagged, then spat into her cupped hand. The shard of china fell into it, glistening. A strand of saliva threaded through with red still connected it to her mouth. She wiped her lips with the back of her hand, causing it to snap.

"My God, are you all right? Did you just take a bite out of that cup?" Sarah asked.

"I didn't mean to," Lucy said thickly; blood had pooled into her mouth. She swallowed. The blood had mixed with the tea, leaving a bitter, metallic taste behind.

Sarah dumped the contents of her cup back into the teapot

and held it out for Lucy. "Here. You shouldn't swallow blood. It'll make you sick."

She spat and spat. She felt as if she were at the dentist, being asked to rinse after a cavity had been filled or a tooth extracted. All she lacked was the smell of gas and antiseptic. Soon, she had spat out enough blood and saliva to fill the bottom of the cup. Her tongue throbbed. The tip already felt raw and swollen. She pressed it against the ribbed roof of her mouth.

"Has it stopped bleeding?" Sarah asked.

"I think so."

"Let me look."

"I'm sure it feels much worse than it is." Her tongue touched the back of her teeth as she spoke, and she winced.

"Let me look."

Lucy stuck out her tongue. Sarah cocked her head, took hold of her sister's tongue with her thumb and index finger, and pinched it. Tears sprang into Lucy's eyes. The cut began to bleed again. A drop ran down Sarah's thumb.

Now it was Sarah who shuddered violently. She thrust her thumb into her mouth and sucked it. When she extracted it, she fixed her eye on Lucy. So strange was her stare, so unlike Sarah, that the blood drained from Lucy's hands and feet and face, leaving her cold.

The only warmth came from the cut on her tongue, which throbbed very fast, echoing her heartbeat.

When Sarah fell upon her, Lucy let out a choked scream and tried to scrabble back. Her heels found little purchase on the waxed floorboards. The chair's legs screeched as they ground against the wood, which made the hairs on Lucy's body rise.

She's going to bite me! She's going to rip out my throat and drink me up like she tried with Arthur. She—she—she will drain, will empty me...

Sarah's fingers closed around her wrist. Her nails had been broken as she clawed at the lining of the coffin—three had come away altogether; the remaining ones Lucy had cut and filed down. She felt the hard press of those two nails against the tender inside of her wrist, felt the soft wrinkled flesh of the fingers where the nail had been ripped out completely. How intimate to feel what was normally hidden, yet how deeply unpleasant, too, like brushing against a cut of cold meat that had been skinned and lay ready to be chopped and put in the pot.

Sarah tightened her grip. She needed only to press down a little, and the skin at Lucy's wrist would split, exposing the thick veins and the thread-thin capillaries that ran underneath. Sarah could tear those open with her teeth, and then the blood would flow fast and freely, and then...

Sarah wrenched the cup from Lucy's hand, then let go of her wrist and retreated, clutching the cup to her chest. Sarah's gray teeth—*save for that porcelain one; God, how incongruous it looks; we should have gone with a different hue, not so horribly white*—were bared. Her gums seemed almost lavender. She brought the cup to her mouth and tilted it, causing the mixture of blood and saliva and dregs of tea to dribble out.

She drank, licked, sucked.

Her eye rolled back into her skull, and her eyelids fluttered; the tattered one rustled against the eye patch like a nail being dragged over velvet.

For a moment, it looked like she might faint, yet Lucy did not take her by the elbow nor put an arm around her waist to steady her. Instead, Lucy sat frozen, little chills swimming up and down her back. The blood she had swallowed churned in her stomach.

When not a single drop remained, Sarah sank back, panting but smiling. Without opening her eye, she wiped her mouth with the back of her hand, then sucked the skin, her brows knitted. Her cheeks were flushed prettily.

Oh, she's beautiful, Lucy thought. Rationally, she knew her sister was not—Sarah was emaciated, her skin a sickly gray, her shorn scalp mottled with bald spots—yet she *was* beautiful, if one could only lift away the veil and *see*, just as Sarah had been able to do with the bog woman…

Horror took Lucy by the throat with such force, she squawked. Her stomach cramped, and she burped softly, painfully. Her heart pounded, each beat like being thumped in the chest. Perhaps a person truly could be scared to death, and this was what it felt like.

Sarah opened her eye. Her smile faded. "Oh, Lucy," she whispered. She got up and crawled to her, and Lucy was too weak to flee, to fend her off. Sarah pressed her cheek against her sister's knee. "I'm sorry. Please don't be afraid. I love you. I don't want to hurt you. I'm just so terribly hungry and thirsty all the time." Speaking of it must have had her salivating; she swallowed twice in rapid succession.

"Then why don't you eat?" Lucy managed to whisper.

"I can't. I know you don't believe me, but I truly can't. I wish I could. It would make things much easier."

Lucy hesitated, then touched her sister's shorn head, placing her fingers in the bluish hollow where skull and vertebrae connected. Even her scalp was cold. "I think there's something very wrong with you, Sarah."

"I know. Please don't tell anyone else about what you saw me do. People have been sent to asylums for much less."

"You aren't Aunt Adelheid, and I'm not our parents." Lucy dropped a kiss on her head. The short hairs were deliciously soft, but there was a smell that clung to them that Lucy realized rose from Sarah's skin; it was far from delicious: stale, earthy, bitter, and sweet, like fruit molding, like mold fruiting. "I would never just send you to an asylum."

"It wouldn't be 'just,' though, would it? It would be the sleepwalking, and what I did when Lucille died, and my morbid obsession with Marianne…" Sarah let out a desperate sob.

"Who is Marianne?"

Sarah was quiet for a moment, then murmured, "The bog woman."

"Saartje, what is happening?" Lucy asked.

But Sarah did not answer, only swallowed thickly.

Chapter 12

THE NEXT MORNING, LUCY ASKED Katje to join her for a walk.

Her reasons were simple: Firstly, she wanted to discuss her sister, which she couldn't do with Michael, since that would be a kind of betrayal. It would also be somewhat useless because Michael had barely spent any time with his wife ever since she had risen from the dead. He claimed he was simply swamped with work, and though Lucy did not think that was a lie per se, she did think the real reason for his lack of visits had more to do with Sarah's unattractive current state and his powerlessness to change it. Lucy couldn't talk about Sarah with Arthur either because he would inevitably slip into his role of doctor. Besides, she was still avoiding him in the hope that his proposal would disappear, a hope she knew was utterly delusional but couldn't quite shake.

That had left either Katje or Mrs. van Dijk. Because Mrs. van Dijk was unsuited to her second reason (Lucy wanted to walk fast and far to tire herself out in an effort to quiet her thoughts), she asked Katje, who had been delighted to be invited for something.

It was a fine morning for a walk: cool but dry. The sun bathed everything in that beautiful warm light so particular to autumn. The trees looked like royalty in their mantles of scarlet and their crowns of gold. The recent rain had left behind the famous pools of dark water for which the estate was named. This day, uncharacteristically windless, they were utterly still. Lucy had the strangest feeling that, if she were to try and dip her hand into them, the surface would not break, and it would be like trying to submerge her hand into black glass.

She told Katje, smiling disparagingly at herself.

To her surprise, Katje said, "I know what you mean. Ever since I've come to live here, I've thought things like that. I never used to. I think there's something strange about this place. It feels realer than other places I know."

Lucy picked up a pebble. It was flat on one side and veined all over. She rubbed it for good luck, then tried to skip it on one of the puddles. It bounced once, then sank, revealing the puddle to be no more than water after all. "Funny. I myself am never sure if Zwartwater is realer than other places or less so."

"Perhaps it doesn't matter. Either one would suffice to cause ripples in the mind." Katje shivered and huddled deeper into her coat. It was one of Sarah's old ones, beautifully woven of fine wool.

"'Ripples in the mind.' I like that. Very poetic. It is of such ripples I wanted to talk to you today."

"Sarah."

"Sarah," Lucy agreed. "Does she not seem changed to you?"

"In what way?" Katje asked cautiously. She looked pinched and pale today, Lucy noted, but they had all had a tough few weeks of it.

"Well, for one thing, she doesn't want to eat." Not the things she should be eating, anyway.

"Perhaps there is a reason for it," Katje said. "Some months ago, Sarah told me of a soldier who had some rotten human flesh flung into his mouth during a battle, which he swallowed accidentally. It made him horribly sick. The whole episode made him afraid to eat afterward."

Something seemed to slither from her mouth into mine, something cool and soft. It tasted sweet and strong and rich, like blood, like rot. I felt a deep sense of revulsion so strong that I gagged. She clamped her hand over my lips and nose. She stroked my throat until, convulsively, I swallowed what she had spat into my mouth.

Could that explain it? Sarah suffered from a horrible nightmare at the onset of her brain fever, which had amplified and anchored it to the point that it made it impossible for her to eat. Why hadn't she told Lucy of it, though?

For the same reason she tried to destroy that diary entry: it made her feel distressed and ashamed. That, or she didn't remember it and now didn't understand herself why she couldn't eat. But why, then, did she crave blood? The thing she had swallowed had tasted of it; would that not make her particularly averse to it?

Lucy pinched the bridge of her nose. "I know that story of the soldier. She read it in a medical journal Arthur gave to her. I didn't know she had shared it with you, too."

Katje flushed. "I was closer to her than you may suppose. And her loss of appetite doesn't have to be caused by something so acute and horrible as what happened to that soldier. I talked to Doctor

Hoefnagel about it. Apparently, some girls and women starve themselves on purpose. It's a documented disease of the mind."

"Sarah has never had much trouble with eating. Even when she lost her tooth, she still ate her buttered bread just fine." Sarah and Arthur had pretended to be knights, with Lucy the fair maiden to be fought over, preferably to the death. They battled each other with wooden swords. Arthur had a distaste for violence, but Sarah fought with a viciousness and anger particular to little girls. That he hit her in the face with such force that her lip split and one of her teeth broke clean at the root was partly her own fault; he had only meant to deflect her blow.

"You forget that time after Lucille died, when Sarah brought her home for a little bit," Katje said. The words came carefully, each pronounced slowly, like a child still learning how to read feeling their way through a text or a foreigner who hadn't yet realized that words in a running sentence were pronounced differently than when taken in isolation.

Oh, but that's a very gentle way to describe a very disturbing thing, Lucy thought.

A few days after they had entombed Lucille, Sarah had become convinced her little girl was still alive. Because no one else could be convinced of this, she broke into the family crypt and took the body home.

A memory rose: Sarah clutching her daughter still wrapped in her shroud, now stained. She had removed the fabric from the little face, which was gray and pulpy. Mold in shades of fantastical orange and yellow had grown in the corner of her mouth. Unlike the flesh of her cheeks, it didn't jiggle as Sarah rocked the small corpse.

"I told you," she said, smiling, her eyes glittering in triumph. "I told you I could hear her call for me."

Lucy locked the door against the servants and against Michael. No one could see this; no one could know.

"Oh God!" Sarah wailed, not a quarter of an hour after, when the delusion had broken. "Oh God, oh God, oh God, what have I done?"

It took the better part of an hour to calm her down. Then Sarah became terrified that Michael would have her committed for this, which Lucy had to admit was one of the more lucid thoughts her sister had had in days, and that set Sarah off again. Lucy had to push her to the ground and lie on top of her to keep her from hurting herself. All the while, little Lucille had lain in the room with them, her fluids seeping into the carpet, the smell of her causing Lucy's eyes to water and her stomach to spasm.

"We all struggled with our appetites that day," she said. Zwartwater had a way of blowing the rooms of her mind wide open. She never remembered things so variedly and vividly when she slept in her little room in Mrs. van Dijk's house, which was a sensible place devoid of sentimentality.

To steer the conversation back to where she wanted it, she asked, "But you don't think Sarah has been behaving oddly?"

Katje toyed with one of the buttons on her coat. "Doctor Hoefnagel says there's a logical explanation for everything, even if we can't see it."

How exhausting this conversation was! Did Katje always hedge so? Perhaps it would have been a better idea to ask Mrs. van Dijk after all. The woman was many things, but known for beating around the bush, she was not. "But what do you think?" Lucy asked.

"My uncle told me it isn't my place to think," she said, then laughed. Her laughter ended abruptly. "I'm sorry," she said, looking appalled. "I don't know why I mentioned him. I'm not in the habit of talking about him."

"I'm sorry," Lucy said as she laid a hand on Katje's shoulder.

Katje looked at that hand with a frown. "Please don't do that," she said softly.

Lucy removed her hand instantly. "I'm so sorry," she said. "I didn't know you didn't care for that sort of touch."

"I don't mean that," Katje said. Color bled into her cheeks. "I mean how you are treating me, as if I'm fragile. I'm not!" She stomped her foot in frustration and roughly knuckled at her wet eyes. Her hands, Lucy saw, were balled into fists, and they trembled. "People look at me, and all they see is this abused girl they must pity. It's a hard thing, to be reduced to the abuse you've suffered. People don't understand that I am so much more than what my father and uncle did to me. Even worse is that I can never say that out loud, because what my father and uncle did to me, well, that's not the sort of thing you can hint at, let alone discuss in polite society."

Katje dropped her fists. "Only Sarah has ever seen beyond all of that. That's why I love her terribly."

Shame burned inside Lucy's chest, creating patches of pink

on her throat and cheeks. "Katje, if I ever treated you like that, I'm sorry. I'll do my utmost best to ensure it won't happen again."

Katje gave her a weak smile. The color had drained from her face, leaving it extraordinarily pale. "I appreciate that, truly I do. Now, can we please go back? I don't feel well. It's almost that time of the month again. It afflicts me more than most."

"Of course," Lucy said, chastised.

They had walked for about five minutes when they ran into Mr. Hooiman. Lucy recognized him immediately from Sarah's description: a brown giant with crooked legs. He stared at her, then blinked and took off his cap. "I'm sorry, miss. You gave me a fright. For a moment there, I thought you were Mrs. Schatteleyn. You two are as alike as two drops of water, but you've probably been told that all your lives."

"It's never unpleasant to be told again," Lucy said. "You are the new groundskeeper, Mr. Hooiman?"

"I am."

"I don't envy you your job. So much rain here, and so much mud."

"You get used to it. After a while, you barely feel it. As a matter of fact, I've just come from the fields. I was on my way to see Mr. Schatteleyn. The boys have found something else, and I thought he might want to have a look at it, seeing as he and his wife were so interested last time we found something."

Her mouth turned dry. She swallowed. Something in her throat clicked, as if she were a clockwork toy rather than a young woman. "Do you mean the bog woman?"

"It was a woman? We couldn't tell."

"What did you find?"

He thrust his hand in his pocket, withdrew it, and held it open with the palm up. The inside of his hand was much paler than the rest of him, though the creases were black with dirt. Cupped in his hand lay a golden ring. "There's something written on the inside, but I can't make it out, and most of the boys can't read. We think it's a wedding ring. It might have belonged to the body. We found it in the same field."

Chapter 13

LUCY SWALLOWED AS SHE LOOKED at the ring. She suffered from that ache in her throat again, the one that often rose when she was anxious. "Why don't I take it from you?" she offered.

"I wouldn't want to impose," Mr. Hooiman said.

"And you wouldn't. Katje and I were just about to turn back and go to the house. It would save you the walk. I'm sure you've got plenty of better uses for your time."

Mr. Hooiman hesitated, then dropped the ring in her proffered palm. Lucy knotted it in her handkerchief and took it straight to Mrs. van Dijk. Her husband had been an enthusiastic amateur historian with a particular fondness for the Middle Ages. Though Mrs. van Dijk herself cared more for classical antiquity, she had always assisted her husband in his research and might be able to date the ring.

Mrs. van Dijk locked Pasja into her dressing room, to keep her from interfering. The dog whined softly and pressed her soft nose against the crack at the bottom of the door. They could hear her sniff in violent little bursts. Ignoring this, Mrs. van Dijk washed the ring carefully in a bowl and cleaned it with a soft cloth. "Have you told anyone else about this find?" she asked as she worked.

"Not yet. We thought it best not to talk to Sarah about it. We didn't want to upset her," Lucy said.

"Smart girl. Of course, just because this ring was found in the same field as the bog woman doesn't mean it belonged to her."

"Of course," Lucy agreed, "but it won't hurt to be careful."

"We must tell Michael, though. The ring was found on his land. It belongs to him," Katje said. She fidgeted with her necklace, moving the pendant this way and that.

"And we shall, but first I'd like to know a little better what exactly it is that those peat cutters found," Lucy said.

Mrs. van Dijk held it to the light with a set of tweezers and peered at it through a magnifying glass. "There's an inscription on the inside of the ring," she noted. "Quickly, Lucy, fetch me some paper and a pencil. You, girl, please hold this ring for me, and hold it steady. I need one hand for the magnifying glass and the other to write."

As Katje held the ring, her forehead carved with a frown of concentration, Mrs. van Dijk drew what she saw, then tried to translate the shapes into letters. After a while, she lowered the glass and smiled with satisfaction. "It's a posy ring," she said.

"What is a posy ring?" Katje asked.

"No need to keep holding the ring up. You can place it on that saucer, dear. A posy ring is typically exchanged between lovers and sometimes used as a wedding band. It has an inscription on the inside, usually a motto or part of a love poem; 'posy' comes from the French '*posie*': poem. *Amor vincit omnia, ubi amor ibi fides*, that sort of thing, though inscriptions in French were also common."

She twirled the magnifying glass between her thick fingers as she spoke. "Wearing the words flush against the skin creates a sense of both intimacy and secrecy. Only the giver and the wearer know what the ring says, hence their popularity among lovers. They've fallen out of fashion now but were in vogue from the late Middle Ages until well into the seventeenth century. That's probably when this one was made, though a specialist might be able to narrow the time frame for you. Jewelry isn't my speciality."

"What does the inscription say?" Lucy asked.

"'*Et ipse dominabitur tui.*' He shall rule over you."

"Unto the woman he said, I will greatly multiply thy sorrow and thy conception; in sorrow thou shalt bring forth children; and thy desire shall be to thy husband, and he shall rule over thee," Katje quoted. "Genesis, book three, verse sixteen."

"Not necessarily what I would have chosen for a ring to my beloved. If I wanted to stick to the Bible, the Song of Solomon seems far more suitable, or some of the psalms. Hush, Pasja! I can hear you trying to sniff yourself through that door," Mrs. van Dijk said. The dog whined, then wagged her tail; it thumped hard and fast against the floorboards.

"It does clear some things up, though," Lucy said.

"Such as?"

"Firstly, the giver and wearer must have been Catholic, or they wouldn't have chosen an inscription in Latin. Secondly, the wearer must have been a woman."

"That doesn't necessarily follow from the inscription. A woman willing to show her submissiveness might have given it to her lover, too," Mrs. van Dijk said.

"But it does follow from its size." Lucy picked the ring up from its saucer. The gold was cold against her fingertips. She slipped it on the ring finger of her left hand, which was where Catholics wore their wedding rings. "It fits, but only barely, and I've got small hands. You'd be hard-pressed to find a man who can wear this comfortably. Besides, it's more common for a man to give a woman a ring than vice versa." She removed the ring, having to tug at it gently to make it slip over the joint. Already the gold had taken on the warmth of her skin, as if eager to please.

"What will you do now?" Katje asked.

Lucy knotted the ring into her handkerchief. "I'll show it to Michael, and I'll ask him to take me to the local archive whenever it suits him best." She'd need him to help her gain access; many archives required women to bring a male chaperone.

"Why the archive?"

"If I go through the records there, I might finally figure out the bog woman's identity. If this ring does indeed belong to her and it indeed hails from the seventeenth century or thereabouts, Mrs. van Dijk has just given me a time frame for her murder. Such a thing must have been noted somewhere."

"Are you sure?" Katje asked. "You're assuming her contemporaries knew she'd been murdered, but how could they if we were the first to find the body? When she disappeared, they might have assumed she'd simply left."

"A woman doesn't simply leave on her own. Maybe you're right, though. Maybe no one thought anything of it when she disappeared and I won't find anything in the archives that'll tell me who she was and why she was killed. I have to try, though."

Mrs. van Dijk took hold of her cane from where it rested against her chair and placed it in front of her, her gloved hand caressing the handgrip, which was made of lacquered wood. "Katje, would you be a dear and please leave us? There's something I must discuss with Lucy here."

Katje sprang up, made a little curtsy to Mrs. van Dijk, and left, though not before shooting Lucy a curious glance. When her footsteps had died away, Mrs. van Dijk placed the pencil back on the table, gave Lucy a small smile, and said, "My dear, where does this sudden fascination for that bog body come from?"

Lucy found she couldn't look her employer in the face. She focused her eyes on Mrs. van Dijk's wayward curls instead, the ginger shot through with gray. "Aren't you curious yourself, then?" Lucy asked, doing her best to keep her voice light and bright.

"I am, but I don't have a sister whose temporary insanity had that very same bog body at its heart, so you'll forgive me if my own curiosity doesn't worry me but yours does. What do you hope to accomplish by solving this mystery?"

Lucy looked at her hands. The ring had left a little white circle around her finger. She pressed her nail against it, watching it blanch even more. "If I solve it, I might discover how to cure my sister."

Mrs. van Dijk sighed and clutched the handgrip of her cane tighter. The fabric of her gloves produced a soft, silky sound as she did so. "You're assuming her illness is connected to the bog body. Sarah believed that, too, and see what good it did her."

"Don't you see that's exactly why I must know more about that bog body? What if she grows obsessed with it again? If we know who she was and why she died, it'll take away the air of mystery, which is what obsessions thrive on."

"Your love for your sister does you credit, but here's a harsh truth: getting to the heart of her insanity shan't solve it. That's why it's insanity—there's no rhyme nor reason to it for those who don't experience it. Besides, knowing something isn't the same as solving it. I may know all there is to know about polio, but that won't cure my leg, now, will it?"

"I don't think you can compare those two things," Lucy whispered.

"Perhaps, but I urge you to be very careful. You are playing with fire here. Your sister may not be well now, but who's to say she won't heal of her own accord? Time is the best doctor there is. Your meddling might harm her more than doing nothing would; it might, in fact, also be harmful to yourself. Still, because I care for you and for your peace of mind, I shall come along to the archive with you. The sooner we get this bit of unpleasantness out of the way, the sooner we can go home."

Startled, Lucy dug her nail so hard into her skin that it tore. "Home?" she asked.

"Of course. I came to attend a funeral. Mercifully, we did not have one, but it does beg the question of why we are still here."

"Because I can't leave my sister. You said it yourself: she's not well." Michael had been unbelievably patient with Sarah, but there would come a point when it would be impossible to hide how disturbed she was, and then he'd have no choice but to send her to a private asylum.

"Why not? She has all the care in the world she could want," Mrs. van Dijk said.

"She needs me," Lucy hedged. She pressed the edge of her handkerchief against her finger to catch the exudate that leaked from the cut.

"You may not be outstaying your welcome—God knows Michael is fond of you, perhaps overly so—but I am. It's horrible manners, and my mother didn't raise me to have horrible manners. Besides, this house is drafty and damp. It's playing havoc with my leg."

Lucy closed her fist around the handkerchief. The ring lay knotted at the heart. The gold was hard and unyielding. "Then go home and leave me here, if only for a little while longer."

Mrs. van Dijk let out a harsh little laugh. "My dear, I know you've had a lot on your plate lately and are probably not thinking clearly, so let me be utterly vulgar here for a moment and tell you how it is: you are my companion. I pay you to be companionable to *me*, not to your sister, nor your brother-in-law, nor his poor relation, nor your childhood friend the doctor. If that isn't to your liking, then perhaps we should reconsider our arrangement. I'll give you until after our trip to the archive to consider. Please let me know when it suits his lordship to go—*if* it suits him."

"Mrs. van Dijk, if I have made you feel…" Lucy began.

The older woman raised her hand and said, "Please leave me. Pasja will start scratching at the door if she has to stay alone in the dressing room for much longer, and as I've said, I have been raised to be a good guest. Pull the bell rope on your way out; I wish to let the housekeeper know that I shall eat my dinner in my room. Good day to you."

Chapter 14

LUCY FEARED MICHAEL WOULDN'T WANT to accompany her to the archive or, even worse, that he'd forbid her from going. Instead, he rested his chin on his hands and asked, "And if you do find out who the bog body used to be, then what?"

"Then I'll know. Not that it matters much to me. I only want to know in order to nip a revival of Sarah's obsession in the bud, should it ever occur."

"Preventing is better than healing, and all that?"

"Yes."

"All right. We shall go tomorrow. The sooner this bit of business has been taken care of, the better."

That night, Sarah was irritable and rude. Lucy had brought some books from the library, but Sarah didn't care for the South American travelogue; she complained she had already read the treatise on Fibonacci and said she had lost all interest in the beautifully illustrated book on botany that had been a wedding gift from Arthur. The prints made by Piranesi couldn't interest her either, and the newspaper print was too small for her and hurt her eyes.

"Saartje, what's the matter with you?" Lucy exclaimed after another stack of books was rejected. "You used to love to read about ferns and moths and all sorts of things from the natural world!"

"Those things don't interest me anymore."

"Maybe you should try and interest yourself in them again, then. You can't just lie here and look at the ceiling. You'll…" *Go mad,* she thought but couldn't say. She might as well have said it out loud, though, for Sarah shot up like one stung.

"Leave me alone, will you? All this talking about what I used to do and didn't do when I can barely think, it makes me faint and sick!"

You didn't use to shout at me either, and you feel faint and sick because you won't eat. But Lucy was always quick to appease her sister, and fighting with her wasn't in Lucy's nature, especially not when her sister felt so poorly that her yellowed eye brimmed with tears.

"I'm sorry. I don't mean to nag; I just worry," she said, then tried to take Sarah's hand in hers, but her sister balled her hands into fists so she couldn't.

She had once read about the case of Phineas Gage, an American who'd had a steel rod blown clean through his head. It entered through his cheek and exited at the top of his skull, destroying part of his brain. Miraculously, he had survived this, but his personality had been much changed. *Perhaps the pen that destroyed her eye and penetrated her brain caused Sarah's personality to change, too,* she thought.

But perhaps it hadn't, and the answer lay within the archive and the tough strips of meat that were all that was left of the bog woman.

The next morning found Lucy waiting in the drawing room with Michael for Mrs. van Dijk and the carriage to be ready. Michael prowled the room, picking things up at random, fingering them for a bit, then placing them back. He was always restless in rooms he found feminine; he did not stalk about so in his study nor the library, which were dark, the furniture large and heavy, everything smelling of leather and wood and smoke.

"I don't see why you had to bring Mrs. van Dijk. You don't need a chaperone," he said.

How sinister he looks when he scowls. Quite the villain. "She's not coming as my chaperone. She only wishes to make herself useful, and useful she shall be. She knows her way around an archive much better than I do and will have a better idea what to look for."

Michael picked up a china dog, then rubbed its painted snout with his thumb. "Perhaps you no longer care to be alone with me."

She turned her face away from him to hide the flush that spread across her face like wine. How easy to deny it, to point out that she was alone with him right now, but she lacked all desire to be drawn into an argument with him. He could be vicious and tenacious when he felt he was wronged. She had once seen him and her sister fight, and the intimacy and violence of it had so shocked and frightened her that she had tried to keep him from anger ever since. "I don't much care to be alone with anyone, at times not even with myself," she said instead. "Of course, Sarah is the only exception. It comes from being a twin, I suppose. She loves company, too."

"I disagree. I've found she has a childish passion for being alone."

"Only so she can work. She's nothing if not committed. She was like that even when we were little. If something piqued her fancy, she'd obsess over it for days."

Michael put the china dog down and cocked his head at her, smiling. *He looks even more like a rogue when he smiles than when he scowls,* she noted. The thought was devoid of emotion; she had entertained it often before. "I've always thought she loves to be alone because she's supremely at ease with herself," he said.

"That, too. It's what makes her such an attractive creature. It's a rare quality. I've never possessed it and don't think I ever shall."

"It would be unusual if you did. With twins, you often see that one of them is the dominant one, the leader, the instigator. The other submits and follows."

"And what of it?"

"I've often thought that Sarah dominates you."

She smiled to hide her discomfort. It always startled her when people saw the truth of her relationship with Sarah so clearly. "And what of it?" she repeated. "Some people wish to rule, others to be ruled. If both parties are agreeable, there is no fault."

"A desire to rule isn't normal in a woman."

She knew the bait for what it was but took it anyway, partly out of guilt for discussing Sarah with her brother-in-law and partly because she always defended her. "Do you mean to say my sister is unnatural?"

"Your sister has many faults."

"As do we all."

"I've often thought she has more than most. Of course, they count more heavily against her because she's my wife."

When they had just begun their affair, he had told her that Sarah was frigid. She hadn't wanted to know that—Sarah had never told her about this part of her marriage, and Lucy had never asked—and yet it had made her feel guiltily triumphant. Though she was used to being compared to her sister, it had never made her feel anything but uneasy and inferior. At least this was one area in which she outshone Sarah.

Lucy said, "That's uncharitable of you. You know very well she has many virtues, too. She's passionate and brilliant. You'd be hard-pressed to find a defender as staunch as Sarah. She can champion you like no other, and she's much more besides: kind, interesting, lively. Oh, and funny, too. She often makes me laugh."

He stopped his prowling. "You talk as if one has no choice but to love her, once one knows her."

"You must agree. If you'll remember, you lost all interest in me once you met Sarah," Lucy said softly.

She had met Michael on a trip to the university's library. Sarah often went there to peruse tracts and books on whatever subject obsessed her at the time. Because women were not allowed there without a male chaperone, Arthur had to accompany her. Lucy often went with them, and they'd make a day out of it: first the library, then tea and sandwiches.

The day Lucy met Michael, Sarah was home sick with a head cold, so it was just Lucy and Arthur in the library. She would never forget the first time she saw Michael. He sat bent over a medieval surgeon's handbook, a piece of paper next to him on which he copied out lines, a deep frown carved into his large forehead. He looked up when Arthur gently tapped his shoulder, and his face was so strange, so unlike anyone she knew, it impressed itself greatly on her mind, like a seal pressed into wax.

Arthur must have introduced them to each other, but she had no memory of this, only of the way Michael took her hand and kissed it, of how soft his lips were and how rough his mustache; her hands had been bare because gloves sometimes snagged on the priceless manuscripts. He still sported a mustache then, though he shaved it off not much later when Sarah had mentioned she did not care for mustaches. As he and Arthur had talked in hushed voices, she rubbed at the spot he had kissed as if she could spread the feeling.

When Lucy was done at the library, Michael accompanied her and Arthur for a while, talking about the paper he was trying to write. "The whole ordeal is damnably more difficult than I thought it would be."

"Language, my friend. There is a lady present," Arthur said.

"Excuse me, Miss Goedhart. I meant to say 'dreadfully more difficult,' of course."

"Of course," she agreed.

"Part of the problem," he went on, "is that half the manuscripts I require must be procured from other libraries, which seems an awful lot of trouble because, during my research, I have found that medieval manuscripts are actually bloody boring." He glanced at her, a mischievous twinkle in his eyes. "Apologies, Miss Goedhart. Very boring, naturally."

"Naturally," she said.

"And the other part of the problem?" Arthur wanted to know.

"That I'm a bloody bad scholar. Ah, I do apologize, Miss Goedhart. I meant a 'very poor' one, of course."

Had she been more daring, better equipped at flirting, she would have teased him and asked whether he hadn't meant to say *a damnably, bloody poor scholar*; that was what Sarah might have done. But in this she wasn't like her sister, so she just blushed and murmured, "Of course." She could still feel the back of her hand throb where he had kissed it, which confused and delighted her in equal measure.

Arthur frowned at him. "Michael, please. Lucy here must think I keep terrible company if you insist on talking like that. As for your problem: I don't think you truly have one. You're not at university anymore, and your job as a gentleman does not require you to write any papers."

"You're wrong there, dear chap. I'd like to be a gentleman-scholar, and I'm afraid I must write several papers a year if I want to call myself one."

"Then find yourself a different subject, one that might actually interest you. May I recommend medicine or botany?"

"You may, though I can't guarantee I'll actually take your advice. Now, you must excuse me. I've got an appointment to keep. Arthur, I shall talk to you soon. Miss Goedhart, it was a pleasure to meet you." He took her hand, the same one he had kissed before, and kissed it again, curling his fingers so they slipped inside her glove and could brush the delicate skin on the inside of her wrist. She felt as if she had been branded, and a thrill ran up her spine, making her twitch. Michael looked at her through his lashes, then slowly grinned.

She knew then there was a natural affinity between them, and the knowledge of it glowed inside her.

The next time she saw him was during a trip to the botanical gardens in Leiden. Arthur had taken her and Sarah because he wanted to show them all the spring flowers. When she spotted Michael bent over a cluster of ferns, his lean fingers stroking the green fronds, her heart began to beat so fast inside her chest, she feared it might bruise, for she had thought of him almost incessantly ever since they had met at the library three weeks before and had fervently prayed that she would see him again.

"Dear Michael, I see you have taken my advice to pursue botany rather than manuscriptology?" Arthur called out to him.

Michael looked up, stood, smoothed his crumpled trousers, and laughed. "Not at all, dear Arthur. I've simply come down with a case of pteridomania. I heard it's very catching."

"I might know a cure for that."

Lucy didn't know what *pteridomania* meant, but Sarah did. "Oh, Arthur,"—she laughed softly—"you know very well there's no cure for fern fever! I've been afflicted for years, and you've yet to cure me."

"A lady specialist?" Michael asked. He had ripped off a bit of fern, and the air around them, thick with the bitter scent of earth, now smelled green and fresh.

"Merely an amateur, I'm afraid."

"Nonsense. You're much more than a mere amateur, Saartje!" Lucy said, wondering why she suddenly used the diminutive of her sister's name. It was not something she usually did in public. She turned to Michael and said, "My sister has just written a paper about the impact of soil alkalinity on how well ferns grow. It's brilliant. I should know. I've proofread it to catch any grammar and spelling mistakes."

"Is that so?" Michael said without taking his eyes off Sarah.

Sarah smiled sweetly at him. "It certainly is. I've kept detailed notes. Would they perhaps be of interest to you, seeing as you are a pteridomaniac like myself?"

"I think they would interest me very much, but only if you are willing to explain them to me yourself."

Something arced between them. Lucy, always sensitive to her sister's moods, felt it vividly. Normally, it would have filled her with pride to see her sister's beauty and brilliance acknowledged, but that day, it filled her with something painful and sickening that she would only later recognize as a mixture of jealousy and despair.

She had wanted this man the moment she had clapped eyes on him, something she could neither explain nor defend, for she did not know him, and with his heavy brow and crowded teeth, he wasn't handsome. But she had wanted him all the same, and over the past few weeks, this wanting, though she had kept it a secret, had suffused her entire being until it had become both pleasure and torment. Now he did not even glance at her. He looked at Sarah instead with a hungry intensity that was almost obscene while she talked to him about ferns, smiling softly at him, showing him the graceful arc of her long white neck and the shapeliness of her wrists as she brushed a fern at their feet carefully to the side to expose the dark earth from which it sprang and illustrate a point she was making.

Lucy had never felt more like a shadow than that day when she stood and watched the man she loved become enamored with her sister, and had been powerless to stop it.

"Lucy," Michael said, ripping her from her reverie. "If I have ever given you the impression that…"

Mrs. van Dijk arrived before he could finish his sentence, and he swallowed the words. Lucy hoped they stuck in his gullet, choking him.

Sometimes, she hated him.

They took the carriage into town. Overnight, a thick fog had crept over the land. It pressed heavily against the windows, swallowing both light and sound. It tasted sour and coated everything with a thin layer of moisture. If only the wind would come and tear the fog apart! Lucy had grown up near the coast, where the wind blew all day long and carried with it the smell of the sea and the shrieks of seagulls. This windless weather where even the birds were hushed unnerved her.

Luckily, Mrs. van Dijk rattled almost as much as the wheels

did on the cobbles. She had thought extensively about the best method to tackle their investigation, she said, so she told them in great detail the plan she had come up with to give their research the highest chance of success.

Michael scowled and turned his face to the window, then wiped at the condensation with his sleeve.

Undeterred, Mrs. van Dijk ploughed on. "We mustn't be discouraged if we don't find something today. It all depends on the size of the archive. Because this is a small town with a small population where usually not a lot happens, it shouldn't be too hard to find what we are looking for, but you never know. And even if we can't find anything useful, not all hope is lost. We can always consult the local church's records. They're very good at noting down who was born, who was baptized, who was married, and who was buried. Of course, the burials pertain to those that took place on church ground, but one never knows." Her eyes glittered with excitement.

Lucy felt a pang of self-hatred. She had shamelessly neglected Mrs. van Dijk. Worse, Lucy had been curt with her when she had pointed it out. Perhaps Michael's senseless dislike for the widow had begun to rub off on her, but that was no excuse. She vowed to do better, no matter what they found today.

The archive was located in a wing of the local library. It smelled of damp and old books. The windows were kept shuttered to protect the fragile paper from the daylight, leaving only the dim light of the gas lamps.

The attendant fetched the texts Mrs. van Dijk asked for: prison records, court documents, pamphlets, broadsheets, and surveys.

Though the archive was small, as Mrs. van Dijk had predicted, she cast a large net. The attendant brought back stacks of books and papers.

"Right," Mrs. van Dijk said, rubbing her beringed hands together. "Let's begin, shall we?"

They spent the next few hours reading through the materials, looking for anything that might show them who the ring had belonged to, who the bog woman was, and whether they might be the same person. Lucy skimmed lists from the local prison, Het Gevang. There were lists of nearly everything: supplies bought (mainly kegs of beer, sacks of flour, and sewing thread, though one entry was for a set of imperfect delft blue tiles, which she supposed had been used to tile the wall of the torture room; china was easy to scrub down), the money paid by the inmates for their upkeep, the causes of their deaths (fevers and agues and the bloody flux, no doubt caused by those who were too poor to afford the beer and had to make do with the water from the moat), etc.

Soon, her eyes glazed over when looking at the numbers. She switched to a report written by an official from the Hague then. He had been sent to assess the land and had deemed it very fit for farming if only it was drained properly. Though he mentioned the peat as a source of fuel, there was nothing in there about bog bodies.

A little after one, the three of them took a break and ate a hasty lunch in the local tearoom. Michael had been reading agricultural reports and had found nothing. Mrs. van Dijk had found a collection of court documents she had sunk her teeth into. "Nothing to help explain the wedding ring nor the bog body yet, but I still think these documents are promising," she said.

When they had eaten their fill of buttered bread and emptied the teapot, they went back to work. For two more hours, Lucy wrestled her way through more prison lists, until Mrs. van Dijk lay a hand on her shoulder and said, her voice smug and face radiant with triumph, "I think that I may have found what we've been looking for. If you'll follow me, please."

She escorted Lucy to her table, on which lay a huge tome bound in leather. "This, my dear, are the proceedings from the court in Murmerwolde from 1558 till 1594. They tell us who got convicted for what and when. This particular entry,"—she tapped a column of text at the bottom of the left-hand page—"tells of a certain mister named JW, who killed his wife because he believed her to be a changeling. He did so by suffocating her in a rather unusual manner: he forced a rock into her mouth, then threw her body in the bog. It was never found."

———————

Next was a hourrible and strange case, the Tryal of J.W.,
a farmer and a bloudy and inhumane Villaine, who,
together with the blacksmith R.J., now dead of a fever,
kild his Wife M.W. The fact was proved against him by
divers witnesses to whom he confest it, and by examination taken before a Justice upon his apprehension. Neither
did he deny it at his Tryal, but seemed to feel justified to it
by both his words and carriage, for when the Court asked
him if he did not find Remors in his Heart and Horror in
his Conscience for his bloudy crime, as there is no Crime
in the world that cries louder to Heaven than the sin of
Murther, he replyed that he did not, for it had not been
his Wife whom he had murdered, and his true Wife would
surely thank him for it.

When asked if he cared to explain him self, the man
told the Court that he had married the aforementioned
Wife some five Yeers ago and that their union had not
been a happie one, for she proved to be strange and

foul-mouthed and often depressed in Spirits and when not melancholic was enraged and cursed her husband and her life and even our dear Lord him self in so foul a tongue it made any one blush to heare it; three Years ago or thereabouts her spirit had grown so heavie she had tried to murther herself through hanging and would surely have succeeded if her Husband had not come in from the fields early that day, and some months after that, she had again attempted to destroy herself by drinking poison, only her constitution being strong it did not kill her but merely sickened her; after that she did not trie to do away with her self anymore but remained melancholic.

That is until seven months ago or thereabouts, when she disappeared for two weeks during which no one saw neither hair nor hide of her. Her Husband believed she had succeeded in murthering her self until she came home; she said she could not remember what had happened to her, which he did not believe but she did not tell him anything and so he tried to forget that it had ever happened, only his Wife soon began to behave in a strange manner.

When pressed to explain what that meant, the Husband said she spooked the animals, knew things she should not, and had unnatural appetites which were to him so disturbing that he enlisted the help of the local Priest who performed several exorcisms everie day over the course of a week though with little result and so at great expense the local Doctor was consulted and offered to bleed her, but she was so opposed to it that they had to bind her down to do so. The Husband alleged that the Doctor was much perturbed by her for she seemed impervious to pain and stank like one several days dead and indeed had begun to show many signs of the Corpse but because the Doctor has since died of the bloody flux, this could not be verified.

The Husband was at this time convinced his Wife was not truly his Wife but a changeling, and having heard that the Good Folk find mistreatment of their kin unbearable to watch, he starved, beat, burnt her in the hope they would give back his Wife but to no avail; desperate, for the animals went into a frenzie when near to his Wife causing the chickens to stop laying, the dog to kill their only goose, and the cows to stop giving Milk, he resolv'd to rid him self of her, and together with his neighbor and friend the Blacksmith, he took his Wife to the bog, a place fit for his hellish purpose, where taking their opportunity they fell upon her and in a Barbarous manner murthered her by forcing a rock into her mouth and keeping her nose pinched shut until she died for lack of breath, then threw her into the dark waters of the bog.

Afraid of Discovery, they came back the next night and brought the bodie to a different bog and drove stakes through it to keep it from floating and to keep it from wandering, but it had already been spotted by a Shepherd who had gone to a Priest, and the Priest having seen the bodie for him self and having recognized it as being the Wife of J.W. whom he had exorcised repeatedly, he alerted the Authorities, though by the time they went to look for it, J.W. and his Devilish Accomplice had hidden it and it remains hidden to this verie day.

By the providence of the Divine Justice, the Murtherers were found and discover'd and one of them now put on Tryal, the other having since died in gaol of Fever, and even tho it is a rare thing indeed to be brought before the Court on charges of Murther when there is no bodie, the proof of it was evident and he for it was condemned to be hang'd, as in such cases of Fellony and Murther is accustomed. J.W. did not attempt to satisfie Heaven, believing he did no wrong, and so went to the hands of Justice impenitent and a Sinner through and through.

Chapter 15

AFTER LUCY FINISHED READING, SHE sat feeling sick and chilled. Her mind, usually so active, flitting from thought to thought, was painfully focused on one thing and one thing only.

MW.

The initials of the murdered wife.

M could stand for *Marianne*.

Sarah had claimed Marianne was the bog woman's name.

According to the husband's testimony, Marianne knew things she shouldn't or couldn't. It had been one of many symptoms—*symptoms that afflict Sarah, too, like the fear she inspires in animals and her lack of appetite, and like Marianne she suddenly cusses like a sailor*—that had made him believe she was a changeling and had led to him murdering her.

Did this mean Sarah was some sort of changeling, too? It would explain everything, wouldn't it?

There was only one small problem: changelings didn't exist, and those who believed in them were either very young, very superstitious, or very mad. Besides, the idea that something had taken her sister's place and was mimicking her in such a convincing manner that she had almost everyone fooled, well, that was too horrible, too dreadful, to even contemplate.

Lucy found her mind rejecting it even before she had properly entertained it. Much better to put her faith in logic and reason. Her sister was behaving strangely because she was recovering from a fever of the brain and the terrifying ordeal of almost being buried alive. The fact the bog woman's name began with an *m* and Sarah had claimed she was named Marianne was a coincidence. A disquieting coincidence, yes, but a coincidence nonetheless.

Lucy desired to slam the book shut and ask the attendant to take it back to whatever dusty shelf it had come from so she could forget all about it. Instead, she smiled at Mrs. van Dijk and forced herself to say, "I think you're right, Mrs. van Dijk. The bog woman must be the wife of this man. It would be very strange indeed if there were another woman buried on Michael's land with a stone in her mouth."

Under her employer's watchful gaze, Lucy copied the entry four times: once for Arthur so he could use it if he ever wanted to write a paper about the case, once for the university currently in possession of the sad few remains of the bog woman, once for Michael in case he ever needed it to treat Sarah, and one final copy for herself. This one she folded and tucked into the pocket of her dress.

When she went to fetch Michael and tell him they had very likely solved the mystery of the identity of the bog woman, he stood and stretched, the joints in his shoulders and elbows popping.

"Pity," he said, looking genuinely disappointed, "I was just gaining steam. I found some very interesting pamphlets. One had some truly filthy limericks. I'll tell the attendant to keep that one from visitors of the fairer sex; we don't want to offend your delicate sensibilities." And he bent close to her and whispered in her ear, a grin on his face.

"There was a girl who made a poor wife,

"Her lovers and dalliances were rife,

"She was always wet as a duck,

"Truly a sweet little fuck,

"Much better suited to the prostitute's life."

She flushed spectacularly. "You're lying about those limericks," she said. Had she not been so perturbed by the document currently burning a hole in her pocket, she might have laughed.

"Of course. I made it up just now. Still, I did find myself thoroughly immersed in this project. I'd almost forgotten how much I enjoy it."

"The writing of limericks or the reading of documents?"

"Both, though I was aiming for the latter."

At the start of their marriage, he and Sarah had been almost inseparable and had created projects to do together. Lucy had boxes of her sister's letters in which she talked in great detail about the butterfly nursery they'd built together, the plants they grew in the hothouse that had come all the way from the Dutch Indies on creaking ships, the hare Michael had shot and they had dissected with Arthur's help. The number of projects and expeditions they had undertaken together had decreased sharply when Sarah found herself pregnant. By the time Lucille had died of scarlet fever, they had become almost nonexistent. Sarah had explained this away by saying she had some projects she'd rather do alone, but Lucy suspected it was Michael who no longer wished to work with her, perhaps because he had discovered Sarah's intelligence far exceeded his own. He did so very much hate being corrected. Lucy had once done so unthinkingly, and he had been sullen and resentful even after she had apologized. Only after they'd had sex had he been nice again.

He would never do anything like that to Sarah, probably because he knew, instinctively, she would not simply stand there and take it like Lucy would.

Sudden tears fell from her eyes.

Startled, Michael lay a hand on her arm, searching for his handkerchief with the other. "Are you all right?" he asked in a low voice.

"Don't mind me. I don't even know why I'm crying," she said, stepping away from him. But she did know.

She wanted her sister. It didn't matter that she was now a sick, sullen creature with only one eye. Lucy felt overcome with love for her twin in all her demanding, obsessive, insufferable imperfection.

This desire to be with Sarah grew steadily on the drive back to Zwartwater. By the time the carriage drew up in front of the house, Lucy had been clutching her own hand with enough force to discolor the skin, first to white, then to pink, now to almost purple. She made herself thank Michael and Mrs. van Dijk for accompanying and helping her, then excused herself, saying she was anxious about her sister and wished to check on her.

She half walked, half ran up the stairs. The paper in her pocket rustled softly as the lifting of her legs creased it. At last: the thick oaken door leading to her sister's bedroom. She opened it without knocking. Until Sarah had gotten married, there had been no need, and old habits die hard. She had taken two steps inside before her brain registered that something was wrong.

Sarah was not alone.

In her bed lay Katje, her nightshirt rucked up around her hips, her head thrown back, her eyes closed but her mouth open. Sarah lay on the bed with her, her hands gripping Katje's thighs with such force, the skin was white and dimpled underneath her fingers, her face between the other girl's legs, held there by Katje's hand.

The room smelled of sweat and sex and blood and something rotten.

Shock nailed Lucy to the ground. The blood drained from her face and limbs, whooshing as it went. Black spots danced in her vision. *Dear Lord, I've never been much of a fainter. Please don't let me start now*, she thought. Her hand—cold, weak—clutched the back of a chair. She stumbled heavily against it as her knees gave out, clung to it, and somehow managed not to let go and fall to the ground.

Though she couldn't hear a thing over the hollow thumping of her heart, her feet dragging over the floorboards and the screech of

the chair as she clasped it were loud enough to disturb the pair on
the bed. Katje opened her eyes. They were glassy, the pupils overly
large from the drugs Arthur had given her to make the stabbing
pain in her womb bearable. They fixed upon Lucy. She frowned
as she struggled to focus, seemingly on the cusp of saying something. Then her eyes simply slid off Lucy. Her back arched, and
she whined and twisted her face against the pillow, her damp hair
rasping against the fabric.

Sarah had looked up, too. Her eye patch had ridden up,
revealing the tender hole underneath that Lucy still cleaned for
her every day, the cotton wool damp and yellowed from where it
had absorbed the fluids that leaked intermittently from the skin.
Her remaining eye was empty, the way it used to be when she was
sleepwalking. The lower half of her face was smeared with blood.
It coated her mouth and cheeks; it had dripped down and stained
the collar of her nightdress, plastering it to the white skin of her
throat. She swallowed. Then she, too, looked away. She bent over
Katje and resumed her drinking.

Lucy's heart contracted fiercely, painfully, and the blood
returned to her hands and feet, suffusing them with heat, extin-
guishing the motes of black that had speckled her vision. She
blushed so furiously, her face and throat felt scalded. To witness
something so private and intimate and then to be ignored, as if
she were so insignificant, it didn't matter that she had seen, was
seeing it still…

Lucy got to her feet. Once in the hallway, she closed the door
softly. Her face still burned. She lay the back of her hand against

her cheek to cool it, but her fingers throbbed with warmth, too. Sweat prickled under her armpits, in the hollows of her knees. She went to her room in a kind of daze, seeing nothing, feeling nothing.

She sank into a chair and sat motionless. Yet, underneath the surface, her mind was in turmoil. It only had so much room for unwanted things. If she kept cramming in more, it would flood like a cesspool. Some things had to be dealt with straightaway, like finding her sister committing adultery with her husband's poor female relation.

But her motives aren't sexual, at least not completely, something within Lucy whispered. *She thirsts for blood and found a way to slake it.* And Katje would let her because she was an invert and thus enjoyed it. Hadn't she told Lucy often how she loved Sarah more than anyone else?

Back to Sarah. This wasn't normal. So little had been, these past few weeks, and now, thanks to her work in the archive, Lucy might finally have an explanation for it all, no matter how strange and inexplicable, no matter how much she wished it weren't true.

She took the copy she had made of the court document out of her pocket, smoothed the folded paper, and feverishly read through it again. Her eyes snagged on certain words and phrases that she had rejected before as too strange and horrible to be true.

When pressed to explain what that meant, the Husband said she spooked the animals, knew things she should not, and had unnatural appetites... The Doctor was much perturbed by her for she seemed impervious to pain and stank like one several days dead and indeed

had begun to show many signs of the Corpse... The Husband was at
this time convinced his Wife was not truly his Wife but a changeling...

She lowered the sheet and pinched the bridge of her nose until her eyes watered with the pain of it, but still the words reverberated inside her head. Now that she had forced herself to contemplate them rather than reject them outright, she could no more deny them than she could fly, and the more she thought about it, the more convinced she became.

Her sister wasn't her sister.

Oh, it looked like her sister, talked like her, and moved like her, but though the imitation was convincing at first glance, perhaps even at the second or third, as soon as one kept looking, one saw through it.

And whatever had taken up residence inside Sarah, it had lived inside the bog woman first.

Lucy let go of her nose. The blood flowed back into the bit of skin she had pinched, causing a sense of heat that brought even more tears to her eyes. She rubbed them away with her sleeve.

What she needed now was a plan. If only she hadn't been so rash as to burn Sarah's letters, her diary entry, the treatise on ticks! Evidence, all of it, that Sarah was possessed by something. Without it, who would believe her? Until an hour ago, she wouldn't have believed it herself.

"And I know Sarah better than anyone," she muttered. She stood and began to pace in an effort to get rid of the desperate, manic energy that had taken possession of her.

No matter if it was sickness or a parasite that currently played puppeteer with her sister, it was convincing, and for the areas where it wasn't, people would find reasons to explain away its strange behaviors. Already Arthur had found explanations for Sarah's— *Not-Sarah's*—lack of appetite and the changes in her personality. As for everything else, well, there was always the excuse of madness. Once one had been deemed mad, anything and everything could be interpreted as a symptom, especially if one was a woman. A desire for sex, sullenness, cursing...

"Hell, if we go by those criteria, I am as mad as my sister. Even madder, because I talk out loud to myself," Lucy said, then laughed, or perhaps sobbed; even she couldn't be sure.

She didn't want to be thought mad, but neither could she stand idly by and do nothing. The real Sarah might still be alive and trapped somewhere inside her body, waiting desperately for someone to notice what was going on, for someone to save her. The thought of her sister frightened and helpless, perhaps in pain, was maddening, sickening, and, above all, more than Lucy could bear.

This could not wait.

She'd go and confront Not-Sarah right now. Didn't the best attacks have an element of surprise to them? "Of course, Not-Sarah will probably deny being Not-Sarah," Lucy muttered to herself as she nervously smoothed some stray hairs against her scalp.

Demons were famous for lying.

Not-Sarah might not be a demon, but she was probably just as tricksy. Any creature with a certain level of intelligence would be, if only out of self-preservation. What Lucy needed was irrefutable

proof even that thing couldn't deny when confronted with it. She
kept pacing as she forced herself to think.

When inspiration struck, it sent an electric shock down Lucy's
spine and raised all the hairs on her body. She opened her sewing
kit and drew a pin from the cushion inside, which was shaped like
a hedgehog, the pins and needles his spikes. Sarah had made it for
her when they were children. The pin Lucy selected was almost
as long as her little finger. She touched the tip to her thumb, then
withdrew it. A drop of blood beaded from the puncture. She sucked
her thumb, doing her best to ignore the taste of salt and metal, and
stuck the pin just below the waistband of her skirt, where she could
withdraw it easily but the folds hid it from view.

Before she could lose her nerve, she went into the hallway and
almost ran to her sister's room. Yet, once there, she faltered. She
rested her forehead against one of the windows. It had begun to
rain. Drops ran down the glass. The rain came so thick and fast, it
formed a layer of distortion; when Lucy looked outside, the world
warbled. She closed her eyes, trying not to feel sick. Nerves writhed
in her belly like snakes.

Don't be a coward, she admonished, then forced herself to close
the short distance between the window and the door to her sister's
room. This time, she did knock.

"Enter," Sarah called.

Chapter 16

SARAH WAS SITTING AT HER writing desk, her diary open before her. Her shorn head was covered by a cotton cap. She had opened the window, dispelling the smell of sweat and sex until only the lingering reek of sickness that permeated everything around her nowadays and the cool, soft scent of rain remained. The rain drummed on the sill and pooled there until the puddles grew too large and the water ran down the wall to be sucked up by the carpet. Despite the cold and the wet, Sarah sat in a thin nightgown and nothing else. The collar had turned brown with crusted blood. If not for that, Lucy could almost have told herself she had imagined everything; Sarah had scrubbed away any trace of blood from her hands and face.

For a moment, neither said anything. They simply looked at each other: Lucy straight on, Sarah from the corner of her eye.

Does she know that I know? I mustn't let on.

Lucy tried to force her mouth into a smile, but the muscles felt taut and her lips trembled. "Why aren't you wearing your dressing gown? You must be cold. You must take good care of the body that was given you, don't you know that?" She picked up a shawl from the back of a chair. As she walked to her sister, she felt for the pin with her other hand. Just the fabric of her skirt against her fingertips, rough and thick. What if it had fallen out without her noticing? Her mouth turned dry.

Sarah turned to her, one jaundiced hand on the pages of her diary. It must be an old entry; the pages were covered in her neat copperplate. No doubt the creature that possessed her was studying it to more accurately impersonate her. That was why Lucy had to confront it until it had no choice but to confess. She would, if only she could find this fucking pin…

And then, mercifully, she felt the smooth hard head of the pin as her nail brushed against it. Quickly, she plucked it from her skirt, then folded her hand around it. The shaft lay hot and hard in a crease of her palm. "Here," she said, then threw the shawl around Sarah's shoulders. Lucy fussed over her, smoothing the fabric over her shoulders, trying to knot it at her throat without touching the crusted fabric of her collar, all the while looking for the right moment to strike. Up close, her nose almost pressed against her sister's throat, the sweet smell of rot was so thick, she had to fight not to gag.

Her hands trembled, and no matter how she tensed them, they wouldn't still. She held the pin between her fingertips with such force, the pink of her nails blanched to a sickly yellow.

"Enough!" Sarah said, laying her hand on Lucy's. It was cold and strangely smooth; the top layer of skin still hadn't grown back. "I know why you've come."

Without looking, Lucy struck. There was no resistance as she drove the pin deep into her sister's hand, doing it at an angle for fear she'd hit the bone. She didn't want to hurt Sarah any more than necessary.

What am I doing? I'm acting like a lunatic, driving pins into my sister because I believe she's possessed, Lucy thought suddenly, and panic squeezed her heart. She took two large steps back, her mouth so dry that it hurt.

But Sarah hadn't noticed the pin. She took hold of the edges of the shawl, held them closed at her chest, and turned to look at Lucy. She didn't look as sickly as she had the previous few days; her eye was clear where it had been cloudy before, and her skin had lost its grayish tinge.

And yet, even without those signs of the corpse—though the fact she was marked with them before proves something, and she still smells like one—there was still very clearly something wrong with her. She must be impervious to pain, else she would've realized her sister had stuck a pin into her, and that was a sign.

Lucy glanced at Sarah's hand and saw she had thrust the pin as far as it would go. Only the head—red, shiny—remained. Afraid of drawing attention to it, she averted her gaze and began to wring her fingers instead.

"I know you must hate me, that you must think me vile and ungrateful and horrible and mad, but is it so bad that you can't even look at me?" Sarah whispered.

Lucy stared at her in surprise. Was her face that naked? It took her a moment to realize Sarah wasn't talking about the fact something had eaten her brain and now lived inside her head, but that Lucy had caught her with Katje.

"There's no need to keep this secret from you anymore. I'll make a clean breast of it now," Sarah went on, oblivious still. "Katje and I are in love. We have been…intimate for a few months now. We have tried to resist it, but there's only so much you can withstand until you must succumb. I've always found unhappiness unappealing, and before her, I was unhappy."

Lucy stood, tongue-tied. The insane urge to laugh brewed in her chest. This whole conversation had the unreality of a dream to it.

"Please say something, Lucy dear! I know how all this must sound to you who have loved Michael for a long time."

Sarah's words struck Lucy like a railroad spike. She had been so careful, guarding her love for Michael even before Sarah knew of his existence; perhaps Lucy had known even then to keep him from her sister. She felt faint. "I have to sit down," she mumbled, then did so on the chair next to Sarah's desk. Still, she was dizzy. She stuck her head between her knees so the blood could rush into her head and dispel the weakness she felt.

Sarah stroked the back of Lucy's head. "Did you think I didn't know? You're my twin; there's not a lot you can keep from me. You must think me very selfish, to chance throwing away all I have here for a few stolen moments of happiness with someone you probably consider poor and disturbed. Almost everyone does, you know. They can't see past the abuse, which is a damn shame because Katje is tremendously interesting. She's much smarter than most people think, much more passionate. Stronger, too. I consider her a fully realized person."

How did she know about Michael and me? It's as if she can read my thoughts. Didn't Marianne's husband say she knew things she couldn't possibly have known? Fear stroked its icy finger down her spine. She realized Sarah was waiting for her to say something. She managed to choke out, "I don't think Katje is just a disturbed girl."

"But you do think that you'd have made Michael a much better wife than I have. You are probably right, though I must say you've got no idea how beastly Michael can be."

"He can be surly, but he's no brute," Lucy said. The blood throbbed in her temples, and she sat up straight. For a moment, black dotted her vision. Then everything looked as it should. She no longer felt faint. Now she just felt insubstantial again, less than half a person. Everything seemed so strange, so *thin*, as if one wrong word or move could tear reality apart like tissue paper.

"It makes sense that you would think that," Sarah said. "I've kept most of his cruelty from you because I didn't want you to worry and didn't want you to think less of me. What's more shameful than a failed marriage?"

"How can you think of your marriage as failed? He loves you terribly," Lucy exclaimed.

"So much that he barely spends five minutes a day with me now that I'm ugly and ill."

Lucy winced. It was true that Michael didn't know what to do with Sarah in her current state. One evening, he had sat down with her and tried to play a game of chess, but she had unnerved him so much that he had gotten up halfway through and left. "He's a man. They never know how to behave in a sickroom."

"How you defend him!" Sarah marveled. "Let's see if you can defend this: he's unfaithful to me."

She knows, Lucy thought. Panic blanched her. *She knows somehow. Oh my God, she knows what Michael and I did, but she never let on…*

Sarah registered Lucy's shock, and her face twisted with triumph. "That's right," she said. "He is unfaithful. I wouldn't mind that so much if he didn't flaunt it so brazenly. I once walked into his study and found one of the maids sucking him silly. They're not his mistresses, just girls he ruts with. Do you know what he said when I confronted him? That I should be pleased. He told me men often have certain needs that are really quite unsavory, and I should be grateful that he respected me too much to use me to sate those needs."

Her mouth puckered in distaste, and she shuddered once, violently. The contraction of the muscles made the pin in her hand move; Lucy could see the shaft twisting slightly, like the hour hand of a clock.

Not-Sarah went on. "All that is horrible and vulgar in and of itself, to treat our staff as if they're no more than napkins for him to frig in, but to do it right under my nose, too? That it matters so little to him that he does it in our home and doesn't bother to hide it from me… Well, it's degrading. It's one of his many infractions against me."

She doesn't know after all, Lucy thought. Shame and relief mingled until she wasn't sure anymore what, exactly, she felt. "You could've told me," she said.

Hypocrite, hypocrite, hypocrite.

Sarah chuckled without mirth. "And have you hate me for making such a mess of my marriage when I knew full well you desired to marry him? No, thank you."

"I wouldn't have hated you. I could never hate you. Don't you know that I would choose your happiness over mine, always? That you matter to me more than any man ever could?"

"You don't even hate me now?" Sarah fixed her remaining eye upon her, and Lucy experienced the horrible sensation that something else was looking through it, not her sister, but something sly and intelligent.

She's toying with me, Lucy thought.

For a moment, she had forgotten it wasn't her sister she was talking to.

Anger rose in her like heat. She did hate then, both the creature possessing her sister for manipulating her and herself for being manipulated so easily, for forgetting what it was she had come here to do.

To gain the upper hand, she looked pointedly at the pin in her sister's hand. The blood, having no place to go, had begun to pool underneath her skin, discoloring it. Sarah followed her gaze and finally, finally noticed the pin. She frowned at it, took it between her thumb and index finger, and extracted it. The shaft was coated with black blood, dulling the otherwise shiny surface. Blood now beaded from the wound, and this, too, was black. It rose sluggishly because it had the consistency of tar. It had a smell to it, not the healthy, normal blood smell of wet coins and salt but a sweet thick reek, like overripe fruit. *That is old blood,* Lucy thought, *stagnant blood, blood gone to rot.*

Sarah looked at it, then at the pin in her other hand, then back at the puncture wound. A trickle of blood crept down her hand, following the dip between two veins. "Did you do this to me?" she asked, her voice threaded with disbelief.

"Yes."

Her face was contorted with sadness and bewilderment. "But why?"

"Oh, stop it!" Lucy snapped.

"Stop what?"

"Stop pretending to be my sister!"

A range of emotions flickered over Sarah's face: hurt, fear, uncertainty. "Lucy, what are you talking about?" she asked, and her voice was small and frightened. It ate away at Lucy's resolve.

What am I doing? Oh God, what on earth am I doing? A voice inside her wailed, but she could not give in to it.

She sprang to her feet and yelled, "Don't try and manipulate me with that look! You are not my sister! I know you're not!"

"You're frightening me. You're acting like Aunt Adelheid," Sarah whispered, her lower lip trembling.

What am I doing? Am I mad? Lucy thought. She began to pace wildly. "I'm not mad! No, no, not mad at all. I know what you are, and I know you have possessed my sister. You're trying to confuse me with lies about Michael, and..."

"I never lied!" Sarah cried. "He truly is a beast sometimes. You know how firmly he believes women should be one thing and men another. Do you really believe he can be courteous and gentle with a woman he deems unnatural? Worse, a woman who is more intelligent than he is?"

"Don't!" Lucy screamed. She tore at her hair, and the burning pain this produced grounded her a little. She took three heaving breaths, then continued. "Stop trying to distract me. I know you are not my sister."

Sarah bent over as if stabbed. "Oh, Lucy." She sobbed. "How can you say such a thing? Of course I am your sister, your twin, your Sarah. How could you not know me, you who have known me since the womb?"

Lucy looked at her, at that darling face that had been altered so much by disease, and this, too, calmed her a little. "Don't you understand? Precisely because I've known my sister as long as life itself, I can tell you aren't her."

Sarah began to cry. "Why would you say something like that to me when you know that I'm not well, both in mind and body? Why would you be so horrible to me when I need your love and compassion more than anything else right now?"

It took everything Lucy had not to break down and apologize and move to comfort her, but she managed.

When Lucy didn't move, didn't even lower her eyes, Sarah's face changed. The best thing Lucy could compare it to was as if the muscles had snapped like bands of India rubber. Sarah's face relaxed almost to the point of slackness, and Lucy wondered how she could ever have thought this was her sister.

"What gave me away?" Not-Sarah asked.

Chapter 17

SHE DOESN'T DENY IT.

The thought was curiously devoid of feeling. It was like Sarah's death all over again: soon, emotion would grab Lucy by the throat, but until it did, she was cool and calm and collected. She swallowed, then ran her tongue over her dry lips to wet them. "A lot of little things," she said.

Not-Sarah brought her hand to her mouth and sucked at the clotting blood. "Feel free to elaborate."

"The fact Pasja is terrified of you. Your thirst for blood. How you smell and look as if you're decomposing. Little things you said and did that Sarah wouldn't have, like your sudden bouts of cursing."

"And yet it took you a while."

"Even in the face of so many small clues, it's not an easy thing to believe. Now, tell me: What are you, and what did you do with Sarah?"

Not-Sarah brought the pin to her mouth, then delicately licked at the blood with the tip of her tongue. It was a healthy pink again, no longer dull and coated in plaque. "I'm sure you've got your theories already. Why not share them with me?"

"Why would I?"

"I like to be entertained."

Another spurt of anger. "I'm not here to entertain you! I just want my sister!" Lucy hissed.

Sarah—*but she's Not-Sarah; why do I struggle so to understand and remember this?*—cocked her head and said gently, "I know. Come, tell me what you think you know, and we'll start from there."

Lucy licked her lips again. They were dry to the point of pain. If she were to smile now, the skin would tear. "All right. Others might have called you a changeling, but I think it's more accurate to say you're a kind of tick."

Not-Sarah laughed. "A tick? Have you ever seen a tick do what I have done?"

An ugly flush crept up her throat, then pooled in the soft tissue of her cheeks. "Don't be pedantic. I didn't come here to talk semantics. I don't know what to call you, but the word 'tick' certainly isn't far off."

"Darling Lucy. Don't lose your temper. I was only teasing. Sarah used to tease you often. I'm not quite Sarah, but I'm close enough. I'm in your blood, and you are in mine." She tried to take hold of Lucy's hand. Lucy jerked back.

Wounded, Not-Sarah let her hand fall. She cleared her throat and said, "You aren't far off by calling me a tick. There's some affinity between that species and mine. We can stay alive for years without fresh sustenance simply by staying very still. When something edible comes along, we attach ourselves to our prey and drink our fill. Of course, a tick only needs a little blood. Then, pearl-like in its bloatedness, it will let go and live up to another decade off the blood it has taken into its body. My kind, once properly sated, can go without sustenance for much longer."

"Is that what you did to the bog woman? Attached yourself to her and drank your fill? Or did you take a little bite here and there, too?"

She gave Lucy a frank stare with her remaining eye. "Funny," she said. "Many would think you a dull little creature, friendly but quite insipid and a little slow, perhaps. They've got you all wrong, don't they? You're much brighter than you let on—and much meaner, though perhaps that's simply because you're unhappy, and you're unhappy because you desire fiercely what you can't have. You yearn and crave and want with such force, it seems to eat you up from the inside. Sarah knew, and therefore, so do I."

Lucy looked away so Not-Sarah wouldn't see the tears in her eyes, but, of course, the act of looking away in itself was already admitting that her words had found their mark. Did all her kind have such an uncanny way of dissecting those around them, of flaying them till nothing remained but the core of who they were? Being emotionally peeled like an orange by something that wasn't even human yet did wear her sister's face was not a nice feeling. But Lucy wouldn't be defeated quite so easily, nor let the creature distract her.

"I used to have terrible temper tantrums as a child," Lucy said, as if that would explain all of it. "I don't think people think me very dull, just insecure or else cold and reserved. Funny you should say my feelings eat me up from the inside, though. That's what you literally did with the bog woman, isn't it? Ate up all her organs, leaving her an empty husk, sucked dry? I suppose you're right; you're not quite a tick after all. Perhaps I should've compared you to a spider instead."

"Similes are rarely perfect," Not-Sarah said lightly. "You are right, though. I did eat her organs. I wouldn't normally—human bodies very much do need their lungs and hearts and what-have-yous to keep functioning even when I'm the one steering the ship, so to speak—but I was in a bit of a bind."

"Because Marianne was dead?" Lucy asked.

Not-Sarah inclined her head. "Indeed. My host was dead, and I hadn't had time to vacate the premises and find a new place to live before she and I were thrown into the bog. There my options were rather limited. I knew I could only get out and find a new host if someone dragged out Marianne's body. Until that happened, I simply needed to survive. So I hibernated. I ate Marianne's organs till I was filled to bursting, and then I slept. I slept for a long time."

Lucy looked down at her hands. They had gone numb. She balled them into fists to get the blood flowing again, then asked, "How did you take possession of my sister?"

"A happy accident, that. By the time those peat cutters unearthed Marianne and me, I was weak. I hadn't eaten nor moved for a long time. I think that, had Sarah not cut her hand on my teeth and thus given me a little of her blood to drink, I might well have died before I could have taken possession of another host. Her blood replenished me."

How matter-of-factly she talks! Lucy thought. A chill swam up her spine. "And then you inhabited her?"

"Not straightaway. I couldn't; that stone obstructed my way. It had to be removed, and when that was done, I had to draw her to me."

"Draw her how?"

Not-Sarah made a slow plucking motion, as if pulling on a thread, and Lucy felt a twinge in her breastbone. "I just *drew* her. It's hard to put into words but not so hard to do. When she cut her hand, a little bit of her entered me, but a little bit of me entered her, too. I drew on that bit. It helped that she was susceptible."

"Because she had a propensity for madness?"

"Because she felt both tenderness and affinity for that leathered, broken body. The way Marianne looked after centuries in the bog, well, that's how Sarah felt sometimes: all twisted and old and strange."

Lucy refused to take the bait. "So you drew her."

"Yes. I drew her and entered her, and that's where the easy part ended and the hard part began. You see, she really did *not* like that I tried to make my home inside her skull. Hosts usually don't, but she fought me with a vehemence I hadn't expected. Of course, it didn't help that I was weak and out of practice, nor that she was on to me. I have to give her this: she was much more cunning and tenacious than I expected. I admire her for it, really." She smiled begrudgingly. With her face no longer slack like that of a dead woman, she was indistinguishable from any normal person.

"The treatise on ticks," Lucy breathed.

"Indeed. She knew something was trying to take possession of her. Not a demon nor a ghost, but something of the natural world, small and tough and tangible. She also knew I was weak; merging with her made me privy to her memories and thoughts and feelings, but that connection worked the other way, too. She came up with a plan to get rid of me. She knew she couldn't destroy me without causing herself grievous harm, so she tried to starve me out."

I felt ravenous, but I knew somehow that it was imperative I didn't eat, as if a headache is something you can starve into submission. Pain rose in Lucy's throat. "Is that why you bit Arthur?"

"Yes. I needed blood and meat."

Lucy realized she was wringing her hands again. She balled them into fists once more and pressed them hard against her thighs. "Why didn't you just give up?"

"Giving up meant dying. I had invested too much of my energy in merging with Sarah to try and find another host, and I can't help wanting to live. Like other creatures, I am hell-bent on surviving." She shrugged almost apologetically.

"Why not ask Sarah to help you? Why not strike a deal?"

"I couldn't trust her. Who was to say she wouldn't grind me to pulp under her boot the moment I left her body? My kind is vulnerable without a host. We are small and soft, easy to kill. No, I couldn't run the risk. I'd take control of this body, or I'd die trying." Her mouth twisted into a bitter smile. She touched the velvet eye patch. The tips of her fingers were wrinkled and discolored like those of someone who had been dead for some days. "Of course, Sarah didn't play fair."

Lucy admitted, "She never could abide losing. She always did cheat when we played games as a child."

"I know."

"And then? After she took the pen...?"

"I was wounded. It's a good thing I do not reside in the optic canal, or I'd have been killed. As it was, I needed time to recover. It would have been much faster if I'd had access to fresh blood and meat, but I had to make do. That's why this body isn't looking so good anymore, but you've seen and smelled that already. What that journalist wrote about me was true, you know: I could still hear and feel and smell, but I couldn't move. I didn't play dead nor wait till the last moment to let you know I was alive out of malice."

Lucy looked at her sister's hands, at the missing nails and fingers pockmarked with little wounds from where splinters had bitten deep into the flesh. "What would you have done if I hadn't heard you scratching?"

"Lie low like I did with Marianne, I suppose."

"Crypts aren't very good places to find healthy live hosts."

"Neither are bogs, and yet here we are."

"And where is Sarah now?"

"In here," Not-Sarah said, then tapped her temple with the pin.

Lucy felt pain shoot through her head, as if Not-Sarah had stabbed her with the pin. "Do you mean she's inside your head, talking to you?"

"No. She died when she stabbed us. But I absorbed all her thoughts and memories and feelings right until she died, so she's still with us, in a way."

Lucy thought for a moment, then asked, "How am I to know this is real?"

"Do you not believe me?"

"Perhaps you're just plain Sarah after all, and you're playing a cruel trick on me."

Not-Sarah gave her a small, sorrowful smile. "You don't believe that. Sarah loved to tease, but she was never cruel."

"Then perhaps you are sick. You truly believe you are a parasite, but that doesn't make it so. People can believe all sorts of things when they're mad. No one would blame you. You suffered from a fever of the brain and then catalepsy so strong that we thought you were dead and almost buried you. Anyone would come out of that a little mad." She realized she was pleading.

Not-Sarah sighed and pricked the pin that had pierced her hand moments before through the pages of her diary. It stood crookedly. "You know, if you all hadn't insisted on Sarah being insane, you might have noticed sooner that something was wrong. She did write you a letter telling you all about me and my intentions for her, didn't she? Though I concede her handwriting was atrocious by that point, you must have been able to read at least some parts of it."

That one cut Lucy deep. "Please," she whispered, "please, Saartje, please tell me none of what you've just told me is true. I won't be angry, I promise."

Pity softened the features that starvation had thrown in such sharp relief. "Poor Lucy. You're grasping at straws now, don't you think? You seemed so certain when you began this confrontation. Why have you changed your mind?"

"Because I don't want it to be true after all," she whispered.

"You'd rather have me mad?"

"I'd rather you were like you were before."

The emotions arrived at last. They swept over her, pummeled her. She began to shake, not with the cold shudders traveling up and down her spine that she had experienced before, but with a full-body palsy that made her teeth grind together. She couldn't remain standing and fell to the floor, where she lay convulsing, gasping for breath. Her chest hurt as if it were being chewed on.

Why had the phrase *to break a heart* ever become popular? It likened this onslaught of pain to the clean break of a china cup, when in reality it was much closer to being mauled.

A thought came to her, clear and horrible: *I shan't be able to keep on living.*

Through the veil of tears and agony, she felt Not-Sarah sit next to her and draw her head into her lap. She rocked her, stroked her hair, made little shushing noises.

When the horror and the grief petered out—for nothing human was final, only death, and perhaps not even that—Not-Sarah was still stroking her with cool peeling fingers.

"You poor little thing. Come, dry your tears," she murmured. "It isn't all bad. I don't think you've been listening properly to me, and for that I don't blame you. Let me repeat it for you now that you're a bit calmer. When I merge with a host—I don't really eat the brain, just parts of it—I don't merely take over the body; I consume their memories and their emotions, too."

When Lucy did not respond, Not-Sarah went on. "So, you

see, it really is as I said before: I'm not *quite* Sarah because I have Marianne's memories and some all my own, but I am really close to being her. I love you and know you just as well as Sarah did. And because I am partly Sarah, I hope you'll be able to love me, too. Life would be quite unbearable if you couldn't, you know." She knitted their fingers together in much the same way Sarah had always done.

Lucy pulled her hand away. "How can you claim to be my sister when you just told me you're a conglomeration of everyone you've ever eaten? How many have you devoured over the centuries? A dozen people, a hundred?"

Sarah looked both hurt and offended at this, almost as if Lucy had accused her of being a slut. "Don't you think someone like me would think twice about merging with another precisely because it alters us so greatly? Do not think we use you up lightly. You are precious to us, and we maintain your bodies so carefully that you live decades beyond your ordinary lifespan if inhabited by us. With some flesh and blood, we can repair damage and wear and tear that would normally cripple or kill you, and then we live ordinary lives, blending in so perfectly that you would normally never know we were different from you at all."

"How many?" Lucy persisted.

"Marianne was my first, if you must know," Not-Sarah said rather primly. "I was inexperienced, and that made the changes I caused in Marianne particularly noticeable to her husband. Luckily, I didn't absorb too much of her personality; we hadn't merged fully when her husband tossed us in the bog, and once she was dead, her body was just meat to me."

Lucy groaned softly, helplessly.

Not-Sarah touched her face, smoothing her hair from her brow. "Don't worry, Lucy. It's not all bad, of course. Poor, angry, unhappy Marianne with her sailor's mouth did give me extensive practical knowledge: what mushrooms to pluck and which ones to leave, when to sow and when to reap, how to assist a sheep when lambing—that sort of thing. Not directly of use to me in my position as mistress of Zwartwater, but you never know."

This is without a doubt the strangest conversation I've ever had, Lucy thought. She suddenly had the insane urge to laugh or perhaps to cry.

"Had you merged fully with my sister when she stabbed herself in the eye with that pen?" Lucy asked.

"Yes. So you see: I truly am her—or at least as much like her as is possible."

It was too much, too soon. Lucy couldn't think about it yet, not properly. She felt drained. This violent purging of her emotions was a relief of sorts, but it left her head aching and her eyes smarting. She sat up and rubbed them. "You took a huge risk in telling me all this. Why? Why trust me?"

"Because you are my sister, and I know you'll help me."

Lucy did not say that the matter of their sisterhood was still pending in her mind. Instead, she asked, "Help you how? By keeping the fact of your adultery a secret or that you are a parasite? Does Katje know?"

"In her own way, she does. She thinks I'm a kind of revenant: Sarah restored to her from the dead. Hers is a tender and romantic soul. Of course, she knows that what is dead must stay dead and that I am therefore a transgression against the laws of God, or nature, or both. There's a price that must be paid for such a transgression, and that price must be paid in meat and blood. Every demon wants its pound of flesh and all that."

That explained the girl's utter reluctance to talk about Sarah's strangeness. Anger once again took possession of Lucy; that she had been made a fool of by this creature was bad enough, but that the same had happened to a girl as brutalized and defenseless as Katje, well, that was truly vile. "And you've been abusing that belief, haven't you? Having her pay this price for you."

For the first time, Not-Sarah looked remorseful. "This you must believe: I would not have fed from her, had I the choice. Sarah was in love with her, and therefore, so am I. Any harm she suffers pains me terribly, but I'm desperate. I've only taken the smallest amount of blood, barely enough to sustain me, let alone heal me."

"Heal you?"

She pulled the cap off her head, revealing her scalp riddled with bald patches, then held out her mangled hands. "Look at me, Lucy darling! I am rotting where I stand. That is why I so desperately need your help. If I don't feed soon, I'll die."

That sense of unreality had returned, making everything feel thin and flat. "What, exactly, do you mean by 'feed'?" Lucy heard herself ask.

Sarah's tongue darted from between her lips, licking them. "I need human meat and blood, and it must be fresh, and it must be plentiful, or I won't be able to repair the damage done to this body. Concretely, I suppose that means I must eat someone."

Part III

"I sometimes think we must be all mad and that we shall wake to sanity in strait-waistcoats."

Bram Stoker, *Dracula*

Chapter 18

"AND HOW," LUCY ASKED, "DO you suppose to get someone you can eat?"

"I was hoping you might help me with that."

Lucy laughed. "Of course you were."

Not-Sarah frowned. "You know I'd do the same for you if our positions were reversed. I'd help you hide any infirmity."

"Of course," Lucy said gently.

Her eye blazed fiercely. "Don't mock me! You know I speak true. For you, I'd lie and cheat and kill and damn myself straight to hell. I'd do all that and more, again and again and again, as long as it took to ensure you were safe, because you are my twin, my half, my more."

That's something Sarah would say. A pain unfurled just behind Lucy's breastbone. She pressed her palm hard against her chest, but the pain stayed, softly pulsing, running up her throat until that, too, ached.

The gong rang, signaling that it was time to get changed; dinner would be served soon. Lucy had never been so grateful for food. She rose. "I must go now. If I don't appear at dinner, they'll think something is wrong."

Not-Sarah pawed at her hand. "You must help me."

"I need to think."

"Please help me," she begged, worry carving lines between her brows, her eye wet and large.

Instinctively, Lucy laid a hand on her shorn head to comfort her. "I will," she promised.

Not-Sarah leaned hard against Lucy in relief, and it was easy, so easy, to imagine it was just Sarah doing it. "Thank you," she murmured. "Now don't forget: you mustn't tell anyone what I've told you."

"I won't."

God, if only Lucy could be left alone for a little bit, have the time to order her thoughts. She pinched the bridge of her nose. Her crying had given her a headache. It throbbed behind her eyes, soft but insistent. She needed to press a cold cloth against them, or they'd still be bloodshot and swollen by the time the first course was served, and that would prompt questions.

No rest for the wicked, though, and apparently no time to tend to the small pains and needs of the body either, she thought grimly as she made her way to Katje's room. The girl slept on the other side of the house, not quite with the servants, though very close to them, in a room originally meant for inferior guests. It was cramped and always dark because the windows were small and north facing.

Katje stood at one of those windows, one hand convulsively

rubbing the curtains, the other at her mouth. Her eyes were still glassy from the laudanum she had taken, her belly swollen, her skin, normally such a beautiful creamy white, now chalky. She had been tearing at her lips, leaving them raw and bloody. Slivers of skin stuck to her fingertips.

Something more for Not-Sarah to suck on, Lucy thought. The thought wasn't accompanied by any feeling; everything had become flat and strange again.

"My sister has told me everything," she said.

Katje swallowed. "Everything?" Moving her mouth caused the scabs on her lips to tear. She winced, then wiped at her chin as a drop of blood ran down. How gladly Not-Sarah would have licked that up.

"Everything," Lucy confirmed. "About you, and about her, and her current…needs."

"And?"

"And I need to think."

"But you won't betray us?"

"No." Perhaps she might have been more shocked had she found out at any other time that her sister was an invert—not that she thought inverts were sinful or deranged; she simply had not expected her sister to be one—but now that she knew her sister was a parasite…well, the whole matter of sexual inversion rather paled in comparison to that, didn't it?

Katje slumped in relief, then came to Lucy and embraced her. "Thank you, oh, thank you," she whispered with a tear-choked voice, over and over again.

In the dining room, Lucy greeted Mrs. van Dijk and Michael, then sat down to eat. As she worked her way through the courses, chewing her food mechanically and tasting nothing, her mind plodded through everything she had just learned. She stripped the matter down to its core, and that core was this: Could she consider Not-Sarah her twin or not?

Yes, because she had all of Sarah's memories and emotions, and what was a person if not the sum of all they had ever thought and felt and lived through?

Then again, all those things that made Sarah herself were now mixed with Marianne's memories and emotions—and perhaps with those of other people, too; Not-Sarah might have lied about Marianne being the only one she'd devoured previously. But even if she had lied and Not-Sarah was a conglomeration of all these feelings and thoughts of her previous victims, did that mean she couldn't be a sister to Lucy? People changed all the time. Not-Sarah wasn't exactly Sarah, but what did that even mean? Sarah wouldn't have been the same today as she had been a month ago. Lucy would still have loved her. Hell, she would've loved her even if a witch's spell had turned her into a toad, or a worm, or a wood louse because having a toad or a worm or a wood louse—or a parasite that had eaten her twin's consciousness and wore her rotting corpse as she might wear a dress—was still infinitely better than having no sister at all.

But she killed Sarah, she thought. She swallowed the piece of potato she had been chewing. It seemed to stick to her esophagus, so she took a sip of wine to dislodge it. It was strong, heady, suffusing her cheeks with heat.

Yes.

That was the crux of the matter, wasn't it? Not-Sarah was directly responsible for Sarah's death. There was no denying that. She had killed to survive, true, but that didn't make it any less awful.

Yet what use would it be to hate her for it or to retaliate? Lucy thought as she moved her food aimlessly around her plate; a lady never finished all the food served to her because she was not a glutton.

Lucy didn't even think she could hurt Not-Sarah, not while Not-Sarah continued to wear her sister's face and speak with her sister's voice, and wasn't that clever of that parasite, to use the love people held for the host as a defense mechanism?

Though if Lucy really wanted to, she didn't have to lift a finger to kill Not-Sarah. If what she had told Lucy was true, she could simply let Not-Sarah starve to death. She couldn't, though, because she would've loved her sister even if she had been turned into a toad or worm or wood louse, so why not love her when she was a parasite…?

When dinner finished, Arthur arrived for Sarah's daily examination. Lucy accompanied him to her sister's room. Katje was already there, sewing in front of the fire, her face pinched with pain. She held a hot brick wrapped in flannel on her lap.

"You are up," Arthur said to her in surprise.

"I'm feeling a little better," Katje said, then gave him a wan smile. Her mouth puckered as another stabbing pain tore through her womb.

"You must rest. This time of the month is trying for you. I'd feel much better if you'd take to bed."

"I shall, in a minute."

"Have you been taking those drops I prescribed you?"

She nodded.

"That's good. Now, for the main patient. How are you feeling, my dear?" He turned to Not-Sarah, who was sitting up in bed, pillows propped behind her back, her hands hidden in the folds of her shawl.

"A little better, thank you."

During the next ten minutes, Arthur examined her. He felt the lymph nodes in her throat, took her pulse, listened to her breathe. He made Not-Sarah stick out her tongue, then peered into her mouth. When he stuck his fingers inside, Lucy took Not-Sarah's hand and squeezed it very hard, warning her not to bite down.

"Do you still find it difficult to eat?" he asked as he washed his hands in a bowl of hot soapy water.

"Very."

"I think you may have reached a point where you're afraid to eat because it makes you nauseous, but you're nauseous because you haven't eaten properly for a long time now. It's a damn conundrum, I know, but you must try and eat. Your body can't heal itself if it doesn't have any fuel. I'll give you something to help soothe your stomach."

He dried his hands, then began to pack his bag. Lucy placed her hand lightly on his arm. The muscles stiffened. Even the tendons in his hands drew taut. "I want to talk to you," she said softly.

He took her out into the hallway. "What is it you want to talk about?" he asked, smiling at her.

She told him of the small golden ring they had found in the same field as the bog woman, then of her trip to the archives to discover if the ring had belonged to her. "We found this," she said, handing him the copy she had made of the court document. He did not read it there and then but folded it and tucked it into his jacket.

"Thank you for this," he said, his eyes shining. "I'm sure it'll make some excellent reading for when I'm home and in front of the fire with a glass of brandy. Now, if I'm not mistaken, you said there was something you wanted to tell me?"

Lucy spoke slowly, feeling her way through the words. She had not known what, exactly, she'd tell him until now. "My sister has been acting quite strange lately, don't you think? Very much… Not-Sarah."

Oh, but she mustn't laugh now. If she began, she wouldn't be able to stop, and nothing made a woman's sanity and logic easier to question than hysterical laughter. She pinched the bruise on the back of her hand made by Not-Sarah to kill the giggles before they could climb up her throat and damn her.

She cleared her throat, then tried again. "She told me why that is, and I need to know what you think of it because I don't know how to feel."

He frowned. "What did she say that has disturbed you so?"

Careful now. There was no saying what he might do once he knew the truth about Not-Sarah. It all came down to who he was first and foremost: Doctor Hoefnagel or plain Arthur. The doctor would think Not-Sarah insane and have her sent to an asylum, where she would surely die; her friend might help her in the way she needed. Which one was she talking to now?

She said, "I can't tell you, not unless you promise you shan't have her committed."

"I can't make such promises. I'm to do what is best for my patient," he said.

She could not give up on him helping her, not yet. "And I must do what I think is best for my sister, or else my loyalty means nothing. You know being committed to an asylum is her worst fear. As my friend, I beg you, please promise me you will not tell anyone nor send her away."

Arthur rubbed his mustache, the hairs bristling against the cuff of his shirt. Then he sighed and said, "All right. I promise I won't have her committed no matter what you tell me. Now, please, tell me."

Lucy hesitated, then decided to make as much of a clean breast of it as she could. "She doesn't think it'll do her any good, because she…she doesn't quite know whether she's alive or dead. Of course, if she won't eat, she'll soon truly be dead, so you can understand that this is quite a predicament."

"If she truly believes that, then she's much more ill than even I suspected."

Lucy persevered. "Sarah may, at times, struggle to understand the limits between 'alive' and 'dead,' as she did after poor little Lucille died, but surely it isn't so strange of her to think it now? You must've felt how cold she is, must've noticed the smell. Could you even find a pulse?"

"Just because her pulse is very faint and she is perpetually cold doesn't mean she's dead."

"Of course, and I'm sure this belief will pass, like it did last time, but until it does, we must find a way to get her nourished. Maybe we can give her another blood transfusion? I've talked to her, and not only is she not averse to it, she even desires one. She thinks it'll heal her, make her current state less..."

Arthur shook his head, cutting her off. "A transfusion is the last thing we should give her."

Her heart sank. A transfusion would have been the only acceptable way to provide Not-Sarah with what she needed to survive, at least for a little while, long enough for Lucy to order her thoughts and decide what was to be done. She tried not to let the disappointment show on her face when she asked, "Why not? It worked a charm last time, didn't it? Sarah is adamant that blood is the only thing that will help."

"Transfusions are risky endeavors, Lucy. I've told you before that they are as likely to kill the patient as to cure her. Sarah's situation isn't dire enough anymore to warrant such a dangerous procedure. More importantly, we must never encourage a patient's delusions," he said patiently.

Doctor Hoefnagel through and through, she thought, and her heart ached softly because she could not trust him, could never tell him the truth now. Already she regretted telling him about the ring and the bog body, regretted giving him a copy of the court document, regretted telling him about Not-Sarah.

He would not help her.

No one would.

Once more, Lucy was alone.

The realization made her stagger.

Arthur took hold of her arm to keep her upright, his face lined with worry. "Are you well?" he asked, then shook his head in answer. "You poor thing. You are overwrought, overtired…"

"I'm fine. A moment of weakness, nothing more. It's passed already." She tried to pull her arm from his grip, but he would not let her.

"You're not fine. You must rest. I'll take you to your room."

"Please don't fuss. I don't want to go to my room. I want to stay here, with my sister," she said.

He made her look at him. "You can trust me. You know that, don't you, Lucy?"

But I can't. She forced herself to smile. "Of course."

Slowly, he took hold of her hands. He had honest hands, square, dependable. Little scars from where he had cut himself patterned the skin, which was dry and tight because he washed his hands so often. A working man's hands, now trembling a little at her touch. "Before you go and become the faithful sister and nurse once more, I must ask you this: Have you thought about my offer?" he asked, his voice low and hoarse.

In that moment, she didn't pity him. She just felt exhausted. She pulled her hands away. "I can't think," she said, "with Sarah being as sick as she is."

There was no tightening of his face, no hardening, as there would have been with Michael, had she rejected him. Instead, disappointment made his shoulders droop and tugged the corners of his mouth downward. "Of course. I shall try and be more patient. Good night to you."

At the mouth of the stairs, he turned back and called to her. "You must try not to fret as much as you do. I'm a capable doctor, you know. She doesn't need a transfusion; she just needs to eat. As soon as she does, you'll find her much improved."

She smiled, said that he was probably right, then went back to Not-Sarah and Katje.

As soon as Lucy closed the door behind her, Not-Sarah launched a volley of questions. "What did you have to talk to the doctor about? Did you tell him what I told you? Did you show him that court document to try and convince him of what I am?" Fear and suspicion warred on her face. For all that she was a parasite with her host actively dying, her mimicry was eerily accurate.

Lucy hesitated, then took her sister's hand in hers and squeezed it. The skin was cool and unpleasant. She forced herself to keep holding it. If Not-Sarah was deprived of blood for much longer, perhaps the flesh would turn gray, and swell, and then fall off her bones. Roses of rot would bloom on her cheeks, and...

Lucy pushed the intrusive image away. "None of that. I only wanted to see if I could get Arthur to help us with our little... problem. I thought I might convince him to give you another blood transfusion. It's the only non-sinister way I can think of to feed you."

"And?" Katje asked.

"He won't. I can't convince him of the necessity without

being honest about your being a parasite, and that I can't do."
Not yet, at least, not when she hadn't made up her mind about
Not-Sarah herself.

Defeated, Not-Sarah slumped in her chair. A foul tear ran
down her cheek. She rubbed at it tiredly. "I'm so tired and so
hungry..." she murmured.

"We won't let you starve!" Katje cried out. She knelt at Not-
Sarah's side, her hands squeezing Not-Sarah's bony knees through
the covers. "I'd kill for you, if it came to that. I'd kill someone, and
gut them, and cut them, and..."

Lucy began to talk over her. "We're not quite as desperate
as that just yet. There are other things we can do than resort to
murder, at least for now."

She took the bowl Arthur had washed his hands in, threw the
dirty water out of the window, and rubbed it clean with a cloth.
Then she took the embroidery scissors Not-Sarah had used to cut
her hair. She rolled up her sleeve, took a deep breath, then forced
the tip of the blades into her arm, aiming for one of the thick blue
veins that snaked underneath her skin. When she extracted the
scissors, it took a second before the blood came. It hit the porcelain
of the bowl with a soft sound, oddly muffled, not at all the clear
plink of a drop of water bursting apart in the sink. It didn't take
long for the blood to stop coming. Lucy stabbed herself again, this
time using the handles to open the blades a little, widening the cut.
She hissed at the pain.

Katje helped her bandage her arm when the flow slowed to a
trickle. She wiped the scissors on her handkerchief, then used them

on herself. She stabbed at her wrist, where veins lay as purple and abundant as a cluster of grapes.

Together, they managed to fill the bowl roughly halfway. Not-Sarah sat fidgeting all the while, plucking at the sheets with her ruined hands until another nail came away. She salivated; Lucy could hear her swallowing.

When Not-Sarah was handed the bowl, she ignored the spoon Lucy also gave her. Instead, she placed her lips on the rim and tipped back the dish. Her thin arms strained against the weight; Lucy had to help her hold it. The last thing they needed was to soil the sheets with blood and worry Magda, who had become impatient and sullen of late. Lucy couldn't blame her; Not-Sarah's rotting body combined with her foul moods and cursing made her a deeply unattractive mistress.

Not-Sarah drank, her throat quivering. With a crust of bread, she mopped up the blood that remained, then poured in a little water to get the clotting blood sticking to the porcelain to come away and turn liquid again, and she drank that, too. By the end, the bowl was licked clean. Not-Sarah sighed with pleasure and lay back against the pillows, her hands folded over her distended stomach.

The whole affair had a fever-dream quality to it, no doubt exacerbated by exhaustion and blood loss. It left Lucy feeling light-headed and weak. Katje, already faint and sick from menstruating, looked as if the slightest push could knock her over.

"Oh, but you took a lot of laudanum, Katje darling," Not-Sarah murmured, then giggled softly.

"Don't get used to it. Katje and I won't be able to give you any more for a long while now, not without damaging our own health. This is just to tide you over until we can find a better solution for our problem. I'll bid you both good night now," Lucy said.

Not-Sarah's eye fixed on Lucy. Already it had taken on the same glassy quality that Katje's eyes had. "Why have you decided to help me?" she asked, her voice soft.

Lucy twisted the doorknob in her hand. "It seems the most logical thing to do." She sighed, then elaborated: "I'm not sure whether it's better to have a parasite for a sister than no sister at all. I will need some time to make up my mind about that. I need for you to stay alive until then, because wouldn't it be silly if I decided I'd rather have you than nothing, only for you to be gone as well?"

"I *am* your sister, Lucy," Not-Sarah said.

Lucy just smiled, then closed the door behind her.

Chapter 19

LUCY WAS SO TIRED, SHE could weep with it. She thought wistfully of her room—not the silver one upstairs but the one in her parents' home that she had shared with Sarah when she was still a child. She missed her bed with the carved legs, her little desk in which certain words were scored from when she had written too forcefully on a thin sheet of paper, and the heavy damask curtains she and Sarah had sometimes draped around themselves as they sat on the windowsill at night, looking at the sliver of sky between the roofs of the houses. She wished she were a girl again, listening to Sarah murmur stories in her ear as they held hands under the covers, their heads so close together that their hair tangled.

No use in wishing, though. Better to focus on the task at hand. Once it was complete, she could try and sleep a little.

Mrs. van Dijk sat in the parlor with a book on her lap and Pasja at her feet. The dog showed the whites of her eyes as soon as she caught Not-Sarah's scent clinging to Lucy's hands and clothes. When Lucy came closer, Pasja trembled and hid behind Mrs. van Dijk's chair, showing her little white teeth.

"Poor Pasja. We used to be such good friends," Lucy said as she seated herself opposite her employer.

Mrs. van Dijk closed her book and smiled. "She'll be much improved once she has spent a day or two at home with no one to shout at her and nothing to frighten her."

"She's coming with you, then?"

Mrs. van Dijk snorted. "Of course she's coming with us. Did you think I'd leave her here for your brother-in-law to put down whenever she gets on his nerves? She's a good dog, aren't you, Pasja?" She twisted to pet the dog, her withered leg dangling from the chair, her shoe rasping against the velvet upholstery. Pasja whined and licked her hands.

"I'm glad you found such a friend in her." Lucy took a deep breath, then went on. "I'm glad because that means you won't be going home alone."

Mrs. van Dijk looked at Lucy from the corner of her eye, her upper body still twisted, one finger stroking the beautiful dip in the skull that ran between the dog's eyes. "Am I to understand you're handing in your resignation?"

"I suppose I am. I'll be forever grateful for how you opened your home to me when I needed it and for everything else you've done for me, but I can't come with you. My sister needs me, and I need her."

Mrs. van Dijk turned to face Lucy. "After all this time, you are still under your sister's thumb," she said, then shook her head in disbelief. "I won't ever understand it. Perhaps that's because I've got no siblings of my own. More likely it's because I'm a proud woman.

If I could, I'd be utterly self-sufficient. Alas, I'm not. I, too, need company, and since I've got no kin, I've been reduced to having to pay for it."

Lucy opened her mouth to contradict her, but her former employer raised a hand to silence her and spoke steadily on. "I won't debase myself by begging you to stay. You're not a good enough companion to warrant it, and there are other girls who'll be glad to take your place. There are always girls of good families fallen on hard times. Yet I'd be remiss if I said I didn't enjoy having you around. Still, I would've liked it if you'd made up your mind a little sooner. No one likes to be strung along, not even an old crippled widow such as myself."

Chastised, Lucy swallowed against the tears and flush that both rose from her throat. "It was never my intention to hurt you, and if I have in any way, I apologize for it."

"It is what it is," Mrs. van Dijk said, then smoothed her skirts over her legs, looking suddenly tired and old, her skin papery, as if the mere touch of a nail could rip it.

Lucy's sleep was fitful and restless, her dreams twisted things, bleak and claustrophobic. Her sister—white, cold, dead—crept over her and sat on her chest so she could scarcely breathe. Sarah tore the fabric of Lucy's nightgown and pressed her mouth to Lucy's belly, then tore at the flesh with her teeth till the blood came hot and quick. She drank. She ate. The pain was excruciating, enough to make Lucy break out in a cold sweat, but for all that she wished she might die, she couldn't move, couldn't even whimper. When enough organs had been consumed, Sarah dropped something cool and soft into the cavity she had made, something that would in time travel up, find its way into her skull, and worm its tendrils through her brain until nothing remained...

She woke gasping, the sweat-soaked sheets twisted around her like a straitjacket. That horrible stabbing pain from her dream lingered. When she lit the lamp next to her bed, she found her period had arrived. She threw the soiled sheets on the ground and wrapped herself in her dressing gown for warmth. The sky was blush red by the time she managed to fall asleep again.

"Whatever we decide to do, we *must* be careful," Lucy said.

She was sitting on the windowsill, a flannel-wrapped brick in her lap, which she moved about occasionally, pressing it harder against her tender belly, willing the heat to relax the cramping muscles of her womb. Katje lay on the carpet in front of the fire with her own brick, her eyes large and bright, her mouth slightly slack.

"Naturally," Not-Sarah agreed. "The last thing we need is to be committed to an asylum because they think we're absolutely mad. We don't want to end up like Aunt Adelheid." She lolled on the sofa. She had the heel of one slippered foot planted firmly on the carpet and swished the foot around from left to right. The intake of blood had done her well. Overnight, her skin had lost its jaundiced look, and her eye was clear and bright. The cuts on her hands and face still showed no sign of healing, though, and the room still stank despite the bags of lavender Katje had sewn into the hems and cuffs of Sarah's nightgowns.

"What happened to Aunt Adelheid?" Katje asked, a little stitch of a frown marring her forehead like a thumbprint pressed into cooling wax. Her voice, like her movements, was laudanum languid.

Lucy looked at Not-Sarah, who was looking down at her feet. The constant swishing of her foot seemed to mesmerize her. Weren't revenants said to be entranced by certain movements or heaps of small things spilled, like seeds and crumbs and beads? Katje took hold of the foot to still it, breaking the spell. Not-Sarah blinked, then gave Katje a soft smile, bent over, and kissed her tenderly.

When she was done, she said, "Aunt Adelheid, you asked? The long and short of it is that she went mad, or at least was considered to have gone mad, was committed to a private asylum, and died there within a year."

"And just the long of it?" Katje asked.

Not-Sarah caught Lucy's eye and nodded at her.

"The long of it," Lucy said, "is that she was always unconventional. She was brilliant and headstrong, and she simply didn't give a damn about what others thought of her. That's why she never married, I think. Most men don't want a wife like that."

"It didn't help that she was a raging sapphist, of course," Not-Sarah added. She had found a loose thread and was playing with it.

Lucy stared at her in shock. "What?"

Not-Sarah looked up from the thread, which she had twisted around her wrist and fingers. "Didn't you know? She wasn't exactly subtle about it. All those hushed conversations with Vera, the hours they spent together in her little room to work on her *various projects*... Scientific research can be thrilling, but not so thrilling to warrant all that. Then again, I suppose it takes one to know one." She extracted her foot from its slipper and gently touched Katje's shoulder. "You would've loved her, darling. She was quite a character."

"Is that why your parents had her locked away? Because she was like us?" Katje asked.

Not-Sarah shook her head. "They could have, of course. They could have had her committed for half a dozen other things: her obvious aversion to marriage, the obsessive pursuit of the masculine area of entomology, her argumentative nature. All things I am guilty of, too. But you must understand that, in her own small-minded way, my mother loved my aunt and didn't want to be parted from her. That's why she lived with us: my mother needed her."

"Why, then?" Katje asked.

"Vera left. We were told she had to go home and look after her sick mother. I don't know if that's true. Maybe someone had found out about her and Aunt Adelheid or something had happened between the two of them. Whatever the reason, she left, and my aunt did not take it well. She couldn't sleep and she often cried. When she wasn't crying, she picked fights, especially with my father, whom she had never liked very much. Of course, that was before he took to locking her into her room for hours at a time. He found it all very embarrassing, very unseemly, do you remember?"

Oh, Lucy remembered all right. She remembered all of it: her mother slinking through the house with swollen eyes, her father's mouth set so hard that it seemed carved into his face, the sounds of her aunt kicking the door until it seemed to rattle in its frame, her screams as she demanded to be let out, saying she was not a small child to be locked in her room until she could behave.

Not-Sarah went on: "My father called our family doctor. He diagnosed her with hysteria, which he thought he could cure by turning or massaging her womb twice a week."

When he entered Aunt Adelheid's room, there was always, at first, the screaming and sobbing, followed by pleading. Then silence.

"Of course, that didn't cure her. If anything, it made her worse. She began to have these fits where she'd fall to the ground and convulse, her eyes rolling back." Not-Sarah wound the string around her finger, cutting off the circulation. The tip turned white. Even the small puncture wounds left behind by splinters blanched. Her fingers, Lucy noted, were not quite steady, but it would have been strange if they had been.

"Did you see her have such a fit?" Katje asked Lucy, which made her realize that, though she had begun this story, she had only said a few sentences before Not-Sarah had taken over. She had not noticed because it was not unusual. Her sister had always been eager to talk and Lucy eager to sit back and listen.

"Only once. We hadn't been allowed to see her ever since our father had begun to lock her into her room. Our mother was afraid it would be too upsetting."

Not-Sarah snorted with derision. "Afraid we might catch Aunt Adelheid's madness, you mean."

"She did stab the doctor with a pen—and then herself." A family habit, Lucy supposed.

"That she did." Not-Sarah sighed. "Of course, she had to be committed then. Even our mother agreed with that. Madness, attempted self-murder, and the falling sickness are all horrible taints and can damage a young female relative's prospect of marriage considerably." Her fingertip had turned red now. She unrolled the string. It had striped her finger.

Lucy vividly remembered the day the wardens had come to take her aunt away. She had been so emaciated, she had to be carried out. They had put her in a straitjacket to prevent her from lashing out and hurting anyone, but she screamed, and she spat, and she thrashed until the attending doctor gave her something to quiet her; their parents hadn't wanted the neighbors to hear.

After, all her things were thrown out, the floors scrubbed, and the sheets washed. Even the walls of her room were papered over. With time, the animal smell of her, thick and fecal, dissipated, and all that was left of her was a tooth Lucy found in her room. It had rolled under her dresser and was cracked clean through the middle. Lucy still had no idea how it had ended up there.

"Is that what killed her eventually? The falling sickness?" Katje asked. She stroked her brick as if it were a cat, carefully and with great delight.

"That's what the asylum doctors said," Not-Sarah said.

"But you don't believe that?"

"They wouldn't let us see her body. We went to collect it because our mother wanted her buried in the family plot with their parents, but they said they'd already buried her in their private cemetery. The institution was forced to close down two years later because of general malpractice and mistreatment of its patients. Maybe Aunt Adelheid died of a fit. Maybe she was beaten to death, or she choked while being bound to the wall, or they forced too much food down her throat and her stomach burst. Perhaps it's nothing as sinister as all that. It could be that she died of natural causes and the reason the institution wouldn't release her body is because they had performed an illegal autopsy on it. We won't ever know now."

"Please let's talk of something else," Lucy whispered.

They were all quiet for a moment, until Katje said, her voice forcefully bright, "Are there any others like you, Sarah?"

Not-Sarah dropped her thread, bent to pick it up, and wound it so tight around her hand that the thread bit deeply into the skin. "Not a lot of others, no, and fewer every year, I fear."

"Why is that?"

"We don't reproduce easily, and when between hosts, we are extremely vulnerable. When Arthur and Doctor Rosenthaler were autopsying Marianne and they cracked open her skull, I fell straight into Arthur's hand. I was utterly helpless then. He could've killed me simply by balling his hand into a fist. I was so scared..."

She shuddered, then smiled. "Funny, isn't it? He saw my true form and had me at his mercy, yet he'll never know the intimacy of that moment." She jumped up and threw her thread into the fire, then began to pace around, moving from one side of the carpet and back again, holding the cotton of her nightgown in one hand to keep it from swishing into the hearth.

"You're restless today," Lucy remarked.

"Your blood has given me some of my energy back. I feel like tearing something small apart with my hands or walking a great deal, anything but this endless lying about. I think it might have given me bedsores, though with the general splitting and rot of my skin, it's hard to tell."

Lucy said, "That brings us back to the issue at hand rather nicely, I suppose. You need to feed. More specifically, you said you need to eat someone. What I'd like to know is whether that's true. Our bit of blood has already done you a lot of good. If we give you a little blood and meat every day, never mind for now how we are to get it, won't that help you heal over time?"

Not-Sarah shook her head. "If you feed a starving man a little food every day, you prolong his starvation but don't cure him. Only copious amounts of food for weeks on end could do that. It's the same for me." She shuddered. "God, what I wouldn't give for a big meal!"

"Does that not feel strange to you? I still hear our mother's voice in my head whenever I'm about to eat telling me that what distinguishes a lady from a maid is how much she eats. A true lady must always leave the dinner table a little hungry. If her stomach isn't grumbling an hour after, she has eaten too much."

Not-Sarah made a face. "Don't put that in my head, please. Eating a human while trying to suppress Marianne's and Sarah's rather negative emotions related to what they view as cannibalism shall be challenging enough without adding in Mother's distaste for a big meal. I need all the calories I can get."

"You're still a growing girl, after all," Lucy said.

Not-Sarah picked up a pillow that had fallen to the ground and threw it at Lucy's head.

"Must those calories come from human meat and blood?" Katje asked.

"Yes."

"Why is that?"

"Why can't you eat belladonna without dying, yet cows and horses and hares can eat it just fine? What is poison to one species is another's daily fare. I must have human blood and meat, or I'll starve," she said, then yawned till the tears ran down her face.

"We could take a leaf out of the book of the resurrection men and find you a body recently buried," Lucy said, and marveled at the ease with which she proposed common body snatching. Not-Sarah was easy to talk to. It felt exactly as it had when she and Sarah had spoken. Only, instead of talking about child-rearing or a treatise on moss or the pair of gloves Lucy had embroidered as a gift for Mrs. van Dijk for Saint Nicholas Day, they were talking about cannibalism.

It ought to have felt odder than it did, more horrible. Instead, it felt both easy and natural.

"I can't eat a rotting body nor diseased meat," Not-Sarah said.

If all her kind were such picky eaters, it wasn't to be wondered at why they were going extinct. Lucy said, "Are you picky about what kind of person you put in your mouth, too?"

"How do you mean?"

"You ate my sister and became her. If that's the case for everyone you consume, I think we should be very careful about your next choice of meal."

Not-Sarah shook her head. "There's a difference between merging with a host and eating someone for sustenance. I could eat everyone in this house, and my character would remain unchanged."

"I'd rather you didn't," Lucy said. She shuddered and wrapped her hands around the brick in her lap to warm them, but it had cooled.

Not-Sarah saw. She gripped the poker and beat hard at the fire in the grate, releasing a cloud of warmth that smelled vaguely sweet; in a previous life, the logs had been fruit trees. "A girl needs to eat," she said simply.

This Lucy could not deny. "Someone might die in an accident. The body would be fresh then," she tried.

"There's no saying when that might happen though, and I must eat."

"That only leaves murder," Lucy said. "I don't think I can commit murder."

"Why not?"

"Because it's horrible, and a sin, and unnatural…"

Not-Sarah let out a little laugh. "Unnatural? It happens every day." Her voice was shrill, the laugh forced, and Lucy knew her sister was getting angry. Unlike Lucy, who had left her tantrums behind, Sarah's anger was still a hot, passionate, volatile thing.

"I know," Lucy said gently, "but that doesn't make the matter any easier for me. If I could…"

Not-Sarah interrupted her. "You'll be committing murder if you don't feed me. Have you thought of that? Neglecting to help someone and thereby causing their death makes you responsible."

Lucy looked away from her sister. Her reflection in the window was frowning. She tried to smooth her brow—her mother had told her that lines on a woman's face were unbecoming—but the frown remained. She breathed hard on the glass until it misted over, obscuring her.

"Maybe we can find someone who isn't so bad to kill, like criminals or people who don't want to live anymore?" Katje piped up.

"How would we find someone like that? We might as well wait for someone around here to die of an accident and keep our hands clean," Lucy said.

"Clean hands? God, you're infuriating," Not-Sarah snarled.

Lucy chose her next words carefully in an attempt to douse the flames of her sister's fury, though she feared she was already too late. Once her sister got riled up, there was often no placating her. "That was an unfortunate phrase for me to use. I didn't mean it like that. What I meant is that we shouldn't be hasty."

"Not be hasty? Can you hear yourself talking? I need to eat, Lucy, or I'll die. Do you hear me? I'll DIE. We can joke around about our mother's silly ideas regarding food all we want, but that's the harsh truth. No more miraculous resurrections. Your sister and beloved twin will be gone then, forever."

"Please don't fight, my love." Katje pleaded. She sat trembling on the floor. "Lucy will help you, of course she will. She loves you terribly. You know this."

They ignored her.

Lucy curled her fingers hard into the flannel wrapped around the brick. Her palms were wet with sweat. "I know that. I'm merely trying to find a way to get you fed without having to resort to murder. It's not as easily done as you might think, and…"

Not-Sarah talked right over her. Her eye blazed in her face. "Sometimes, you need to get your hands dirty for the things you want. I thought you understood that. I thought you'd be willing to do that for me. You wept over my corpse and said all these pretty words when you thought me dead, all these things you'd do to have me back. Well, here I am, but when push comes to shove, those words are nothing but hot air. Don't you see your promises don't mean anything if you're only willing to help me when it doesn't inconvenience you?"

That stung horribly, but Lucy knew better than to retort. There was no reasoning with Sarah when she was like this; Lucy had known that ever since she was little. Once her anger had spent itself, things would soon be well again. If she could just sit here and pretend to be of stone, let it wash over her…

Not-Sarah snapped her finger in front of Lucy's eyes, startling her. "Are you even listening, or do you care so little for me that you can't even be bothered? A fine sister you make! I'm starting to think you wouldn't mind me dying."

Not-Sarah was goading her. *Do not rise to it*, Lucy told herself, but she couldn't help it. "How can you say that? If only you'd stop interrupting me, I could explain. I could…"

"I'm not interested in anything you have to say. You know why, Lucy? Because you're disloyal, and spineless, and utterly weak. You've so little strength, so little character, you might as well be only half a person!"

The words were as deliberate and agonizing as a brand. Blood rushed to Lucy's face, tears to her eyes. She got up, put the brick on the windowsill, and took exaggerated care to smooth her skirts in the hope the color would have left her face by the time she turned around to face her sister. What use was it, though? Not-Sarah's words had found their mark. No one could wound Lucy like her sister could, and right now, she had wounded her to the quick.

"If that's what you really think," Lucy said coolly, "then I don't see what use it is for me to stay here."

She made for the door, but Not-Sarah wouldn't let her. "Don't go," she said, and her voice was no longer choking on anger.

"Let me pass," Lucy said, doing her best not to look her sister in the face.

"Please don't be like this," Not-Sarah pleaded.

"Like what?"

"So cold and reserved. I didn't mean what I said. You know I say the most horrible things when I'm angry, but I never mean them. I'm just so hungry, I think I'm going mad with it. I could tear out dour Magda's throat or take a bite out of Michael's cheeks. Sometimes, I think I might even be able to eat you." She tried to take hold of Lucy, tried to kiss her cheek, but Lucy tore her hands from her grip and averted her face.

"Do what you must," she said. "Eat the maid, for all I care, or your own feet, but leave me out of it. I've always been at your beck and call. No more. It's brought me nothing but grief."

"You don't mean that." Not-Sarah laughed. "Come. You're upset by what I said, and that's fair, but there's no need to retaliate. I've apologized, haven't I?"

"I do mean it. Sometimes, I think of all the things I might have been and might have done and might have had if I didn't have you to care for, and it makes me sour with regret and longing," Lucy said, her words as cold as the ice that bloomed on the window where she had breathed on it.

"Is this about Michael? I knew I should never have let on that I knew you wanted him," Not-Sarah said.

"Not everything is about Michael!" Lucy snapped.

Not-Sarah laughed bitterly. "But for you, it is! You wanted him, but he chose me over you, and that has made you jealous and spiteful. You blame me for your unhappiness, but all the time you spent pining over my husband, you could've used to find some meaning in your life, like I have with my many interests and Katje. You could even have found a husband of your own if only you didn't lack initiative and perseverance."

The little voice in Lucy's head told her to hold her tongue, to leave and let Not-Sarah rot. Everything she'd say now, she'd come to regret bitterly.

But the words stuck in her gullet, and she needed to hack them up or else choke on them.

She took a deep breath and said, "I may be all those things you said about me, but you are greedy and possessive and can't stand for me to have something for myself. You were a parasite long before one ate your brain."

She didn't wait for Not-Sarah to respond, rushing outside, where her sister could not follow.

Chapter 20

HOW DARE SHE? LUCY THOUGHT as she marched down the lawn and into the woods. The grass, stiff with hoarfrost, crunched under her buttoned boots. *How dare she talk to me like that? How dare she think those things of me? After all I've done for her!*

When she had been little and still beset by tantrums, she would throw things and scream till she threw up. She hadn't done so in a long while, but her fury needed some sort of outlet, or something inside her would snap and kill her. She broke a branch off a tree and used it to slash at the bracken as she walked, making drops fly around. Already, it had begun to thaw.

To say Lucy was unwilling to help her twin whenever it inconvenienced her was a gross and utter lie. If Not-Sarah believed it, she was completely delusional. Lucy had come to be with her whenever she was needed, hadn't she? And she had done so much besides. She was there to help Sarah pick out her trousseau when she got married, even though her heart felt as if it were being ripped to shreds; she held Sarah's hair when her pregnancy made her vomit several times a day, and she wiped up the sick; she sewed and embroidered little Lucille's baby clothes because Sarah had never had any patience or talent for needlework but wanted beautiful things for her little girl.

A thousand things Lucy had done for Sarah, painful things and disgusting things and boring things, never asking for anything in return.

Besides, even if she discounted all that, it was still absolutely irrational of Not-Sarah to be angry with Lucy for not rejoicing at the thought of murder. Lucy had always believed herself capable of killing someone for Sarah, but whenever she had thought of it, she imagined someone who had wronged her sister terribly, thus justifying the act of murder. She knew instinctively and hotly that she would destroy anyone who dared to hurt her sister. She would rip out their throat and desecrate their body, then dance on their grave and gladly burn in hell for it.

But to kill someone who had not harmed her sister, that was different.

If I can even consider that parasite my sister.

She looked like Sarah, talked like Sarah, acted like Sarah, but that did that make her Sarah?

This philosophical conundrum aside, Lucy was ill-equipped for murder. She had never managed to conceive of the act beyond abstract terms. To balk at the reality of it was only natural. Truly, Not-Sarah should have been far more concerned if she had found Lucy willing and eager, but then her sister could be unbelievably delusional and selfish.

Lucy gave an oak tree a sound thrashing with her stick until the heat beat off her face and hands and her breath steamed from her mouth in great quick plumes.

Delusional and selfish, yes. How dare Not-Sarah say Lucy was responsible for her own unhappiness? How dare she even think it! She had taken the one man Lucy had ever loved and wanted for herself, hadn't she? And after their parents had died and left her penniless, all her prospects had been dashed.

Well, not quite. Michael could have given her a dowry and put her back on the marriage market, had she asked. She hadn't because she was too proud to take his money. But even if it weren't for him, Arthur had still proposed to her. The only reason she hadn't taken him up on his offer was out of respect, both for herself and for him. She didn't love him. She'd rather be a spinster than wedded just for the sake of it. To think, though, that her sister felt she wasn't responsible for Lucy's current situation, as if it hadn't been absolutely cruel of her to snatch up and marry the one man Lucy had ever loved...

Though perhaps she didn't know that at the time, a little voice piped up. Not-Sarah hadn't told her when, exactly, she'd realized Lucy loved him.

No! She must have known from the start. Lucy hadn't told her, but that didn't mean Sarah couldn't have known. They never kept secrets from each other.

Except for the fact you were Michael's mistress for a while. That Sarah still didn't know and did not suspect.

Naturally.

Lucy wouldn't expect something as vile and underhanded as that of her twin either.

And it *was* vile and underhanded. She knew that. She had known it from the very beginning but had shoved the knowledge aside because she had wanted him. Oh, she could pretend she had merely wanted to comfort him and one thing had led to another, but lifting your skirts and bending over for a man again and again was a choice, not a natural law. Yes, she had done it partly so she would know what it was like and she and Sarah could be alike again, but the truth of the matter was that she had wanted Michael to love her, to desire her, to prefer her over Sarah, as if love and life were competitions.

She was spineless after all, then—and rotten and selfish, too.

Lucy twisted the stick in her hands, scraping her palms raw. The wet bark peeled away in strips, revealing the smooth wood underneath, pale as bone.

Why did it always keep coming back to Michael? Her life did not revolve around him. God knew Sarah's never had; she had her insects to study and her books to read and her papers to write and her Katje to kiss. As children, Lucy and Sarah had rarely ever fought. There had been little frustrations, of course, small squabbles. Naturally; they were only human. These feelings of resentment and envy, though? They hadn't come about until Michael stepped into their lives.

It would've been better if he never had.

No man was worth hating and despising your sister for, nor yourself, for that matter. That was why she had broken things off between them after Sarah had gotten well again, then taken the position as Mrs. van Dijk's companion that Arthur had found for her when she had let him know she no longer wished to live at Zwartwater.

All the same, Not-Sarah shouldn't have raged at Lucy like she had, shouldn't have said such awful things. Lucy allowed herself to be inconvenienced by her sister all the time, for instance…

And so her thoughts went around and around in circles. She was too hurt to admit to herself what she knew deep down: that, in some things, her sister had been right.

———————

That night, it stormed. The wind stripped trees of their bark and branches. It howled, threw things, like a child having a tantrum. Raindrops cold and hard as bullets smashed against walls and windows and wormed their way into every nook and cranny. Soon, rain trickled down the walls and ruined the wallpaper or dripped from the roof. The maids had to bring buckets and bowls to catch the drops.

By morning, the storm had spent itself. The only movement among the trees came from the occasional raindrop falling to the ground and rippling the pools. The ground, already sodden and waterlogged, had been unable to drink up the rain. A sheet of water lay across the land, reflecting the bruised sky and flagellated trees overhead. Young trees had been ripped from the soil and lay helplessly draped across the roads, their roots washed clean of clods of earth and raised to the clouds as if in supplication. The air smelled of water, of churned-up mud and broken wood.

There was no question of Mrs. van Dijk leaving now. Even if the roads had been passable, which they were not and would not be until at least some of those trees could be cut and removed, no sane man would send out a horse in these conditions. The risk of it stumbling and breaking a leg was simply too great.

Lucy spent the day in her room, the door locked against her sister. The next day, too, she refused to talk to her. Not even Michael could persuade her to do otherwise. In the end, he threw up his hands and exclaimed, "I don't much care what has caused this rift between you, only that you make amends. Nothing fouls up a house's atmosphere the way women fighting does."

"Then tell your wife to apologize to me and mean it this time, and I shall do the same!" she snapped, then went back to her diary. She had filled page upon page with her thoughts on her sister, on Not-Sarah, on Michael. Her fingers were smeared with ink, the tips of her thumb and index finger dented from where she held the pen. It wasn't the one Michael had given her for her birthday—God knew where that one had gone once it had been plucked from her sister's socket—but one Sarah had bought for her when she was about fifteen, just because she could. They had given each other little gifts often: a pretty ribbon, a dried flower, a drawing the size of a stamp dabbed with scent. Over time, the pen's nib had split too far, doubling every stroke, twinning each word.

By the third day, the water had gone down in many places, and most of the fallen trees had been cut and dragged to the side of the road, making them passable again. That morning, Katje knocked on Lucy's door and begged to talk to her. Lucy ignored her and would have gone on ignoring her, had there not been a heavy thump. When she opened the door, she found the girl had fainted.

Lucy cursed softly, then dragged her inside and placed her feet on the chair to let the blood flow to her brain. Soon, Katje moaned and tried to move her head away, rubbing her cheek against the carpet until it looked raw. The other, by contrast, was smooth and white as the inside of a shell. It took about five more minutes before she regained full consciousness. "I'm sorry," she mumbled. "I think I fainted."

Lucy looked down on her, her arms folded across her chest. Her mouth, she knew, must have been an angry line, pale from tautness, but she couldn't help it. "You've been letting her feed from you, haven't you?"

"No."

"Don't lie. I can see the marks on your wrist. Those are fresh. You look pale as well, and your pulse is much too fast. You let her feed from you even before I knew what she was."

"Maybe I have," Katje admitted.

Lucy began to tap her foot in annoyance. "You want her to drain you? You want her to kill you, then eat you up? Don't be stupid. She'd never be able to eat you without others noticing. Besides, where would she be without you? Do you think others would let her live if they knew the truth of what she is, let alone help her? Dying for someone is easy. If you really want to help her, stay alive."

"Then help me. I can't do it alone," Katje begged. Tears rolled from her eyes over her temples, beading in her hair. One fell into the whorl of her ear. She rubbed it away with her little finger.

"I am trying to help! Why can't you see that?" Lucy realized she had raised her voice. She swallowed, then forced herself to speak calmly. Katje tended to cringe whenever she was shouted at, which she didn't deserve.

"I am trying to help," Lucy said, quieter now. "I've been thinking the matter through these past few days,"—she had, during those moments when she wasn't stewing in anger or pity or self-hatred, whichever one had her gripped—"and I don't see an easy solution. A good murder is complicated. Even if we disregard the ethics of it, there's still the logistics to consider. If we are caught, we will be sent to jail, or worse: the madhouse. Why must my carefulness be seen as cowardice?"

Katje said, "If she eats the body, there's no body, and without a body, there's no crime."

"We don't know how long she needs to consume an entire body, and even if she could do that swiftly, we still need to get the body, then get the body to her or her to the body."

Katje took hold of her hand. Her fingers were cool and clammy. "Whatever we do, we must hurry. She's getting frantic. She's *famished*, Lucy."

"I know that. I…"

Down the hallway, where Not-Sarah's room was, Pasja began to bark hysterically. Lucy's heart thumped against her ribs like a bird throwing itself against the bars of its cage. She swallowed, feeling the veins in her throat throb as the blood was forced through it at great speed. She locked eyes with Katje. "Did you leave my sister in the care of a servant?"

Please, she thought, *please tell me you didn't. Please tell me she is by herself right now.*

Because if Katje hadn't, and Not-Sarah—starving, desperate— had been left in the same room as a highly edible member of the staff she had no emotional attachment to…

"No," Katje said.

Lucy relaxed. Of course, Katje wouldn't let Not-Sarah close to a servant, for all their sakes. "Thank God for that," she said.

Katje smiled weakly. Her eyes were soft, dreamlike. Perhaps she had taken a drop of laudanum to help numb the pain of Not-Sarah biting her. "I left her with Mrs. van Dijk."

Whatever relief Lucy had felt evaporated. "You left her alone with Mrs. van Dijk? Old, frail, defenseless Mrs. van Dijk?"

Her eyes lost some of that blurredness. "Mrs. van Dijk asked me to. She said she was leaving, and there was something she had to say to Sarah, something private."

"Oh, Katje, how could you!"

She trembled. "I didn't think… But she wouldn't, surely she wouldn't, not when I promised her I'd go talk to you, and we'd help her…"

But she would, and if Pasja's manic barking was anything to go by, she already had.

Fuck.

"Stay here," Lucy ordered. "If you get up now, you'll just faint again."

"But I…"

"Stay!" Lucy yelled. She was already halfway through the door, her hands holding up the slippery stuff of her skirts so she could run without tripping over the hem. Pasja stood in front of the door to her sister's room, her hackles raised, her lips pulled up so far that her snout looked like a crumpled piece of paper. She barked incessantly, the sound echoing between the thick walls, so loud as to be painful.

"Easy, girl!" Lucy said. When she reached for the door handle, the dog whined and butted her head against the wood in her eagerness to get in. Lucy gripped her collar to hold her back, but she thrashed and screamed.

Lucy had never heard a dog scream before.

It was a nerve-shattering sound, high and panicked, the sound a terrified child might have made.

"Hush, Pasja!" Lucy pleaded, trying to soothe the dog by laying a hand on her trembling haunches, but Pasja wouldn't be consoled. She struggled against Lucy, her nails scrabbling against the floorboards, scoring the wood. The collar bit deep into her slender throat, cutting off another scream.

They struggled until Pasja went limp. Lucy threw an arm around the dog's heaving chest to hold her back and eased the pressure on her throat. Pasja let out a horrendous honking cough, her tongue lolling from her mouth. It was flecked with foam and blood.

"Hush, girl. It'll be all right. You mustn't get so worked up," Lucy said, then rubbed her under her chin with a trembling hand, taking care not to touch the bruised part of her throat. The fur there, usually so soft that it was almost impossible to tear herself away from fondling it, was stiffening from all the drool.

Lucy righted herself. With one hand still clasping the leather collar, she opened the door at a crack. Pasja stiffened, her nose trembling. A smell wafted through the crack, cloying, so thick that Lucy tasted it at the back of her throat with every breath.

It was the smell of the abattoir.

Without warning, Pasja bolted forward, ramming the door with her slender head, opening it. Lucy tried to hold her back, but she hadn't been prepared and wasn't strong enough. She fell to her knees, her arm feeling like it was being ripped from its socket. She tried to pull back, but her fingers were still hooked around the collar. Pasja kept going, choking and whining and growling. Some of her nails had cracked or come away altogether; her paws left bloody lines on the floorboards.

Mercifully, the collar snapped.

Lucy lay where she had been dropped. Her shoulder was on fire, flames of pain licking down her back and arm. Her fingers burned, too, the blood pounding at the tips as if pooling there.

No matter. They were still attached, weren't they? Although wiggling them made it feel as if hot rods were being driven through the bone, she had more pressing concerns. With her good arm, she forced herself up, then looked around the room.

It was in utter disarray.

The little writing desk had been toppled. The inkwell had shattered, leaving a pool of gleaming midnight. Some of it had been sucked up by the stack of diaries that had fallen. They lay bent, their pages creased. The binding had broken in one of them, and pages full of Sarah's meticulous handwriting lay scattered on the floor like leaves in a forest. Some of them had the print of a bare foot on them done in ink.

Lucy followed the trail of footsteps. It led past the writing desk and onto the bed, ruining the sheets. Though if the ink hadn't ruined them, Pasja's bloody paws would have. She had jumped on the bed and half crouched at the end, a snarl rumbling through her thin frame.

Not-Sarah had clambered on top of the bed's headboard to get away from the dog and now stood pressed hard against the wall, the tendons in her feet taut as they gripped the wood. Her mouth was smeared with blood. She bared her teeth at Pasja. The porcelain one had cracked. One of her hands was mangled. Blood dripped slowly from her balled fist and ran down the wallpaper. Some of the fingers stood at an impossible angle. It was a wonder they were still attached, Lucy thought. By all rights, they should have fallen off. At the very least, jagged ends of bone should protrude from her knuckles. They...

They weren't her own fingers.

Chapter 21

LUCY WHIRLED AROUND. AT THE other end of the room, she found Mrs. van Dijk. Her former employer huddled in a corner. She clutched one hand with the other. Both were slick with blood. It covered the front of her blouse, her skirt.

"I only came to tell her goodbye, and to ask her to talk to you, to make you reconsider. She smiled and gripped my fingers. I thought she might kiss my hand, only she didn't. She put my fingers in her mouth and then she bit me," she said in a small voice. She looked down at her hand in disbelief, as if to verify that Not-Sarah had indeed ripped her fingers off and she wasn't imagining it. A little blood spurted from one of the stumps, hitting her in the face. When she looked up at Lucy, the blood had run into one of her eyes, making her blink convulsively.

Lucy knelt next to her. "Let me see," she said.

Mrs. van Dijk shook her head. Lucy peeled away her remaining fingers to assess the damage done, gritting through the pain in her own two fingers that had gotten caught in Pasja's collar.

Mrs. van Dijk's index finger, middle finger, and ring finger from her right hand had been bitten off, the middle finger and ring finger down to the knuckle, but the index finger only partly.

A soft ripping sound behind Lucy, then a crunch.

She's eating them.

Her stomach twisted with nausea. The pain was as acute as being knifed. She took a deep breath and pressed her hand against her belly to calm the organ, but her breakfast rose mercilessly, burning her esophagus, her tongue, the ribbed roof of her mouth. She forced herself to swallow her sick and focus on Mrs. van Dijk instead. Those fingers couldn't have been reattached anyway. Better that Not-Sarah eat them. Though how she was to explain where they had gone once it became known her sister had torn them off with her teeth, she didn't know.

Where were the servants? The dog was making an infernal racket. They must've heard. If they didn't come soon, Michael would fire them all. Another worry for later. First, she had to make sure Mrs. van Dijk didn't bleed out. Three fingers unorthodoxly amputated was a lesser crime than murder.

"Put your arm around my shoulder and hold up your hand as high as you can. That should slow the bleeding," Lucy told her. She dug into her pockets and found her pen, a spool of thread, some needles, a folded piece of paper, and a handkerchief. She wound the handkerchief around the stumps. Mrs. van Dijk let out a little shriek and tried to pull away, then slumped, her eyes rolling back into her skull. The eye where the blood had run into it was no longer white but a dark pink. Lucy bound the stumps as well as she was able, but the blood still came, soaking the fabric. She pulled a blue ribbon from around her wrist and used that to try tying off what remained of the fingers to slow the flow of blood.

Suddenly Magda was beside her. She propped Mrs. van Dijk up with her shoulder, then held Mrs. van Dijk's right hand steady. Lucy wove the ribbon around her stumps and remaining fingers, tying it around the wrist to keep it in place. Still the blood came through.

"We must cauterize the wound," she said.

"Shouldn't we let the doctor do that?" Magda asked, frowning.

"Probably, but it'll be a while yet until he can get here. We can't risk Mrs. van Dijk losing any more blood. Go run down and send someone to fetch him, then come straight back up."

"All right." Magda straightened herself and looked at Not-Sarah. "You stay right there," she ordered. Magda spoke loudly and slowly, as if Not-Sarah were deaf, or very small, or just plain stupid.

When she took off, Lucy looked around the mess on the ground for Sarah's letter opener. Her own fingers had turned blue and would hardly bend. "They're going to crucify you for this," she said. She didn't have to raise her voice; Pasja had ceased barking and now merely stood growling, her eyes tracking every move Not-Sarah made.

"I know," Not-Sarah whispered. "I knew it even as I did it, but I couldn't stop myself. I was so hungry... Have you never done something you knew was stupid and you'd come to regret later, but it was stronger than you?"

Lucy remembered the press of Michael's teeth as he nipped at her earlobe, the wild, animal smell of him as they rutted, his guttural groan when he spent himself. "Yes, but not as stupid as this. How am I ever going to explain this away?" She looked up. Not-Sarah still balanced precariously on the headboard, her eye trained on Pasja.

"I don't know," she admitted.

"Stop looking that dog in the eye. Don't you know that's an act of aggression? She's already this close to ripping out your throat. The last thing I need right now is to lose you, too." Though that was inevitable now, wasn't it? There was only so much that could be explained away and otherwise hushed up.

"I'm sorry. I didn't mean for this to happen. I wouldn't have done it if I knew you'd help me," Not-Sarah said, but her voice lacked conviction.

Tears of frustration and anger temporarily blurred Lucy's vision. She shook her head hard to get rid of them. "Of course I was going to help you, you stupid dolt!" she snapped, her voice high and thick with emotion. "I may at times feel like only half a person when compared to you, but I'm not disloyal, and I'm more than willing to help you even if it inconveniences me! You are my sister, aren't you?"

As she spoke the words, she knew them to be true. If she had thought of Not-Sarah as a mere parasite, their fight wouldn't have hurt as much as it did. Only her sister could injure her so, and she could because she had Sarah's thoughts and feelings and memories, and what was a person if not an agglomeration of those?

"Do you mean that?" Not-Sarah asked, her face torn between hope and doubt.

Lucy nodded grimly. For better or for worse, cannibalistic needs or no, the rotting woman in front of Lucy was her sister now, and she'd do anything to protect her.

A tear ran down Not-Sarah's face, creating a clear track through the blood drying into rust on her chin and cheeks.

Lucy resisted the urge to go dry her tears with the hem of her skirt. Instead, she said, "Not that it matters now. You're in all likelihood beyond help. Fuck!" The last word, she screeched. She gave the writing desk a hard kick in frustration. Then she forced herself to be calm and reasonable again and look for the letter opener. She found it under one of the diaries. It was a small blade, beautifully wrought; Michael had bought it for her sister on their honeymoon in Florence. Lucy heated it over the fire with a pair of prongs, then dropped it on the stones of the hearth, wrapped the handle in a piece of her skirt, and took the searing thing to Mrs. van Dijk, who had started to come around.

"I'm sorry, but this will hurt. Try not to move," Lucy said, and before the other woman could do much more than blink, Lucy pressed the blade against the stub that was left of her ring finger. The raw meat sizzled as it burned. Mrs. van Dijk howled and tried to yank her hand back, but Lucy had her wrist clamped between her knees.

"I know, I know," she muttered as she moved on to the next finger, then the next. The smell of cooked meat made her stomach contract.

Alarmed by Mrs. van Dijk's screams, Pasja began to bark again. The dog seemed torn between keeping Not-Sarah cornered and flying at Lucy's throat. She opted for the latter and might have succeeded, had Michael not run into the room at that moment. He grabbed the dog by the scruff of her neck as she streaked past him. As he hauled her out of the room by the bruised flesh of her neck, Pasja yelped and writhed, the whites of her eyes showing.

Mrs. van Dijk tore her hand from between Lucy's knees and struggled to her feet, using the wall as support, smearing it with blood. She grabbed her cane with her good hand and beat Michael with it. "Don't hurt my Pasja!" she wailed.

Michael raised an arm to defend himself. "Stop beating me, woman! Can't you see the dog is rabid? It attacked you!"

"Pasja didn't bite me, you fool! Your wife did!" Mrs. van Dijk screamed.

I should've let her bleed out. I could've blamed it on the dog then. Why didn't I think of that?

The thought cut through all else like a blade. Lucy tried to push it away as she grabbed the cane and ripped it from Mrs. van Dijk's hand, then embraced her to keep her from falling, but thoughts could hardly unthink themselves.

Michael threw Pasja out of the room and shut the door. He helped ease Mrs. van Dijk down, then looked at her mangled hand. "Give me that pitcher over there and tear off some strips from the bedclothes," he commanded.

Oh, but it was a relief not to be in charge anymore! Lucy did as he asked, then washed Mrs. van Dijk's face and throat and hand for her. The linen soon took on shades of pink and red and brown.

"I can help. Tell me what I must do, and I'll do it," Not-Sarah said softly.

Michael looked at her over his shoulder, his face a fiendish mask. "Stay where you are, and shut your mouth!" he snarled.

"Don't talk to my sister like that!" Lucy said.

Michael locked eyes with her. "Don't you start as well," he said, and his voice was soft and dangerous.

She looked at the ground and was silent, hating herself, hating him.

Pasja kept whining and pawing at the door, her breath coming in great sighs as she sniffed at the crack under it. By the time Arthur arrived, a servant had taken her away. Two other servants helped Mrs. van Dijk to a different room where the light was better, which Arthur needed to more accurately assess the damage done to her hand. Katje was roped into helping him. Before being led away, she looked helplessly at Not-Sarah, her eyes brimming with tears, though from fear or sadness or shock, Lucy didn't know.

Lucy and Not-Sarah were sent to the Silver Room, allowing the servants to clean the scene of the crime. Lucy washed her hands and face, then dabbed at the dried blood on Not-Sarah's chin with a piece of flannel, careful not to damage the skin. They couldn't speak; Magda had come to sit with them at Arthur's instruction. She had locked the door and held the key.

So they don't trust Not-Sarah to be alone with anyone anymore, and they fear she might try and escape, Lucy thought as she dipped the cloth into the basin and wrung it out, then brought it to Not-Sarah's face. She even had blood behind her ears.

Not-Sarah fit her hand around Lucy's wrist and leaned hard into the palm that cupped her cheek, her eye closed. Her fingers no longer felt like ice. They were merely cool now. Her lip began to tremble.

I won't let them take you away, Lucy mouthed.

"You can't stop it. They're coming for me, and they'll take me away, and you'll never see me again. Whatever place they'll take me to, I shan't leave it, not even when I'm dead," Not-Sarah murmured. A tear got caught in her lashes.

"Let them try to take you away from me! Let them try, and they shall see the stuff I'm made of," Lucy growled.

She rested their foreheads together, then stroked a line across her sister's cheekbone with her thumb.

Let them fucking try.

Chapter 22

LUCY WAS STILL GENTLY CLEANING the blood from her sister's body when the knock at the door came.

Please, no, she thought, closing her eyes briefly. She had hoped there would be more time for her to think of something, anything. At the very least, she had hoped she would be allowed to clean her sister in peace, but they would not even give her that.

When she opened her eyes again, Not-Sarah was staring at her, her eye large with fright. Her mouth was trembling so much, her chin wrinkled like a prune.

Magda came to her feet with a grunt. "Stay over there where I can see you," she told Not-Sarah. She spoke in that loud, rough way again, the sort of voice some people used on the very old or the very young, those they did not expect to understand.

This, more than anything, made Lucy's determination reassert itself. "That's no way to speak to your mistress!" she snapped.

Magda stared at Lucy for a moment, then just shrugged and went to unlock the door, letting both Arthur and Michael in. There had been no time for them to clean themselves up, and they stank of sweat, of carbolic soap, of blood. The stuff had begun to dry, leaving hard brown stains on their sleeves, their shirtfronts, and their collars. Despite the gore that had soaked into their clothes and despite the horror they had just witnessed, they came in wearing placating smiles.

Lucy's stomach sank.

They wouldn't be smiling if they didn't mean to disarm her, and what did they need to disarm her for, if not to leave her vulnerable for whatever came next? Instinctively, she moved in front of her sister to shield her.

Arthur opened his mouth, no doubt to utter something meant to soothe. Lucy spoke before he could. "Please don't send my sister away. I know what she has done is terrible, but it isn't her fault. She can't help being what she is, and it shan't happen again. I'll make sure of that."

Because next time Not-Sarah got hungry and decided to eat someone, Lucy would make sure they'd leave no witnesses.

"Lucy, dear…" Arthur began.

She ignored him, looking at Michael instead. His face, always bloodless, always strange, was unreadable to her now, like a mask carved from marble. She couldn't allow herself to be frightened by that, though, not now, not when everything depended on what she said and did next.

"Katje and I can look after her. You must concede that we will do so with infinitely more care and love than some nurse or alienist who has a dozen other patients to tend to, and such love and care will be beneficial to her recovery. We shall watch her every minute of every day. You wouldn't even have to know she was there, if that would please you. No one else need know either. It could be our secret."

Michael gave Arthur a look, and now she could read him very well again. Did he think she wouldn't notice, that she wouldn't understand the significance of that look? Every woman did. It was the kind of look men gave each other when they thought a woman was overreacting, the sort of look that meant to say, *Can you believe how silly she's being?*

She felt the words die in her throat as it locked in anger. Not-Sarah clasped Lucy's wrist with the strength of a snare snapping shut, though whether from fear or in warning, she didn't know.

In response to Michael's look, which Arthur acknowledged with a smile and a soft shake of the head, Arthur turned to Lucy and used that horrible voice of his she knew he used on his patients, the ones who couldn't think straight because of the pain or the fever or the sickness eating through their brain: "Dear Lucy, whoever said anything about sending your sister to an asylum?"

For a moment, she didn't know what to say. Her throat was still locked tight, and when she tried to speak, the words came out a little mangled, as if the speech impediment that had plagued her in childhood had returned. "Then you don't mean to send her there?"

"Of course not. We know how that prospect terrifies the two of you, don't we? And terror is the last thing we need Sarah to experience right now."

Not-Sarah's hand, which still clutched Lucy's wrist like a vise, tightened even further, causing a shooting pain in her hand. Without looking, Lucy pried her sister's fingers away, then held her hand gently, begging the familiar feel of their fingers slotting together to soothe her. But Lucy's hand was numb from the blood flow being restricted by her sister's tight grip, so it felt like nothing much at all.

"What do you plan to do, then?" she asked cautiously.

"I plan to prescribe a rest cure for Sarah. Rest and relaxation restore the mind like nothing else can, especially the female mind."

"What does a rest cure entail, concretely?"

"Six to eight weeks of bed rest supplemented by a hearty diet of milk and meat to allow the body and the brain to heal."

From her place by the door, Magda said, "That doesn't sound at all bad, now does it, Mrs. Schatteleyn? If I had the chance to spend a few weeks in a little cottage by the sea doing nothing but sleeping and eating, why, I'd take it in a heartbeat."

Arthur motioned for her to be quiet, but the harm had already been done.

"What do you mean, 'a cottage by the sea'?" Lucy asked. "Do you mean she can't stay here?"

Arthur laughed in an effort to diffuse the tension. "A change of scene would do anyone good, wouldn't it?"

"He *lies*," Not-Sarah hissed in her ear. "He means to trick us. He won't take me to some quaint fucking cottage but to an asylum!'

Arthur laughed again. It sounded pained, pathetic. "Of course not, Sarah! Why would we do that? You're not thinking straight. It's not your fault. You're very ill. But that's why you must trust those around you who love you and want nothing but the best for you! Now come to me."

"So you can take me away? I don't think so," she snarled.

"To look at you and make sure you haven't hurt yourself. I believe you've lost a tooth," Arthur said. He was still smiling, but it was forced now, this tight baring of the teeth that in any other animal would be a clear sign of aggression.

When Not-Sarah didn't move from her spot, he turned to Lucy. "Come, Lucy, bring your sister to me," he said, then held out his hand, beckoning her.

"No."

Arthur blinked. "Excuse me?"

"I said no."

"For God's sake Lucy, stop being difficult, and do as the doctor says," Michael barked.

She let out a snort of laughter. It sounded more like a scream. "'The doctor'? I've known Arthur my entire life, and I've never called him that, and neither have you!"

"Come!" Michael barked, then snapped his fingers at her.

Anger churned in her stomach, made her tremble like a reed. "I'm not a dog!"

Behind her, Not-Sarah began to pant. Her hand had turned slick. Lucy resisted the urge to let go and scrub her hand on her skirt. If she let go, she feared the unseen force that tethered her to her sister would snap, and they would take her away, and then they'd never meet again.

Arthur said, "We are also doing this for you, Lucy. You don't want to see what comes next, I promise you."

"Then you *are* taking her away from me!" she exclaimed. She could not help that her voice was high and frantic with sudden panic.

"They lie, they lie! All they do is lie!" Not-Sarah wailed.

"Lucy, you're not helping!" Michael snapped.

Not-Sarah began to back away, dragging Lucy with her. "Please," she begged, "please, please, *please*..."

"Where do you want to go? There's no way out of this room!" Arthur said.

"For God's sake!" Michael advanced, reaching for them with those spidery hands.

"Touch her, and I'll scratch out your eyes, see if I don't!" Lucy hissed.

"You're acting like a goddamn lunatic!" Michael shouted. He rubbed his eyes harshly, then turned to Arthur. "Do something, will you?"

"Nobody do anything, or I... I'll do myself an injury!" Lucy screamed desperately.

For a moment, they all stood glaring at one another.

Then Magda lunged.

Lucy had been so busy following Arthur and Michael's every move, she had completely forgotten about her sister's lady's maid, who must have been creeping up on her all this time. Magda was a heavy woman, made strong by years of manual labor. It wasn't hard for her to wrestle Lucy to the ground, no matter that Lucy spat and fought.

"Please," Arthur begged as he bent over her and tenderly brushed some hair out of her face, "please don't struggle, darling."

"Fuck you!" she snarled.

For a moment, he looked appalled. Then he simply sighed. "You don't know what you're saying. Folie à deux, I think. Poor thing. No matter. You'll be right as rain again as soon as we remove you from your sister's influence."

He pressed a cloth against her face. It was drenched with something chemical. She tried to twist her face away, but he had grabbed the back of her head with his free hand, making it impossible to move. She held her breath until the blood pounded in her head and her lungs felt like they had caught fire, but it was no use.

She had to breathe.

Foul fumes filled her lungs. Instantly, her limbs turned heavy, and her thoughts began to drift.

Distantly, she heard Not-Sarah scream.

———

Lucy woke lying in bed with a chemical taste in her mouth. Her head felt stuffed with cotton wool. She had rested her head on one of her arms, and it had gone to sleep. She sat up, then had to hold her head in her hands, she felt so dizzy and sick.

Magda rushed to her side and clasped her shoulders to keep her from falling.

When the nausea abated, she tried to rub her eyes and found her fingers wouldn't bend. Someone, most likely Arthur, had swaddled them in bandages. Her other arm was all pins and needles. She shook her hand to get the blood back into it again, then looked around.

The curtains had been drawn but not all the way, leaving a little gap through which the sun was visible. It hung low in the sky like a peach ready to be plucked, its warm light turning the pools of rain to liquid gold.

That wasn't right.

Or was it?

Her thoughts moved through her skull slowly, like treacle. She shook her head to get them to flow a little faster, but that only made her dizzy again.

"Magda, why am I here?" It hurt to talk. Her throat felt scraped raw. She winced against the pain.

Magda gave her a glass of water to drink. The liquid was lovely against the tortured flesh inside her throat, cool and clear. "You didn't feel well. The doctor gave you something to help you sleep, miss."

To sleep? But it was day, wasn't it? She scraped her tongue with her teeth, then swallowed. The chemical taste still lingered, foul and potent. "How long did I sleep?"

"A few hours."

Then it had been morning when Arthur had administered the drug. Maybe she'd had an accident. That would explain her fingers, the rug burns on her knees, and the general soreness of her body, though not why her wrist was bruised and the bruises held the shape of fingers.

If only she could think clearly! She shook her head again to rid it of that dazed feeling that made her thoughts crawl instead of run. She forced herself to concentrate, to follow her memories like beads on a chain.

Not-Sarah had eaten three (technically, two and a half) of Mrs. van Dijk's fingers. That was too awful not to remember but not awful enough to repress to the point of forgetting. After, Lucy and Not-Sarah had been locked into the Silver Room together with Magda. Lucy had washed her sister's face, then poured perfumed water from a porcelain pitcher into a white bowl, the rim painted with little flowers, and made Sarah soak her hands in it to allow the crusts of dried blood to stop adhering to her fingers and dissolve, but they had been interrupted...

It all came back to her now.

She grabbed Magda's arm. "Where's my sister?"

Magda sighed. "You mustn't worry about that, Miss Lucy. The doctor said..."

"To hell with the doctor! Where is she?"

"You are hurting me, miss," she said, her voice still sweet, but now sugarcoated steel.

"I'm sorry for that, but I need to know where Sarah is, or I'll... I'll have to hurt you."

"There's no need to threaten me, miss." A slow smile crept over her face. "You and I both know I can easily take you in a fight, now, don't we?"

Lucy remembered how easy it had been for the maid to overpower her, how horrible the weight of her had been, pressing the breath out of her. "Please, Magda," she begged, "can't you see I'm desperate? I *must* know where she is!"

"All right, no need to make such a fuss. They've taken Mrs. Schatteleyn to Doctor Hoefnagel's house."

"Why?"

"To treat her."

None of that made sense. Arthur's house lay in the middle of town. If they had been honest about the rest cure, his house was the last place to take her. Lucy rubbed her eyes hard to get rid of the cobwebs in her head. "What does the doctor's house have that Zwartwater can't provide?" she asked.

Magda shrugged. "It's closer to the madhouse."

Chapter 23

THE NEWS WASN'T A SHOCK, exactly, but it still landed heavily in her belly. From there, it sent out little creeping tendrils of dread, as if her veins had been injected with ice water. She swallowed against her gorge rising, somehow managing not to let her grip on Magda's arm slacken. "Then my sister is at the madhouse now?" she asked.

"She might be, unless there's no room for her at the local one. Then they must find a different one for her, won't they? Until they find a place for her, he can keep her safe and asleep in the room where he usually performs his surgeries," Magda explained.

Lucy had to do something, and she had to do it fast. If only she weren't so abominable at performing under pressure! She preferred mulling a question over like a cow chewing cud. No time for that now. Every minute she dawdled, Arthur and Michael took her sister farther away from her and closer to the asylum. She might already be there. Who was to say there wasn't a spot available straightaway for a case as dire as Not-Sarah's, a case where the man who would pay for her stay had deep pockets and every incentive to get the matter over with as quickly as possible?

She forced herself to think fast. "Where's Katje?"

Magda had long since stopped trying to pull free and now stood with an impression on her face Lucy had only ever seen on marble statues supposed to represent long-suffering martyrs. "Miss Katherina is locked in her room. The doctor gave her something to help her sleep, just like you. She was very distressed when they removed Mrs. Schatteleyn. Now please let go of my arm."

"So you can fetch someone to administer another sedative to keep me nice and complacent and knocked out while my sister is taken from me? I don't think so."

Magda's mask cracked. Underneath, Lucy found both annoyance and anger. "Miss Lucy," she said, and she spoke as one would to a willful child, "I like to think I've been very patient with you and Mrs. Schatteleyn all this time, but my patience is running out now. If you don't let go of my arm this instant, I'll scream. Then they'll come running and hold you down and give you another sedative, just as you said. If you let go and promise to sit quietly, I won't call anyone. Miss." The final word was added as an afterthought.

"You shouldn't talk to me like that. It's insulting and improper," Lucy said.

Magda smiled. It was more a baring of her teeth than a genuine smile. "I don't give a damn."

A chill ran down Lucy's spine like a wave of cold water, drenching her heart in her chest. It stuttered, strained through the next beat, then sped up. "Servants who are insolent never stay servants for very long," she tried, but the smile stayed firmly on Magda's face.

"You rich ladies with your fancy ways like to think you're so high and mighty, but you're no better than the rest of us just because you don't have to wash your own bloody rags and unmentionables. Do you think Mr. Schatteleyn will keep on a lady's maid when there's no lady?"

"He won't give you a good reference if he hears you talking like that."

"I think he will. I could tell some tall tales about Mrs. Schatteleyn, couldn't I?"

I should've paid closer attention to her, Lucy thought. Had the circumstances been different, she would have taken more of an interest in Magda.

Too late now.

Another opportunity missed. God, was she cursed to always run after the facts, never ahead of them, condemned to clean up messes but never able to prevent them?

No matter. Crying over spilled milk didn't put it back in the bottle. All one could do was throw a rag in the puddle to soak it up, then give the surface a good wipe to prevent it from becoming sticky and smelling sour.

She loosened her grip on Magda's arm.

The maid stepped away, rolled up her sleeve, and massaged the flesh that had reddened under the pressure of Lucy's grip. "Look at what you've done," she said, tutting.

"I'm sorry, Magda. I shouldn't have done it. I…"

Magda smacked Lucy's temple with her fist. Lucy's head snapped to the side and struck the bedpost, which cut it.

The pain was sickening, sharp and continuous at first, then

assailing her in steady waves. A trickle of blood ran down the side of her face, so soft and slow that it was almost a caress. She looked up at Magda in shocked confusion.

"That'll teach you to grab me, you wicked thing," Magda said. "Now, will you be good and quiet?"

Stunned, Lucy nodded.

"Good. That's what we like to see," Magda said. She smoothed her sleeve down over her arm, did up the button at the cuff, then sat in the chair beside the bed and took up her needlework. She was mending one of Sarah's blouses, a delicate thing of crushed silk. Perhaps she meant to keep it for herself. Not-Sarah didn't need many clothes where she was going.

Lucy fought the urge to cry. Her nose stung with it. She pinched the bridge hard to press the tears down. Crying was something children did—or women who were disturbed in their faculties.

I could cry if I wanted, then.

It wouldn't make any difference. They already thought her hysterical, maybe even mad. But no, she wouldn't cry. She wouldn't give Magda the satisfaction. The cut was small; the bleeding had already stopped. Hardly something to cry about. It would be from surprise more than anything else anyway, and that, too, was already waning.

Besides, Lucy had no time to feel sorry for herself. She had to get out and save her sister from Michael and Arthur. First, though, there was the small matter of Magda, who stood between her and the way out.

"Magda," Lucy said in a little voice.

"Yes, Miss Lucy?"

"I'm sorry, but I don't feel well at all. I think I might be sick."

Magda sighed and handed her the chamber pot. It was made of porcelain and painted green with silver stripes to match the wallpaper. Lucy gripped it, hunched over it, made soft gagging noises. Tendrils of hair had come loose and hung in front of her face.

"For Pete's sake," Magda muttered, then bent close to grab her hair and hold it back.

Lucy swung the pot against Magda's head with as much force as she could. A crack ran through the porcelain. Magda cried out and fell to the ground, holding her face with her hands, and oh, wasn't the sight and sound of it delicious?

No time to dwell on it, though. Lucy jumped over her and ran for the door. If it was locked, she was done for.

Please don't let it be locked...

The knob turned without resistance. She yanked the door open and ran down the hallway, toward the stairs. Behind her, she heard Magda shout, heard the maid's footsteps as she pursued.

Should've hit her harder. Should've cracked her skull till her brains ran out like yolk from a broken egg.

Lucy took the stairs as fast as she was able before leaping down the final dozen steps. Her ankles screamed as she hit the floor, the impact traveling up her shins, but she didn't stop. Through the main hallway, out through the front door, down the lawn, and into the woods. She expected to be grabbed at any moment, but if anyone's hands reached for her, they didn't manage to catch her. She ran until she couldn't anymore. When that moment came, she forced her way into the bracken and crouched there, waiting to see if anyone was still after her.

Her lungs burned. Both her breathing and her heartbeat came with a dizzying speed. She couldn't hear anything over the sound they made. She waited for what she guessed was about ten minutes, then waded out, took hold of a tree, bent forward, and was sick after all. Mucus clotted in her throat. She coughed and coughed until red dots spangled her vision and her throat felt scraped bloody, then straightened herself and leaned against the tree.

"Oh, Lucy, you've been rash indeed," she said to herself. There was no way back now. Better to press on, to persevere. She wiped the sweat off her brow with her sleeve, found a deer trail that would keep her off the main road—if the servants were to look for her, that was the first place they'd search—and began to walk.

In her mad dash, there had been no time to dress properly. She had no coat, no hat, no scarf nor gloves. The lack of a hat would make people think her indecent, and the lack of a coat, mad. All the more reason to get to Arthur's house quickly.

It didn't take long before the heat of the flight left her and she began to shiver. She stuck her hands into her pockets, then clenched and unclenched them to keep the blood flowing, but they turned red with cold.

Her bare hands were less of a problem than her feet. She hadn't run out with nothing on them, but the thin slippers she was wearing were meant to be worn around the house. They didn't even have proper soles. With every step, the twigs and stones sprinkled on the road bruised her feet. A branch ripped from a bush of brambles pierced straight through the embroidered fabric and bit into the soft pad underneath her right big toe. Soon she was limping. When she had to wade through a puddle that had swallowed part of the road, the water reaching her knees, she was almost grateful for the icy mud and water the slippers sucked up; they numbed her feet and thus the pain.

It took three hours to walk to the village. Once she made her way through the thin line of woods surrounding the estate, there was only heathland. Clusters of dead grass long as most women's hair swayed in the wind. The rare lone tree stood naked and forlorn, its thin limbs stretched imploringly to the sky.

By now, the sun had thoroughly set, but she had the light of the stars and moon to guide her. It was a thin pale light, painting everything around her in hues of gray and blue. Thin tendrils of mist crept from the earth and nipped at her ankles. It was said that they heralded the arrival of the *witte wieven*, white women who came out at night from the burial mounds that were everywhere on the Dutch heath, hungry for gold, hungry for souls. They were the restless ghosts of witches, or fairies wishing to lure people off the straight and narrow, or perhaps something else altogether.

They could be the ghosts of those unfortunates who have drowned in the bog.

Once this thought had entered her mind, it would not leave her be. How many had lost their lives here, trapped by the mud that slowly pulled them in deeper until cold black water forced its way into their mouth and lungs? So few had ever been found, yet this land had been hungry since before the Romans had come to conquer. The ground beneath her must be stacked with corpses looking like Marianne.

Perhaps it was a trick of the moonlight as it glided over the wet landscape, or maybe her mind had finally broken under the strain of all the fear of the past few weeks, all that repressed desire and hunger and rage—whatever it was, Lucy could see them now, the veil separating her world from others finally blown away: the bog people as far as the eye could see, all tanned and dyed, lying snugly within the black earth like blankets folded in a drawer, dreaming, waiting.

Just ahead of her, buried beneath the road, lay what she thought might be a woman. She couldn't be sure. To be taken by the bog meant to be altered, and whatever outward signs of a sex this body had once possessed had been erased. This woman—for Lucy could not help but think of her as such, just as Sarah had instinctively known Marianne was a woman—was dressed in rags and wore a rope around her neck, tightly knotted.

Lucy hesitated. Would this woman, unfed for so long, try to reach for her and drag her into her cool leathery embrace? As Lucy quickly stepped over her, she sighed and turned toward her as a child tucked tightly into bed might, slowly and with difficulty.

She's looking at me, Lucy thought.

Not that this woman had any eyes to look with. The bog had eaten those, as well as the bones. All the same, she was watching Lucy.

All of them were.

As Lucy passed the bodies, they turned one by one so as to

keep looking at her. Their muscles, cramped from having lain in the same position for centuries, made soft creaking noises of protest.

It was a curious thing to be watched so carefully by the dead.

She laughed softly. Had this happened to her sooner, she would have been terrified. Not anymore, though.

It was not the bog people who meant her harm.

When she reached Murmerwolde, she was almost sad to leave them behind. In a way, they had made her feel almost safe. She waved goodbye at them, then staggered into town. The paved streets were no easier on her bruised feet than the cold wet earth out on the moors had been. Just like at Zwartwater, the ground here was soft, leaving many of the houses crooked, their bricks cracked. Arthur lived in a little house of dusky pink that looked a muddied brown at night and a roof black shingles. Still wet from the recent rainfall, they glistened in the lantern lights. It made them look as if they were made of licorice.

It's like I'm in the fairy tale with the gingerbread house, if only Hansel and Gretel had tried to eat the witch rather than the other way around, Lucy thought. Why did so many stories for children carry the threat of being eaten? Maybe they had come into existence at a time when Not-Sarah's kind had existed in much greater numbers than they did now. It would make sense for those parasites to go after children. Though not as nourishing as an adult, they were much easier to kill.

She stopped in front of the door, swaying with cold and exhaustion. Her hands had turned red at first, then white. Now they were bluish. She raised the right one, trying to grab the string of the doorbell. The movement was clumsy, and she missed. Control over her fingers had fled at the same time their ability to feel had. She tried again, this time with her left hand, where the fingers remained unbruised and weren't wrapped so tightly that they wouldn't bend, but she missed anew.

She balled both hands into fists, then banged them against the door, not caring that her governess had told her never to knock on a door because it would roughen her hands and make them look servantly.

The door swung open so suddenly, she almost tumbled inside. A pair of beautiful hands with long white fingers steadied her. She looked up into Michael's face, strange and bloodless as always, the brows almost touching in the middle. When he recognized her, his broad mouth opened in surprise, and she could see the little pearly pips of the extra two teeth growing behind the others.

"Lucy," he said. He held her away from him, then noted the lack of a coat and hat and shoes, and now his brows did meet in the middle. He pulled her roughly inside and threw the door closed behind them. "What happened? You look like you were beset by highwaymen and then crawled your way through the woods. Has anyone seen you?"

"Where's Arthur?" Her jaw was stiff with cold, mangling the words again.

"He got called away. A breech birth. He might be gone for hours. God, woman, are you utterly insane? Do you fashion yourself some sort of gothic heroine, wandering the moors at night without a coat?"

"Please don't talk to me like that. I'm dog-tired, so thoroughly chilled that even my marrow feels cold, and my nerves are frayed. I can't be held responsible for what I might do, should they snap," she said. It was no easy thing, to keep her voice even remotely civil when all she wanted to do was watch him suffer.

"We can't have that. There are only so many madwomen I can deal with," he muttered. He wrapped her in his coat, lifted her from the ground, and carried her to the room Arthur had chosen as his surgery. It was an inferior room at the back of the house, rather small and dark because it faced north, but it had a door that led to the garden to recommend it. Patients who wanted their visits to be discreet made grateful use of it. No one could look into the windows either, not even from the surrounding houses. The angle was never right.

Michael helped her to a chair, then rifled through Arthur's cabinets, looking for iodine and bandages and a pair of tweezers. She rested her cheek against the fabric of the chair, trying not to crack her teeth as they chattered. Soon her hands and feet began to burn as the blood forced its way through her capillaries. The pain was shocking. She stuffed the lapel of Michael's coat into her mouth and bit it to keep from groaning. Tears streamed down her face.

"Fuck," Michael muttered. He looked at her over his shoulder. "I'll go to the kitchen to grab some things. Stay here."

She sat slumped in the chair, shivering with such violence, she wondered if she might break her bones. How could she confront him when she was as wretched as this? Yet confront him she must, no matter how infirm she felt. She was Not-Sarah's only hope, her sole defender.

By the time Michael came back with a bowl and pitcher and a towel slung over his arm, her shivering had passed its peak, and she felt a little stronger.

"Are you feeling a little warmer? You've got a bit of color back in your cheeks," he said.

"A little," she said.

"Good. You should drink something hot, broth or tea or coffee, but it's the housekeeper's day off. She's visiting her sister in Apeldoorn and won't be back till morning." He washed her feet. When this was done, he began to pluck thorns and bits of pebble from the soles. She looked away, doing her best not to twitch as he rooted around the tender flesh looking for things. It was clear the housekeeper wasn't here; the curtains weren't drawn. A spider had woven its web at the window. The recent rain had studded each strand with drops that glittered coldly in the light of the moon.

Lucky little spider, Lucy thought. If it had spun its web at Zwartwater and one of the maids spotted it, they would have beat it to death, like the woman on the train had done all those weeks ago.

Not Arthur. Even as a boy, he'd had an instinct for tenderness and preservation of life, which had manifested in him using cups and bits of paper to export bees and ants and even wasps outside whenever they had found their way into his house. People found such kindness unseemly in a boy; they'd rather have seen him pull out the legs of a spider one by one than save it. Yet, despite the bullying of his father, brothers, peers, and schoolmasters, Arthur had remained kind.

It shows an enormous amount of character and willpower, Lucy thought, then wondered why she had never come to love him. Though she could never love him now, not after he had conspired to have Not-Sarah removed.

"Where's my sister?" she asked.

"Don't talk to me. I can't listen and concentrate on your feet at the same time."

Lucy pulled her foot back. "Where's my sister? Magda said you brought her here. Is that true, or did you take her to an asylum already?'

Michael looked up at her, frowning with annoyance. "Don't be a child," he said. He gripped her ankle hard and yanked it back with such force, she would have fallen out of the chair had she not gripped the armrests. Her bruised fingers throbbed in protest.

She bit her tongue and waited. She couldn't afford to antagonize him now.

He was methodical as he worked on first one foot, then the other, laying out all the things he had tugged from her skin on a white handkerchief he had spread out on the ground next to him: bits of twig, sharp little stones, and thorns, all of them blackened with her blood. Perhaps the smell of her blood was what had interested the bog people. Lonely they couldn't be, not with there being so many of them.

"Stop moving. You'll get iodine all over my trousers, and those stains won't come out," Michael snapped.

When he had bandaged her feet, he said, "There. All done. Not as neatly as Arthur would have done it, but beggars can't be choosers." He straightened, the joints in his shoulders and knees popping.

"Where's my sister?" Lucy asked again.

Michael sighed. "You really want to know, don't you? I presume that's why you came running all the way from Zwartwater looking like a hussy?"

"Naturally. I would have preferred to have come along with you in the carriage, but you didn't give me that choice, now, did you?"

Something tugged at the corners of his mouth. Not a smile—distaste, perhaps, or impatience. "We had no choice but to drug you. You were hysterical. You said you were going to hurt yourself. You acted like a madwoman. For a moment, you had me quite worried. I thought we might have to commit you alongside your sister."

"There's no need for that. There's no need to commit her either."

Again, he sighed. He picked up the handkerchief with things plucked from her feet, then idly sorted the twigs and thorns and bits of pebble on the palm of his hand. "She's very sick, Lucy. You know that as well as I."

"It'll pass."

"It won't."

"You don't know that."

"Actually, I do." He pulled a letter from his pocket and tossed it in her lap. "Read that, then tell me again why I shouldn't commit my wife to the madhouse."

LETTER FROM DR. ABRAHAM ROSENTHALER
TO DR. ARTHUR HOEFNAGEL

Veendijk, 31 October 1887

My dear friend Arthur,

Let me begin my letter by thanking you for sending me a copy of that court document. It always gladdens my heart to see your spidery handwriting on an envelope when I come home from another grueling day of work (I am only joking; unlike yours, my patients never complain, though time may occasionally be of essence), so you can imagine my joy when I picked up your latest missive and found the envelope thick and heavy. I can't thank you enough for allowing me to spend an evening with a cigar, a glass of brandy, and a ghoulish murder case.

For it is a dreadful case, to be sure, but I have to admit I chuckled in delight when I had finished reading it. In my line of work, it's rare to know the identity of the body in front of you. Just imagine how much more interesting and complete this information shall make a potential paper written on the subject of the bog body! You must let me know when you can spare the time to sit down and actually write it—I refuse to do it without your help, dear boy, and I also think we simply MUST write one, for bog bodies are a rarity, and to know the identity of the bog body, well, that's practically unheard of.

Also think of how interesting this case could be for the alienists. It's clear that the unfortunate JW labored under the delusion that his wife had been replaced by a near-exact replica, a delusion that is not common but does occasionally occur.

On to a different, albeit related, matter: in your last letter, you mentioned a peculiar case you were currently working on and asked me to consult a number of alienists on your behalf. I agree with you that the case is extremely delicate, both due to the nature of the affliction and the patient's reputation. It's never easy when they are of high rank, is it? Well, I did as you asked. I need not tell you that living corpses do not exist outside penny dreadfuls and the superstitious minds of certain peasants usually found in the Eastern parts of Europe, though there have been some recent cases of New Englanders believing their dead loved ones to be revenants. I'll copy out the newspaper article for you, if I ever find it again. I fear my housekeeper might have used it to light a fire.

I digress. What DOES happen according to those alienists is that a person may come to BELIEVE themselves to be a walking corpse in much the same way that someone may believe their loved one a changeling. Such cases are exceedingly rare and are often found in those with a propensity for insanity, specifically in schizophrenics. This particular kind of delusion is called le derilé des negations, named by Doctor Cotard. He has documented the case of a woman who believed herself to be thus afflicted.

Because it is so terribly uncommon, it's hard to say what might cause it, though I think that, had I been almost buried alive, my mental faculties would be horribly shaken, perhaps even momentarily perverted, to the point where I may have wondered if the world I had woken up to was not perchance a kind of limbo or afterlife, and I myself dead. I suppose it wouldn't help matters much if I had been very sick just before. You and I both know how alien our bodies can feel after a particularly violent illness. If the vigorous and healthy mind of a man can be disturbed to such a degree by such an awful thing happening, I can only imagine what havoc it must have wreaked on the frail mind of a woman with an affinity for madness (not to worry, dear friend: I didn't divulge the details of your poor patient's horrible ordeal, only that it was of such a horrid nature that it gave her delicate nerves a tremendous shock).

As for treatment, the alienists were quite unanimous in their verdict. A patient thus afflicted should be committed to a private institution with all haste. There's no saying what she might do if she believes herself forsaken by both God and the natural laws governing the universe. To prevent her from harming herself and others, she must be entrusted to the care of specialists. Because cases of le derilé des negations are extremely rare (if this is indeed what she suffers from; an alienist should be able to tell you), it is hard to say how long it'll take to subside, if ever. Taking into account the patient's previous episodes of mental disturbance, I'm afraid her chances of recovery are exceedingly small.

Best wishes,
Dr. Abraham Rosenthaler

P.S. Let me know about that paper!

P.P.S. For a potential paper, Mrs. Schatteleyn's drawings and notes would be invaluable. Is there any chance you might secure them? I would write to her husband if the circumstances were different. As it stands, the poor man must have too many worries clamoring for attention to give my small request any consideration. Do give him my sympathy and wishes for Mrs. Schatteleyn's speedy recovery.

Chapter 24

WHEN LUCY FINISHED READING, SHE wanted to crumple the letter into a ball and throw it in the dirty water at her feet. She resisted the urge. Instead, she stood, her teeth gritted against the pain, and dropped it onto the chair, then wiped her hands on her skirt to get rid of the feeling of the oily paper against her skin.

"Remember how you said that journalist was making things up because Arthur would never share sensitive medical information with such a hack writer? I think you should revise that opinion," she said coldly.

"I disagree. A doctor may write to another doctor and ask him for his opinion without harming the confidentiality he owes his patient. In this case, it would've been better if he had broken his oath and told me. Then Mrs. van Dijk might still have ten fingers."

"All the same, you can't send Sarah to an asylum."

"What else am I supposed to do? Hush it up and hope she won't do anything crazy ever again? That's what I did after she brought our daughter's rotting corpse home, and see what good that did!"

"I know. Of course I do, but please, Michael, *please* don't send my sister to an asylum. If you do, she'll die."

He laughed, and in that moment, Lucy understood exactly what Not-Sarah had meant when she had said he could be unbearably cruel. "Could you try for, I don't know, maybe five minutes—no, make that three, five is too ambitious a goal—to not be so goddamn dramatic? This is not the Middle Ages, Lucy! Asylums are places of refuge for the insane, places where they get treated, not places of abuse."

Tears sprang up; she couldn't help it. "But m-my Aunt Adelheid…" she stammered.

"Ah yes, your poor Aunt Adelheid! She died in an asylum, therefore every single asylum on Earth must be dangerous and horrible. God, woman, somewhere in that pretty head of yours must reside a brain. Use it, will you?" he thundered.

She couldn't speak. She looked away, trying not to cry, but that just made it inevitable that she would.

She hated him.

She hated how he treated her sister. She hated those two extra teeth that grew behind the others. She hated his sulking, his intense self-pity. She hated his beautiful hands. She hated his rigid opinions on what was right and what was wrong, what was proper and what was not. She hated how her body smoldered under his touch. She hated how she had loved him, how she had lusted after him, how he had so easily persuaded her to betray Sarah.

She hated, and loathed, and detested.

Everything that had once attracted her to him repelled her

now. Such was the force of this feeling that made her body burn from sole to crown. It raged within her, not the sort of sickly flame that would flicker in the slightest draft but an inferno, the sort that might light people on fire like candles and reduce them to twisted corpses if they got too close, if one let it.

And she'd let it.

She wanted to see Michael burn.

"Besides, who are you to meddle?" he raged on. His cheeks were flushed, and spittle flew from his mouth. "If I decide to have my wife committed to the excellent care of a private institution, then there's no one who can stop me. A man must keep his own counsel or he's no man at all, goddamn!" He slammed his fist on the desk, making her and the papers on top of it jump. He dragged a hand through his black curls, then moved to stand at the window. His breathing was fast and loud.

She could see the exact moment Michael saw the spider from his reflection in the glass. His mouth twisted with revulsion. He unfastened the window and threw it open, tearing the web to shreds, and killed the spider by crushing it with the heel of his hand.

Lucy hated him even more.

When he spoke again, his voice was strained with all the emotion he tried to suppress. "You must see this is the only solution. At this moment, she is a danger to herself and a danger to society. She must be placed where she can do the least amount of harm."

"I'm telling you she'll die if you send her away," Lucy managed to choke out. Either the fear would kill Not-Sarah, or she'd starve.

He turned around, his eyes flashing. "Then she'll die. I've suffered enough!" he said.

"I won't survive losing her again!"

He rubbed his eyes hard. His brows drawing together gouged deep lines into his forehead. "Don't dramatize, please. It's hard enough as it is. I've got my own health and sanity to consider, too, Lucy. These past few weeks have drained and pained me."

"If you send her away, I'll *die*." Her throat felt as if it were laced with thorns; each breath was agony. She balled her hands into fists, letting the pain of forcing her bruised fingers to bend ground her. Her nails dug into her palms; she hadn't had time to file them yet.

"Then so be it. My mind is made up. Sarah will go wherever I deign to send her. She is my wife, and wives must submit to their husbands," he snapped.

I shall kill you first.

The thought came clear and cold, like ice water running down her spine. She shuddered, briefly closing her eyes. Her mind was empty in a way it had never been. When she opened her eyes again, Michael was staring at her.

"Oh, Lucy," he said. His face had softened, as if someone had wiped at a wet window with a sleeve and blurred the glass. "You must see there's nothing else we can do, my sweet. I can't in good conscience leave Sarah where she is. It wouldn't do to inflict such a burden of care on you. Besides, no matter how much you love her, you can't guarantee there shan't be another incident, and if there is, it shan't be on your head but on mine. Any reasonable man can see this is my only option."

I shall kill you first.

He came to her, then brushed the tear tracks from her cheeks with his thumbs. He had a dark scab just below the last joint of his left thumb; it scraped painfully against her cheek.

"And when you think about it," he went on, "wouldn't it be better if she died? She suffers so unbearably, with no hope of respite nor relief. Oh, I know you think she'll recover her wits at some point, but don't you see that would be worse? She shall discover what she has done—there's no keeping such a thing from her—and it shall torment her, as shall the knowledge that she might at any time fall into madness again and repeat the horrors she has already inflicted. I imagine death must be a mercy to such a suffering soul as Sarah. I know it'll be hard on you, Lucy. It'll be hard on me, too, but we must remember that to force her to keep living just because we can't stand to lose her is both cruel and selfish."

I shall kill you first.

She couldn't utter a sound, but that didn't seem to bother him. He tilted her face up, studied her swollen eyes. "Your eyes are all red, you poor thing," he said, then blew on them. His breath smelled of smoke. It made her eyes sting worse, and her lids blinked rapidly of their own volition.

She didn't resist him when he began to kiss her.

"Oh, Lucy," he murmured, "I have a need of you. I know sending my wife away is the only right choice, but that doesn't mean it comes easily to me. To be the sane one, the responsible one, the one others look to for guidance, well, it's a heavy burden. I've been bred to carry it, but it's a heavy burden all the same. I have a need of your comfort tonight more than I ever have before. I imagine you, too, must be desirous of comfort. Let's find it in each other, my sweet little fuck."

He slung an arm around Lucy to pull her body flush against his, and it was like being wrapped in winding sheets. His kisses turned hard; she felt the press of his teeth behind his fleshy lips. He wound a hand in her hair and held the other at her throat, his thumb digging into the tender spot where her lower jaw curved upwards to be jointed with the upper one.

All the while, she stood in his arms like a cold thing, like a dead thing. His touch would have enflamed her with passion once; now it merely stoked the fires of her hatred. He had to die. There was no alternative she could see that would allow her to keep Not-Sarah out of the asylum, and she would damn herself before she would let anyone take her sister from her again.

But how to go about it?

If you are ever attacked, remember that eye gouging is extremely effective at incapacitating an attacker. For someone as small and slight as you, it's probably the best way to defend yourself. Thrust hard and thrust deep. You must crush the eyeball or at least cause severe hemorrhaging if you are to take out your assailant.

She brought her hands to his face. Her heart stuttered in her chest and her throat, still sore from the onslaught of emotions she had experienced throughout their conversation, now felt tight and parched. Her mouth, too, was dry, her tongue lying inside like a piece of leather. How could Michael stand kissing her? Didn't he feel as if he were kissing a corpse? If the bog woman had still had her tongue by the time they'd found her, it might have felt like that.

Perhaps he didn't notice, or he didn't care. His standards were never particularly high when he was in heat, and he was definitely in heat now, the way he was grinding against her, his cock straining against his trousers, his breath punching out of him. She needed to act, or she'd have to couple with him again. Somehow, she did not think he'd stop even if he found her slit was as dry as her mouth, and dry she was.

"Slowly," she whispered, and the tightness of her throat made her voice husky, sensual, even. She put a hand at his throat, pressed hard against his Adam's apple to get him to stop pawing at her. "Slowly," she repeated. She kissed his throat, doing it mechanically, feeling nothing but the thundering of the blood in her veins and the nerves tearing her insides apart. He hadn't shaved very well; his throat had large patches of stubble scraping her lips raw.

"God, Lucy, the things you do to me. It has always been you, do you know that? You I should have chosen. You I should have married," he groaned. He leaned against the desk, his beautiful hands gripping the wood till the tendons stood out. A vein writhed just under the surface of his skin like a snake. Funny, the things one noticed even when one was sick and anxious because one was about to murder someone...

She placed the tips of her thumbs over his eyes, gently, gently, the eyelids flickering at her touch, his mouth twisting into a smile— that's how gentle she was, touching them as if she loved him, that is, barely touching them at all, for she only had one chance to do this right and should position her fingers just so...

She thrust her thumbs hard into his eyes.

She had expected it to be harder, somehow. Perhaps she and her sister had a particular affinity for bursting eyeballs. It was, she thought hysterically, as easy as puncturing a grape with her finger. First, there was the resistance of the cornea trying desperately to keep the eye whole, but once that had ruptured under the pressure of her nails, her thumbs sank into the jelly of his eyeballs just fine.

For a heartbeat—though it felt much longer, almost unbearably so—nothing happened. He stood there, Lucy's thumbs up to the joint into his eyes, and took it in silence.

Perhaps he's a parasite, too.

The thought flashed through her mind, but there was no time for another to follow it, because at that point, Michael found his voice and screamed.

She had only heard him scream once before, when he was told Lucille had died. That had been a scream of grief. This was a scream of pain, and of rage, and of betrayal.

She had known it was coming, but it startled her all the same, so much so that she took a step back, extracting her thumbs from his sockets.

His hands flew to his face. There he encountered Lucy's hands. He managed to clasp her left wrist, squeezing with such force that she felt the bones of her arm buckle. "My eyes! You fucking bitch!" he howled. "You scratched out my fucking eyes!"

She tried to pull away, but though her hands were slick with blood and other fluids, his grip held. "Let me go!" she screamed.

"You bitch!" he roared, throwing a punch. It hit her in the eye, the flesh and bone still tender from Magda's slap, and the pain was both immediate and sickening. She stumbled. He raised his fist to hit her again. In a moment of pure instinct, she jabbed her free hand into his face, raking it with her nails. One of her fingers struck true, tearing his eyelid to shreds and ripping more jelly from his ruined eyeball.

This time, Michael didn't roar.

He groaned, then crumpled.

Lucy tore her hand from his grip and dashed behind the desk, clenching her teeth against the screaming pain of her feet. Her heart was pounding, and her breaths came in ragged gasps. Her wrist throbbed, the pain worse than that of her eye, which felt hot and swollen. She didn't look to see how badly he had mangled her wrist; she didn't dare take her eyes off Michael for a moment. He had already overcome his fainting spell and was sitting up, moving his head from left to right as if to look for her even though there was no chance of him still being able to see.

There was simply not much left of his eyes.

He swung his head from side to side, his nostrils flaring, as if trying to sniff her out. That, more than anything else, terrified her. His head snapped to the side. And he lunged, his arms windmilling as he tried to take hold of her. She hadn't been where he'd thought she was, and he fell hard, his jaws snapping shut.

"You crazy cunt! Where are you? WHERE ARE YOU? I'm

going to kill you, you hear?!" he raged. The words came out slurred, as if he were holding a bit of drink in his mouth and trying not to swallow. A little blood mixed with saliva dribbled from between his lips, and she realized he must have bitten his tongue when he'd fallen and his mouth was filling with blood.

He flung his arms this way and that, trying to find her. She stood as still as she could, trying to get her breathing under control so as not to give away her position. She didn't think he could hear much over his sobbing and raging and spitting, but she didn't want to find out.

I should've pressed down past the occipital bone to damage the nerves there. That would've killed him, she thought. Too late for that now. If she came within reach of him, he'd strangle her or bash her head against the flagstones till they were splattered with her brains.

And she'd come within reach of him. Of that, there could be no doubt. The surgery was small after all, with almost no places to hide, not even from a blind man. If she could get in reach of the back door, she might be able to flee into the garden, and that way out into the street and out of his reach.

Only, she couldn't leave him alive.

Her sister wasn't safe unless he was dead, and neither was Lucy; she couldn't imagine a single scenario in which she could justify blinding him and be believed, at least not while he was living and able to contradict her.

Meanwhile, Michael was still looking for her, crawling through the room. He knocked into the desk with his shoulder. A stack of journals tumbled to the ground, hitting him on the head and back.

He grasped at them, crumpling them in his fists as he gnashed his teeth in rage. Either he was beyond pain, or the pain in his head was all-encompassing, because he bit his lips to shreds but didn't seem to notice. The blood trickled down his chin and stained his cravat. In the faint light of the lamp, it looked as if he were spewing ink.

The pen, she thought.

Her hands flew to her pockets. Here was that spool of thread, and there that wad of paper she still didn't remember putting there. Needles, some pins, and then the smooth case of the fountain pen Sarah had bought for her, the one with the split nib that doubled everything, just as they had been doubled in the womb. Lucy pulled it from her pocket, then took off the cap. It was warm from where it had lain against her thigh, feeling almost like a living thing.

She threw the cap against Michael's head, where it tangled in his curls. He snatched it from his hair and tried to crush it between his fingers. He was beyond words now, grunting and growling and groaning.

Lucy took her chance. As quietly as she could, she climbed on the desk. Her gore-smeared hands almost made her slip on the polished wooden surface, but the bandages on her feet were rough, and that helped. She crouched there, holding the pen aloft so she could strike straightaway.

"Michael," she said.

He looked up at the sound of her voice, exposing his throat. Once, she had loved that throat. How she had kissed it, scraped her teeth over the bulge of his Adam's apple, rubbed her face against the stubble that sprung up during the day. It had seemed like such a common miracle to her, the way his throat could be smooth in the morning and rough as sandpaper by nightfall. He had never grown out his beard, having his manservant shave it each morning. How she had imagined doing it for him: stropping the knife, then scraping it over his skin, smelling the soap and desire thick around them.

Lucy fell upon him, aiming for the artery that wriggled in his throat with every spurt of blood being pumped through. He hadn't expected this and toppled under her weight, which helped to drive the pen in deeply. The nib snapped when it hit bone. She felt it more than she heard it, this soft jolt that didn't travel beyond her fingers.

For a moment, nothing happened. She lay on top of him. He didn't move but still breathed. She pushed herself away from him, crawled to the chair, then dragged herself up. Michael swallowed wetly. She pulled up her legs, rested her chin on her knees, and studied him.

He lay on his back, his eyes ruinous caverns, the pen sticking straight up. He felt his throat with unsteady hands, encountered the pen, shied away from it, then gripped it after all and tried to pull it out. It was too slippery. He kept trying to grip it, then yank it out, but could not. Again he swallowed; again the sound was labored and wet. His swallowing caused the pen to move. Blood welled around it, then ran down the side of his neck. Finally, he shook his sleeve over his hand and grabbed the pen. This time it came when he pulled.

A jet of blood spouted from the wound. Lucy got caught in the spray. It rained down on her, hot and salty, but only for a few seconds. She wiped the worst of it away with her skirt, making sure to keep the muddied hem away from her eyes, then watched Michael bleed out.

He had pressed his hand hard against the cut. The blood spurted from between his fingers in time with his heartbeat. Eventually, it slowed to a trickle. By then, he had lost the strength to keep his hand clapped over the wound. It lay limp in the spreading puddle of blood, which soaked into the carpet and ran down the seams of the flagstones in small rivulets.

I should've brought a flask and caught some for Not-Sarah, Lucy thought. She had to laugh then, softly, hoarsely. Soon the laughter turned to sobs, but that didn't last long either. By the time Arthur came home, she was quiet.

Chapter 25

EXHAUSTION MADE ARTHUR'S MUSTACHE DROOP and had sucked the ruddy color from his cheeks. He smelled of amniotic fluid, perhaps of blood, too, only so much had already been spilled that the scent had gotten stuck in her nose, so she couldn't be sure.

He stared at the wreckage of his surgery, his eyes wide, his hand tightening around the strap of his doctor's bag. He knelt next to Michael to feel for a pulse, then held his fingers underneath his nose to see if he still breathed, doing so without any hurry. When he saw Lucy, he visibly started, then went to her, his scrubbed hands reaching to assess the damage.

"Did he hurt you? Have you any pain?" he asked as he checked for cuts.

She did her best to keep her hands away from him so as not to ruin his clothes. Blood and eye jelly and other fluids had run down her wrists and into her sleeves, where they had begun to crust, caking her cuffs to her skin. This only made him think something was wrong with them, and he bent her fingers one by one, then pulled on them till the joints popped softly, sparing only the two she had bruised when hooking them into Pasja's collar. That done, he placed two of his fingers underneath the joint of her jaw to feel the blood thunder through her veins. Gooseflesh erupted at the spot, rippling down her throat.

He smiled. "Sorry. Cold hands, I'm afraid. Does anything hurt?"

Her limbs from weariness, her feet from being abused by the road, her fingers where she had bruised them, her wrist where Michael had clasped it, and her face where Magda had struck her. Put like that, there was very little that didn't hurt. "My eye," she said. Her voice was dry to the point of hoarseness. She cleared her throat, then repeated herself.

Arthur helped her to her feet and brought her close to the lamp. He brushed some hair from her forehead. It was sticky with blood. He tilted her head this way and that, then gently pulled her lids open, his fingertips ruffling her lashes in a manner she found deeply unpleasant. "Bloodshot and bruised, but nothing that won't heal. That cut doesn't need stitches either, but I'll clean it to stave off infection," he decided. He grabbed his doctor's bag, opened it, and disinfected the cut on her temple. When he was done, he rested the back of his hand against her swollen eye, and the cold was lovely against the burning flesh. She leaned into it, sighing with the simple pleasure.

Certain now that she was relatively well, he began to interrogate her. "Lucy, I must know. What are you doing here? How did you even get here?"

"I walked."

He stared at her in disbelief. "All the way from Zwartwater?"

"All the way from Zwartwater. It's only a few hours. I suppose I would've been faster if I hadn't been drugged."

He had the decency to blush. "You were in extreme distress when you realized we had to take Sarah away. I feared for your health."

"Of course you did," she said bitterly. Since she had only one eye to see him with, Arthur's face looked strange to her, curiously flattened and unreal, as if she were talking to a poorly made waxen cast of him. If she pushed her fingers hard against his cheeks, she was half convinced they'd be forever marked with her fingerprints.

"The best treatment for a patient may not be the most pleasant one, but you know what they say: gentle surgeons make stinking wounds."

This reignited her anger. It rose in her like bile, tearing the gentle fugue of her fatigue to shreds. Her face heated with it, making the feel of his hand against her socket disagreeable. "Will you tell yourself that when you go to sleep at night, knowing my sister lies in some impersonal little room surrounded by lunatics, sobbing her eyes out, terrified and unhappy?"

The color in his cheeks leaked into his forehead and nose until his whole face was pink. "You're too close to her to understand what's good for her."

She blinked hard with rage. Again her lashes brushed unpleasantly against his skin. She pulled away and rubbed her eye on her sleeve, but her eyelid felt cut in places, as if the lashes had been ripped out at the roots. "On the contrary. At the moment, I'm the only one who really understands what she needs."

He sighed. That little sigh made her want to hurt him. He smoothed his mustache with thumb and index finger, then asked, "Where's your sister now?"

"How should I know? I haven't seen her since you forced whatever vile medicine you gave me down my throat."

"I didn't force anything down your throat. With chloroform, you don't have to. The patient only needs to breathe it in. Now, stop lying to me and tell me where Sarah is."

"I. Don't. Know," she said through gritted teeth.

His face in the grips of utter bewilderment looked more than ever like that of a boy with a mustache plastered on. "What do you mean, you don't know? She murdered Michael, didn't she? And by the looks of you, you were right here when it happened. You're soiled with blood."

She chuckled with incredulity; she couldn't help it. "You think Sarah did this?"

"Didn't she?"

She shook her head so fast, the remaining bits of hair plastered to her face with blood and gore tore free. "No! I did, Arthur. I killed him."

"Lying for your sister is admirable, but…"

It was like the funeral all over again, when he wouldn't be convinced she had heard her sister scratch at her coffin. "You're not listening to me!" She thumped her solar plexus with her palms. "I killed him, Arthur. Not Sarah, *Lucy.* I put my thumbs through his eyes the way you told me to, should I ever be assaulted, and then I stabbed him in the throat with a pen. The blood spouted out of his neck with such force, it was like a fountain. That's why I'm covered with it, like the wall, and the window, and the ceiling."

His eyes were large and wet with hurt. Then he blinked, straightened his shoulders, and embraced her. She struggled, but he held her tightly, her arms pinned painfully against their chests, useless. "It's all right," he whispered in her ear. He began to stroke her hair with one hand, as if consoling a sobbing child. "I know why you did it. I know how he abused you."

This close, with her nose pressed against the tweed of his vest, the scent of amniotic fluid was incredibly potent, overpowering the smoke of his cigars, the starch his housekeeper used to stiffen his shirts, and the sweat he must have worked up as he yanked on a small slick shape stuck inside a woman. Again she tried to push away, using her elbows, but there was no space, no leverage.

"Abused me?" she asked. She had to murmur; her mouth, too, was pressed against his vest, a button compressing the soft meat of her lip hard against her teeth.

"Did you think I didn't know? Michael is proud, and selfish, and an insufferable braggart when in his cups. He loved to boast of…of all the times he'd had you. I shan't repeat the exact words he used, but I…I knew."

She felt as if she had been dropped from a great height, the ground slamming all the air out of her lungs. Had Michael not been dead, she would have liked to stab him again and again and again, until nothing remained of his face but a mass of meat and broken bone. Tears burned in her eyes. "You think he abused me, yet you did nothing?"

Finally, he loosened his grip a little in order to look her in the face. He touched her lip, rubbing at the shape of the button the pressure of his embrace had stamped there. "But I did! I secured you a position with Mrs. van Dijk on the other side of the country to keep you as far away from him as possible, didn't I? And when we thought your sister had died, I offered to marry you to keep you out of his clutches. You can't know how relieved I was when your sister proved to be alive after all. I lived in such dreadful fear that Michael would manipulate you into becoming his wife, using your couplings as a reason to wed."

"I thought you asked me to marry you because you loved me."

"I did! I do! Most ardently, Lucy." He tried to kiss her.

She twisted her face away. That weak fleshy mouth he tried to hide with a mustache revolted her. "No! You betrayed me. I told you things about my sister in confidence, trusting you never to relay that information to another. I'd never have told you had I known you'd use it to remove her from my life forever. The worst of it is that you shared it with all your schoolfellows first. You have treated Sarah like she's nothing more than fascinating material for a paper rather than one of your oldest and dearest friends. You've been a bad friend and a bad doctor!"

He clasped her shoulders, then shook her until she had no choice but to look at his imploring face. "If I hurt you, you must understand that was never my intention. Allow me to make amends. I'll take care of all this." He made a sweeping motion with his arm.

"How? I brutally murdered a man, Arthur."

He smiled. "No, you didn't. Your sister did."

"What are you talking about? I just confessed to you that it was me who killed him. Look at my hands! They are coated with bits of him. Sarah doesn't even know he's dead."

He squeezed her shoulders, still grinning at his own cleverness. "But outside of you and me, no one knows that, now, do they? And what story do you think the police are more likely to believe: That you, who have up till now always proven to be a quiet, dependable little creature, killed him, or his insane wife who earlier today ripped off the fingers of a crippled and elderly widow without provocation?"

"No! If you told anyone that, she'd be locked away for the rest of her life."

"And would that be so bad? She may not have murdered Michael, but she very well could have killed Mrs. van Dijk, might in fact still accomplish that if putrefaction sets in."

"I'm not justifying what she did. It was wrong and horrible, but if you send her to an asylum, she'll die. I know you think me dramatic and irrational when I say this, but you must believe me. I know she's unwell. Of course I do. I'm her twin, aren't I? But sending her to the madhouse won't solve this problem."

"God!" he cried out, his face twisting with rage, as if a child had smashed their fist into putty with two pale blue chips of glass for the eyes. She had never seen him angry before. It scared her.

"Sarah, Sarah, Sarah!" he shouted, and his voice was like that of a stranger, too, rough and a little hysterical. "Always *Sarah*! Your whole life, you've stood in her shadow. Don't you see that she's unworthy of your affection? She's nothing but a dissatisfied, spoiled, selfish little girl. She makes you act like a madwoman, has you carry out atrocities. She uses you, Lucy, and will continue to use you unless I put a stop to it. And I will! It stops tonight!" He shook her roughly as he shouted at her. Her head snapped back. Pain radiated down her neck.

She whimpered, and he stopped. She tore herself out of his grip and backed away from him. She stumbled over Michael's sprawled legs but caught herself against the desk with Arthur's leather doctor's bag on top. Inside were spools of bandages, a suturing kit, a pair of dirty forceps, and a used scalpel poorly wrapped in a bit of soiled cloth.

Arthur was breathing hard. He pulled on his vest to straighten it, then wiped a drop of sweat from his temple. His face was still this waxen thing, quite horrible, but when he spoke, he did so with the calm, authoritative voice he used with his patients when he needed them to understand that he was in charge. "It stops tonight," he repeated. "Sarah is like a strangler plant. As long as she has her tentacles inside you, you can never grow. You are too weak to remove her, so I shall do it for you. Then we shall get married, and you need never worry about a thing again."

There's no swaying him, Lucy thought, and she almost sobbed.

He smiled, and it was ghastly. "You'll make a good doctor's wife, Lucy. Not everyone would have found a man's jugular artery on the first try."

He reached for her. She shied away, upsetting his bag with her elbow, tipping it over. Its contents spilled over the tabletop. His face crumpled with pain and disappointment, and suddenly, it was the face she knew again, that of her childhood friend. "Don't be scared of me, Lucy. Come, did I hurt you? I didn't mean to. I'm afraid I got a bit carried away. I'm rarely ever ruled by my passions, though; this you know. Now let me look at you."

He placed his hand on her neck. She gripped the scalpel that had fallen from his bag.

"If you ever think I'd let you hurt my sister, then you don't know me at all," she hissed as she cut across his throat.

The blood sprayed into her eyes, blinding her. It went up her nose and into her mouth, hot and thick. She twisted to the side, wiping her face against the inside of her sleeve to restore her sight. When she looked up, Arthur was staring at her with an expression of complete bafflement, the blood gushing down his throat like a sheet of unbroken dark silk that looked sometimes crimson, sometimes brown. When his legs gave way, he fell heavily. He made a soft choking sound. She had cut so deep that his windpipe had been ruptured. Air came through the rip in his throat, briefly turning the blood into a thin mist that flew everywhere.

She thought of holding his head in her lap and stroking his hair as he died, but she was too angry, too agitated, too filled with the glory and the horror of murder, and by the time she could reconcile herself with the idea, he had already grown slack, his eyes open but unseeing. A tinge of regret made her soften. She hadn't loved him, but she had been fond of him, had admired him, even, for his steadfastness, his kindness, his selflessness. His desire to marry her had been his one selfish act, and it had cost him his life.

She stepped over his corpse, then over Michael's, trying not to tread into their comingled puddles of blood. This brought her close to the window. In its surface splattered with blood, she saw her face reflected. Her eye was already swelling shut where Michael had hit her, the flesh red and puffy. Almost all the white of her eye had turned pink. She supposed it was only fair. An eye for an eye, and all that...

That hysterical laughter took possession of her again. She bent double with it. It tore through her till she felt she was convulsing. Her knees buckled, dipping her hem into the blood after all. She pulled herself along the windowsill, sank down, and laughed till she felt she might hurl again. She only ceased when she heard a heavy thump upstairs, then a sound like something was being dragged.

Someone else was in the house with her.

Chapter 26

LUCY'S MIND RACED ALMOST AS swiftly as her pulse. Who else could possibly be here? Another patient, come to look what all the racket was about? Oh, but she couldn't kill again. The thought made her want to weep. Yet she would, if that was what it took to keep Not-Sarah safe…

They came down the stairs. They did it haltingly and very slowly. There was no steady patter of footsteps, the one-two, one-two of a foot stepping down, followed by the other. It was a heavy thudding, like a sack of spuds too heavy to lift being hauled down bit by bit.

Hardly human at all.

She listened to the sounds with bated breath, the blood buzzing in her ears. By the time they reached the hallway, she was sweating profusely. She had taken the pen from Michael's cooling hand and held it tightly. The nib had broken off, but she had seen the damage a pen might do in great detail twice now, so whatever it was that now crept toward her, she could still defend herself…

Not-Sarah staggered into view.

Thank God. Finally some good fucking luck, Lucy thought. From the moment she had arrived, she had been terrified it had been too late, that her sister had been committed already. She saw now she needn't have worried so; how could Arthur possibly have suspected Not-Sarah of having murdered Michael if she hadn't been here? Funny how Lucy hadn't realized that sooner.

Then again, she had been quite preoccupied with other things, like hot-blooded murder.

Her sister clutched the doorframe. She held herself oddly, as if she were a puppet where some of the strings had snapped, her limbs all angles, her neck and back crooked.

For a moment, they simply looked at each other. Then Not-Sarah rushed to Lucy, her gait weird and dragging. She touched her all over with her long cool fingers. "Are you all right? What did they do to you? Have they hurt you? If they have, I swear I'll tear their guts from their bellies. I'll crush their bones to powder. I'll…"

"Peace," Lucy said, gripping those searching hands to stop them. "Almost none of this blood is mine. I've just got some bruises, nothing more."

Not-Sarah's eyelid fluttered with relief. The tendons in her throat and hands loosened, slinking back into the flesh, turning invisible. She straightened as well as she was able, one hand pressed to her forehead as she surveyed the scene. "You've made quite a mess, Lucy dear." She kicked Michael's leg, then bent down and dipped her finger in the blood that had run down the seams of the floorboards. She brought it to her mouth and sucked on it hard, her cheeks all hollow, her eye half closed with the bliss of it.

Lucy looked away and down at her hands, which lay useless and dirty in her lap like a pair of soiled gloves. It was almost impossible to imagine that these hands, which had braided hair and held the sticky hands of a child and threaded hundreds of needles, had just mutilated a man, then killed him, and killed again, all within the same hour. "Michael was going to have you committed. I tried to talk him out of it, but he wouldn't be persuaded, so I killed him. I couldn't see another way out. Then Arthur found me. He would've had you take the fall for Michael's murder, so I killed him, too."

"Why would Arthur have done that?"

"He thought he could manipulate me into marrying him that way."

"I'd say you've proven adequately that it was a very stupid thought for him to have." She sat next to Lucy with a groan. "I'm feeling awful."

"You're not looking very well. You…your angles are all wrong."

Not-Sarah looked at her crooked legs, then said, "I can't help it. You know I could hear you from upstairs? Not the words, but I heard you and Michael argue, heard him scream. I wanted to help you, but I couldn't move. Oh, Lucy darling, it was awful! I felt as if I were in the bog again, staked to the ground, yet I couldn't even writhe; I could only listen. I willed myself to move, but it took forever, and then my limbs wouldn't behave. I had to roll over and fall out of bed, then drag myself downstairs."

"They drugged you. I'm surprised you're up already. Michael said you wouldn't stir for hours yet." Maybe pills and powders didn't work the same for Not-Sarah's kind as they did for humans.

"Stupid bastard. That makes sense, though. I don't really remember getting here. I think they must have used Arthur's pony trap. My bones feel jolted."

"They gave me something, too. Otherwise, I wouldn't have let them take you. I would've come sooner."

"I know." Not-Sarah patted her hand. "It smells like a slaughterhouse in here." She tilted back her head and took deep gulps of the scent, drinking and drinking of it.

Lucy looked at the bodies. Both lay sprawled, their hands near their throats. If Michael had still had his eyes, they would have begun to cloud over by now. She was glad she had taken them; the idea he could look at her disgusted her. "What are we to do with them?" she asked.

Not-Sarah thought for a while, then smiled and said, "Michael I shall consume."

"Even the bones?"

"Even the bones," Not-Sarah confirmed.

"It would take days. We don't have days, only hours."

"It won't take as long as all that. I'm a fast eater. Don't you know I'm fucking starving?" She gave Lucy a playful push with her shoulder.

Lucy managed a weak smile. It died on her face when she remembered the gravity of their situation. "What about Arthur? You can't eat both of them before the housekeeper comes back or someone else finds us, and then we'll be ruined. Oh God…" She pressed her palms against her eyes until the pressure on her eyeballs became a steady pain. The clotting gore on her hands got stuck in her lashes. When Not-Sarah pulled her hands away, the blood in her lashes framed the world like red curtains.

"None of that," her sister said. "Now, do you know if Arthur contacted any asylums yet?"

"I don't know. I don't think so. He was supposed to do so, but he had to attend a breech birth instead. He did write to one of his doctor friends to ask his opinion about you. He did it in veiled terms, but his friend knows it's about you. The letter is here somewhere." She rubbed her eyes, which made them sting. The adrenaline was leaving her system, and exhaustion settled over her like a blanket. How lovely it would be to take a hot bath and wash herself clean, then slip into bed and sleep for hours and hours… She curled her hands into fists to stay awake, made herself listen to her sister talk.

Not-Sarah thought for a while, a frown etched on her face. "It doesn't much signify whether he wrote to anyone about me or not," she decided, "not when I've made a miraculous recovery and the need for an asylum has passed. And believe me, it shall have passed after I've eaten."

"What about Mrs. van Dijk? I don't think she'll be convinced, not after you ate some of her fingers."

"Oh. That." Not-Sarah said. She touched the cavity where her porcelain tooth had been with the tip of her tongue and saw Lucy look. "I cracked it on her wedding ring. I think I must've swallowed it after. The ring, I mean, though probably also the tooth. Do you think there's a way for us to convince her to keep quiet?"

"I don't know." Her skin felt tight and dry under the peeling mask of dried blood. She rubbed at it. "Oh, Saartje, what are we to do? I don't want you to be committed. I don't much want to be committed myself either, but I don't see how I can prevent it, not after everything that has happened today. God, I feel silly now. All this slaughter, all this gore, and to what end?"

"I think our lives will be much improved without Michael in it, and don't forget I will finally be able to feed now. Once I've eaten him, I won't have to eat for a long time. He's a big man. He'll last me a year, probably longer if I conserve my energy. My kind is snakelike in that way. And once I have healed, I shan't have to eat entire bodies anymore. I can make do with blood then, plus a finger here and there. So, if you ask me, I think all this slaughter and all this gore does serve a purpose."

Lucy leaned her head back against the wall. Now that the adrenaline had gone, all the little pains and discomforts of her body reasserted themselves. She was frightfully thirsty. She pictured biting into a lemon, the sour juice spraying against her soft palate, and that helped a little because it made her salivate. She swallowed, then asked, "What does any of that matter if we both end up in the madhouse anyway?"

Not-Sarah thought for a moment, her brow like the small bumps made by a thread tugged on too hard, wrinkling the fabric. Then the thread broke and her brow smoothed. "We won't. Now, here's what we will do. You'll clean yourself up, then fetch Katje with Arthur's pony trap."

"Katje?"

"Of course. I can't abandon my little love, now, can I? Besides, she's well used to various horrors and very practical. Whenever anyone presses you, just say Arthur has sent for her because he needs someone to stay with me while he tries to sort out the matter of the madhouse, someone other than just you; after what I've done, it would be madness to leave me alone with only one other person, wouldn't it? No one knows yet that Michael and Arthur are dead; we'll keep it that way for much longer if I eat Michael. I won't be able to consume Arthur as well, but that doesn't matter. It'll be easy to make his body disappear."

Lucy softly cleared her throat. Her trick with imagining the lemon had done only so much, and her throat ached with tightness. "How?"

"The bog, of course! It took centuries for anyone to find Marianne's body even though people knew she was in there. No one will know with Arthur, especially not if we clean up properly. We could even leave a note saying he has gone away for a while, perhaps to study a particular case. If we take some of his things, no one will be any the wiser for weeks." She began to laugh. "Hell, we might even make it out that he and Katje eloped!"

"Eloped?" Lucy asked, bewildered.

"Yes!" Not-Sarah said, her one eye gleaming. "It's brilliant, Lucy darling, don't you see? The police won't be looking for a couple who have made it clear they don't wish to be found. They will focus on finding Michael and you and me instead, making it much easier for us to travel unobserved because no one will be looking for three women! Now, for this to work, you must make sure Katje packs some of her things when you go and fetch her from

Zwartwater; that'll make it look like she eloped. You should grab some of my things, too: clothes, jewelry, some shoes. All the little things I might need if I really were staying here for a few days."

"And then we will disappear?"

"Exactly so. It shall be as if we never existed. It'll be the mystery of the century. Now, where's that letter Arthur received from his friend?"

"I threw it on the chair."

Not-Sarah limped over, then felt in the slits of the chair. Triumphantly, she pulled the crumpled letter out. She tore it into small bits. "Open up," she said, then placed a bit on Lucy's tongue. It tasted of wood and something chemical. She rolled it around her mouth until it was a ball of pulp, then swallowed. It took a long time, with her mouth being so dry. Sarah fed her another bit and another, until there was nothing left.

"There. As if it never existed. That might buy us some more time, and if not, no harm done."

"Where will we flee to?" Lucy asked. The taste of the paper lingered on her tongue, making her lips pucker.

"Anywhere that takes our fancy. Paris. Milan. New York. Think about it while you scrub the blood off your face and clothes. In the meantime, I'll eat Michael. Glad to see that snaggletoothed bastard is good for something after all."

"I must tell you something first," Lucy said. She swallowed. Her throat really was frightfully dry, reducing her voice to a whisper.

"I'm sure it can wait. There's much to do, Lucy darling. Time is of the essence!"

"I must tell you first because I think you deserve to know before you decide whether you want to run away with me. You see, I was Michael's mistress."

Not-Sarah said nothing.

Lucy rubbed at her throat to get rid of the taut feeling there, but that served only to redden her skin. The words still came out small, sounding absolutely pathetic to her own ears. "Please say something, Saartje. I know it must come as a shock, and I'm sorry."

"I already know."

Lucy stared at her dear face through a mist of tears. "You do? Since when?"

"From the beginning."

"Oh, Saartje, I'm so sorry. You must have felt so betrayed by me, so utterly forsaken. It shouldn't have happened. All I can say to defend myself is that I was stupid and selfish and weak, just like you said I was. I hurt you, all for a man who turned out to be small and mean and self-obsessed. He wasn't worth my affections, never was. I wish I'd never done it. I wish he weren't dead so I could kill him all over again. I wish…"

"It doesn't matter," Not-Sarah interrupted her.

"But it does! I betrayed you!"

"You destroyed him because he threatened my existence. That makes it pretty clear to me where your allegiance lies."

Lucy brought her hands to her face and dug her nails into her hairline. "But I coupled with him while you were grieving Lucille. You were half out of your mind with it, and rather than look after you, I rutted with your husband, like a common slut, like…"

Not-Sarah grabbed her hands and pulled them down. "Don't do that. Your fingers are filthy. The last thing we need is for you to get sick. And you looked after me very well, I've always thought."

"Even so! I debased myself, I…"

"And I married him knowing you loved him and I did not. Does that make us even?" Not-Sarah stroked a loving little line over the back of Lucy's hands with her thumb.

Lucy looked at their hands together. Hers seemed very dark against her sister's lighter ones. How many colors blood could take on, depending on the light. "Why did you marry him if you knew?"

Emotion bled into Not-Sarah's voice. "Because I couldn't bear you leaving me behind. I thought it would hurt less if I were the one leaving you behind instead."

"And did it?"

She let go of Lucy's hands to dash away the tears; even the cavity underneath her eye patch wept. "I don't know. We all have our regrets. This one is mine. Now, do *you* still want to run away with *me?*"

"Of course. You're my sister."

"And you're mine. Let's waste no more words on my husband. He's dead, and in being so, he'll prove useful after all. Now come. There's much to do."

But she didn't get up, and after a while, Lucy laid her head on her sister's lap. Not-Sarah stroked her hair, softly, sweetly. She was wearing skirts of heavy dark green velvet. Her cheek was still smeared with blood despite her crying and rubbing. If she was to go to Zwartwater and get Katje to come with her, she'd need to put on her sister's clothes. Lucy heavily suspected her own were ruined beyond saving. Though some of the stains might come out if she let the dress soak overnight in a bucket of cold water. Not that she would. There wasn't enough time, and why bother? She'd probably just throw the dress away together with Michael and Arthur's things. She could afford to be profligate. Damned she was already.

"I've murdered two men," Lucy whispered. She began to shiver violently, making her bones and teeth ache. She tried to stop but could not.

"All shall be well now," Not-Sarah promised her and gently took hold of her hand, which was covered with blood also, now cooling and clotting. She licked at the tip of Lucy's index finger, then took the whole digit into her mouth, sucking at it gently till all the blood was gone. One by one she lapped at her fingers, scraping the scab of dried blood out from under each nail with her incisor. She licked Lucy's palm, until that, too, was clean. That done, Not-Sarah toyed with Lucy's fingers, moving them this way and that, then rested Lucy's palm against her cheek and closed her eye in bliss.

Softly, Lucy began to laugh.

LOCAL LADY RAISED FROM THE DEAD VANISHED INTO THIN AIR

On 8 October this year, this paper reported the miraculous case of Lady Sarah Schatteleyn, beloved wife of Lord Michael Schatteleyn. After a short but violent sickbed, she was pronounced dead, yet when her grieving family went to bury her, they discovered only just in time that their beloved wife and sister was, in fact, very much alive. The mistake must have come about due to a case of catalepsy caused by a fever of the brain, which can, in severe cases, mimic the state of death so convincingly that even a well-trained physician may be fooled.

Now this strange case has turned stranger still: since Thursday November 3 no one has seen nor heard from Lady Schatteleyn, *nor* her husband, *nor* her twin sister!

The facts as we know them are thus: the three missing persons were last seen at the local doctor's office, where the Lady

Schatteleyn presumably went to be treated for the lingering effects of the brain fever that almost caused her to be buried alive. The trio left there sometime during the night, though why and whether voluntarily or under duress, we cannot say; when the doctor's housekeeper returned from her day off the following morning, the house was deserted.

Local police officer van Schouten believes they must have left because they had no other choice. "The roads were in a bad state due to the recent storm, and a thick fog had rolled in during the night. We therefore believe that Lord and Lady Schatteleyn's situation must have been dire. Perhaps there was some sort of medical emergency; that would also explain why they had sought out their doctor rather than summoned him."

When asked whether the police are considering foul play, Officer van Schouten said the following: "There are things I cannot reveal to the press without hindering an ongoing investigation. Suffice to say we are currently considering multiple options and are doing everything within our power to find Lord and Lady Schatteleyn and her sister."

He urges the public to come forward if they have any information related to this strange case. They are especially interested in finding Doctor Hoefnagel, who was the last to see the three before they disappeared. Officer Schouten would neither deny or confirm the rumors that the doctor eloped with a poor relation of the Schatteleyns. "But what I do know is this: three people can't simply vanish into thin air!"

Indeed, they cannot, and

there might be a perfectly ordinary, if tragic, explanation for their disappearance. The roads through the bogs can be treacherous at the best of times, but on a dark and foggy night, it is especially easy to take a wrong turn and fall in. With the current temperatures and no one around to hear, drowning is not merely likely but inevitable.

Why, it was only a few months ago that the body of an unfortunate claimed by the bog was discovered on the *Schatteleyn estate*!

If the three are not found soon, yours truly would advise the police to dredge the bogs. There is no saying what horrors might lurk in those black waters.

READING GROUP GUIDE

1. Describe Lucy and Sarah's similarities and differences. How would you characterize their relationship?

2. What draws Lucy to Michael?

3. Not-Sarah insists that as the keeper of Sarah's memories, she *is* Sarah. Do you agree? How else would you define her?

4. As an older unmarried woman, Mrs. van Dijk must pay for a companion. Where does she stand in the social hierarchy? How do others view her?

5. Lucy grapples with the morality of killing to keep Not-Sarah alive. Put yourself in her shoes: What would you do? Was there an ethical way to help Not-Sarah?

6. Explain what happened to Lucy and Sarah's aunt Adelheid. What kinds of dangers did women of that period face?

7. JW, the man who killed Marianne and buried her in a bog, suspected she was a changeling. What made him think that?

8. Define Katje's role in the household at Zwartwater. How do people treat her? Is her relationship with Sarah different?

9. Where do you think Lucy ends up?

A CONVERSATION
WITH THE AUTHOR

In this story—indeed, in history—madness and queerness are often conflated. How did you go about navigating that while writing *Blood on Her Tongue*?

I believe two important rules apply here: 1) depiction is not endorsement and 2) correlation is not causation. Just because some of the characters consider the women in my book mad (partly) because they are queer doesn't mean I agree with them.

Furthermore, the reason why that conflation is harmful is at least partly caused by the stigmatization of mental illness; if we didn't think poorly about the mentally ill, the conflation of queerness and mental illness would bother us less. I am a big proponent of destigmatizing mental health issues, as I hope the book shows; even if some of the characters could rightfully be considered "mad," that doesn't mean they aren't worthy of love and compassion. Indeed, if everyone hadn't been so quick to dismiss Sarah's accusations against the bog body as the ravings of a madwoman, we might have had a very different book!

Lucy feels almost shadow-like compared to the other "fully realized" women in the story. Why is identity such a key theme in this book?

This is a theme that is near and dear to my heart. My sisters and I are triplets. They are identical to each other but not to me. When we were growing up, so many people were obsessed with us and our identities, especially that of my sisters. They gave my parents loads of (unwanted) advice on how to raise us to ensure that we would all become well-rounded individuals: We shouldn't go to the same school, we shouldn't be allowed to try the same sports, we shouldn't have the same friends, etc. Even when we turned eighteen and went to university, people still told us that we shouldn't go to the same university because that would be bad for our personal development.

What fascinates me about this is the underlying assumption that, unless something is done, twins will grow up to be toxically codependent on each other, with very little to no identity outside of their twinness. I don't think this is true for most twins and other multiples, though. When you are young, being a twin or triplet is necessarily a huge part of your identity because you define yourself by comparison to your sibling ("the three of us like Pokémon" or "I like scary stories, but my sisters don't"). This isn't necessarily that different from children who aren't twins, though; they, too, develop an identity by comparing themselves to others, be that their older or younger siblings or their friends.

This is not to say that there can't be any problems with twins. If one of them is both physically and mentally stronger than the other, this can result in physical abuse (more usual for boys) or psychological abuse (more usual for girls). Even when twins aren't abusive toward each other, there is generally one who is dominant and one who is submissive. Though this dynamic isn't exclusive to twins and multiples, it's generally more pronounced and impactful with them. Neither "dominant" nor "submissive" is generally seen as a positive trait (unless you move around in certain conservative or religious circles, though even then both traits are only seen as admirable in a highly gendered context).

This brings us back to Lucy and her fascination with what she terms "fully realized people." With Lucy and Sarah, I wanted to explore a twin relationship from the submissive twin's point of view. Unlike Sarah, who has a fully realized identity outside of being the dominant twin—she is also an avid amateur scientist, a wife, a mother, and a lover, among other things—Lucy's identity revolves largely around being a twin. When that core part of her is threatened, it makes sense that she will go to great lengths to protect it. If Lucy hadn't thought of herself as a shadow, I don't think *Blood on Her Tongue* would be half as wild!

At its core, this is a book about sisters and the unbreakable bond between them. Can you talk a little bit about that?

Within horror, we often find the concept of a "mercy kill": it is considered a mercy to kill someone before they can turn into the Other. This makes sense if this Other is an active threat to your loved ones and your principles. This is why we see a lot of mercy kills within the zombie genre: I, too, would rather be dead than an aggressive corpse. As Stephen King would have it, sometimes, dead is better.

But what if it isn't? What if, for example, your loved one becomes something else yet retains enough characteristics to still feel like them? What if they are dangerous, yes, but not so dangerous that killing them is the only way to guarantee your own safety? When does a mercy kill stop being about mercy to the person you aim to kill and start being about placating your own fear of the Other?

I thought the best way to explore this conundrum would be through sisters. I genuinely believe the bond I have with my sisters is, more than any other bond I have, as good as unbreakable. "As good as" doesn't mean "completely," and because I think good horror comes about when we contemplate horrible scenarios, I dreamed up a situation in which the close relationship between sisters would, at the very least, be horribly strained. What would I do if one of my sisters became a Not-Sister? Would that bond remain, or would it snap? Ultimately, I think my other sister and I would find ourselves googling "how to kill a person and get away with it" in order to feed our Not-Sister, regardless of the two of us being what Lucy would term "fully realized" persons!

In many ways *Blood on Her Tongue* is a vampire story, featuring your own fresh spin on the monster. What was it like making

your own entry into a genre with such a longstanding history? What made you choose to tap into that vein*?

You know what they say: Vampires never get old!** In all seriousness: I have loved spooky stories ever since I was a child, and of all the scary creatures I read about, I loved vampires the most. They just seemed so cool and mysterious. It was therefore a no-brainer that I would one day write my own vampire novel, and I can safely say that it was so! much! fun!

This is your second novel. How was your writing process different between your debut, *My Darling Dreadful Thing*, and *Blood on Her Tongue*?

The process for both was actually quite similar; if anything, I think my third book might be very different. Both *My Darling Dreadful Thing* and *Blood on Her Tongue* were books that I had attempted to write previously and failed at; both are historical gothic mysteries with visceral horror that deal with similar themes such as madness, the supernatural, and how far we would go for those we love. I think we can call *My Darling Dreadful Thing* and *Blood on Her Tongue* twins—if not identical, at least fraternal!

This novel dabbles with body horror, particularly around characters' eyes. Do you ever get squeamish while writing those scenes?

I sure do! I love to tap into things that terrify and upset and

---

*   pun intended
**   pun also intended

disgust me. Not only does it work therapeutically, but I believe it also makes my horror writing more effective.

Bog bodies are featured in both of your books. Why is that?

I guess I wasn't quite ready to let them rest! I think bog bodies are great for horror because they fall so beautifully in the uncanny valley. Bog bodies look either astonishingly human—we can still see the whorls on their fingertips and the down on their faces—or like a deflated football, and anything in between. Some of that is to blame on the fact that bog bodies deteriorate very quickly once removed from the bog, but even so, the bog changes them: It turns their skin into leather, eats away their bones. That's the stuff body horror is made of! To make matters more interesting still: We don't really know why these people ended up in the bog. Some of them were clearly murdered, though whether their bodies were thrown into the water to hide them or because they were sacrificed remains unclear. That means we don't only have some pretty gnarly horror on our hands but a murder mystery, too! Really, I don't understand why we don't find more bog bodies in the crime and horror section of our local bookstores and libraries.

***Blood on Her Tongue* ends on an ambiguous note. Do you know what happens to Lucy and Sarah?**

I do! I think the girls will go on a grand tour through Europe, which will satisfy Not-Sarah's craving for exploration and research whilst also giving her plenty of opportunity to eat in safety. I don't want to say too much in case I ever do end up writing a sequel, but

I can totally imagine Lucy, Not-Sarah, and Katje spending spring in an Italian villa, taking the water at a small French coastal village or exploring the woods of Transylvania and making clever use of the locals' fear of the undead.

ACKNOWLEDGMENTS

The more you do something, the better you supposedly get at it. You'd therefore think that *Blood on Her Tongue* would have been easier to write than *My Darling Dreadful Thing*, but that's not the case. This dark, twisted, obsessive little novel took me about five years to write and leaves in its wake the corpses of many failed attempts. The last time I counted, there were at least a dozen drafts left to rot on my laptop's hard drive, some of them abandoned after only a few thousand words while others were the length of a full novel. At a certain moment, I completely despaired of this story and became convinced I would never be able to get it out of my head and onto the paper in a way that would at least sort of satisfy me.

And yet, I managed it after all and in no small part thanks to the following people: firstly, my editor, Jenna, whose feedback helped make this book as good as it is. Thank you for your brilliant insight. I hope we will get to write many more books together!

Secondly, my agent, Kristina, who is always supportive of my ideas, responds super quickly (my anxious little brain appreciates that more than I can say!), and never laughs when I ask stupid questions, of which I fear there are many.

Thirdly, my sisters, Lieke and Hilke. They say you shouldn't ask family members to critique your work for you because they will invariably be dishonest so as to spare your feelings, but I can assure you that few people are more critical of my work than my sisters, precisely because I am their sister (or maybe because I keep inflicting horror novels on them even though they don't like horror; who is to say?).

I am, of course, also deeply indebted to my beloved wife, Corinna. I said few people are more critical of my work than my sisters, but Corinna may be one of them. She pushes me to not take the easy way out and instead write the best possible version of the story I have in me. At the same time, she is also endlessly supportive of my writing and will fight anyone and anything on my behalf. I love you, babe <3.

There are also a number of people who didn't contribute directly to the writing of this book but whose help and support nonetheless helped me immensely, beginning with my loving parents and my uncles, Anton and Lowie. They have been cheering me on since day one, which is very heartening. I am also grateful for my bookish friends Nita, Nina, Annika, and my Paagman buddies.

Last but not least, I must also thank you, dear reader. Without you, none of this would be possible. I hope you enjoyed reading this novel (and if not, sorry not sorry)!

ABOUT THE AUTHOR

Johanna grew up in the Netherlands together with her two sisters. The three of them are triplets, though her sisters are identical to each other and she's different, a fact she didn't discover until she was five years old; at least, unlike most people, she can pinpoint the exact moment she became self-aware.

She has received an MA in English literature with a specialization in early modern literature, as well as an MA in book and digital media with a specialization in early modern book history, both of them at Leiden University. She currently works as an editor for a big company that sends a lot of reports and letters out every day, all of them requiring a lot of love and attention to make sure that every comma is where it should be (which doesn't mean she's any good at placing them correctly when it's her own work though). This job gives her enough time to write (mostly queer gothic) novels. When she isn't doing any of those things, she enjoys spending time with her wife, her sisters, and her dog, though not necessarily all at the same time.